Advance acclaim

"*Watch the shore*, Graham Holderness's migrant forebear is commanded in his mighty 'Matter of England' saga: *Hold the ness*. So, with *Ancestors*, England's great Shakespearean keeps his family's word. In this hawk-eyed travelogue of Brexit Britain the long march of the post-War Left is transfigured into a pilgrimage, which arrives in a secluded chapel where 'history is now', as a campus novel miraculously converts into a testament of faith. This memoir of the journey of a generation tells our island story with the passion and belief of a true bard."

– Richard Wilson, Kingston University,
author of *Will Power* and *Free Will*.

"From Brunanburh to Brexit, this novel chronicles a millennium of Britain's culture wars, and throws down the gauntlet to political correctness. At last, an anti-woke novel. Graham Holderness is the bravest man I know."

– Roger Lewis, author of
The Life and Death of Peter Sellers.

ANCESTORS
Adventures in a Foreign Country

Graham Holderness

EER FICTION

Edward Everett Root, Publishers, Brighton, 2022

EER FICTION
Edward Everett Root Publishers, Co. Ltd., Chambers, 33 West Street, Brighton, East Sussex, BN1 2RE, England

Full details of our stock-holding overseas agents in America, Australia, China, Europe, Japan and North America, and how to order our books, are given on our website.

We stand with Ukraine.

www.eerpublishing.com
edwardeverettroot@yahoo.co.uk

Graham Holderness, *Ancestors. Adventures in a Foreign Country. A Novel.*

First published in England by Edward Everett Root Publishers 2022.

ISBN 9781913087821 Hardback
ISBN 9781913087838 ebook

This is a work of fiction. Space and time have been rearranged to suit the convenience of the book, and with the exception of public figures, any resemblance to persons living or dead is coincidental. The opinions expressed are those of the characters and should not be confused with the author's.

Cover by Pageset Limited, High Wycombe
Book production by Andrew Chapman, www.preparetopublish.com

The author

Graham Holderness is a writer and critic who has published, as author or editor, more than sixty books, many on Shakespeare, and hundreds of chapters and articles of criticism, theory and theology. His more recent work has pioneered methods of critical-creative writing, exemplified by *Nine Lives of William Shakespeare* (Bloomsbury/Arden Shakespeare, 2011); *Tales from Shakespeare: Creative Collisions* (Cambridge University Press, 2014); *Re-writing Jesus: Christ in 20th Century Fiction and Film* (Bloomsbury, 2014); and *Samurai Shakespeare* (EER, 2021).

He has published several other works of fiction: *The Prince of Denmark* (University of Hertfordshire Press, 2001; EER, 2021); *Ecce Homo* (Bloomsbury, 2014); *Black and Deep Desires: William Shakespeare Vampire Hunter* (Top Hat Books, 2014); and *Meat, Murder, Malfeasance, Medicine and Martyrdom: Smithfield Stories* (EER, 2019). A list of his works is given at the end of this present book.

'The past is a foreign country:
they do things differently there'

– L.P. Hartley

In Memory of Bryan Loughrey
1952–2021

Chapter One

DNA

'Time present and time past
Are both perhaps contained in time future'
– T.S. Eliot, *Four Quartets*

Putney, 2015

It was a noise he had always loved: the sound of the delivery of the early morning post. The loud clatter of the brass letter-box; the scuffing of paper sliding down the panels of the front door; the echoing thud and slap of envelopes scattering across the black-and-white chequerboard of tiles in the narrow hallway. The sound, which invariably invoked in him a quiet thrill of expectation, unquenched by the years of bank statements, circulars and junk mail, was probably recollected from his distant boyhood, when the postman would bring hand-written letters, postcards from the seaside, a bundle of comics from his aunt in America. For him, notwithstanding the long habit of disappointment, the morning post still prompts a counter-intuitive feeling of anticipation, a triumph of hope (to adapt Dr Johnson's cynical view of second marriage) over experience.

As it happened, on that particular day, the mail contained a message that brought the past into violent collision with the present, and altered everything in his future. Initially it had lain there, unobtrusive in the untidy pile of newly-delivered post in the hallway of his Victorian terraced house, or artisan's cottage as he preferred to call it. He had scooped up the whole lot and slapped it onto the stripped pine table in the kitchen. The fittings and furniture had not been changed since the 1980s, but to him the room signified comfort and continuity: the smell of coffee, the worn wooden surfaces, sunlight struggling through the dusty net curtains, yesterday's *Guardian* lying on the worktop. To a stranger the kitchen would have felt neglected, uncared for, unlived-in. But to him it was home.

As he waited for his coffee to brew, he had sifted through the pile of post, looking for anything important or welcome: a royalty cheque, a conference invitation, a hand-written letter from an enthusiastic reader. Finding nothing of more interest than a couple of bills, a reminder to renew his subscription to the *New Left Review*, and a circular from his trade union, he pushed the remainder aside to examine later. As he did so he noticed the envelope: crafted from unusually thick and heavy paper, sporting on the front a fake heraldic crest, but addressed not to 'The Resident' or 'The Occupier', but to himself by name: 'Dr Ralph Ravenswood, 4 Oxford Road, Putney, London SW15 2PD'.

He opens it, and from it releases a train of events that will turn his stable and familiar world upside down. All his old loyalties will come into question. His very sense of his own being will be subject to the harshest scrutiny, the most coercive interrogation. All that is solid will melt into air, all that is sacred will be profaned, and he will at last be compelled to face, with sober senses, his real conditions of life, and his relations with his kind.[1]

---

1 Karl Marx and Friedrich Engels, *The Communist Manifesto*, ed. Francis B. Randall (Simon and Schuster, 1988), p. 63.

Inside the envelope is a neat, flat cardboard box, imprinted with the serpentine image of the Double Helix, and the inscription:

'DNA TEST. YOUR JOURNEY BEGINS'.

Together with the box there is an accompanying letter, printed on heavy embossed notepaper, bearing the same phoney heraldic crest as the envelope, and explaining in painstaking detail how to undertake the test. Interpolated into the text is a personal greeting:

'The truth will set you free. You can spare the spit. Happy 60th Birthday. Your son Martin'.

He has forgotten that today is his birthday. He puts the package down, looks at his watch, and feels the pressure of time, though in truth his first meeting is later in the morning. He stuffs the box and letter into his old leather briefcase, drains the rest of his coffee, and begins to ready himself for work.

Ralph Ravenswood is Principal Lecturer in Cultural History at Blacksmith's College, University of London. He has lived alone for ten years, divorced and irregularly in touch with his son. He still lives in the house he rented thirty years ago, when the area was dilapidated and down-at-heel, the small redbrick terraces still then accurately describable as workmen's cottages. The tide of gentrification had transformed the street, and escalated the property prices. In the intervening period he could, with some financial difficulty, have bought the house with the help of a mortgage. But since capitalism is the root of all evil, and all property is theft, he preferred to remain a tenant. His original landlord never sought to raise the rent; but when he died the house passed to a property company which promptly sought to inflate the rate in line with market prices. Ralph had managed to resist their efforts, by invoking various legal protections, historic rent controls and immemorial rights, and was able to continue as a tenant, at an absurdly beneficial rate of rental, in perpetuity. The house had also been his marital home: his wife had been more concerned to distance herself from him, than to hang around disputing the equity of tenancy agreements. He takes pride in the proletarian legacy of the house, dismissing the acquired £1 million price tag as the result of property speculation and capitalist greed, none of his doing, and bringing him no profit.

He closes the front door and sets off on his walk to the station, which will take him across Joseph Bazalgette's shallow-arched bridge, over the Thames to Putney Tube Station. As he walks, he thinks about the envelope, its contents, and the sender. Martin, the donor of the mysterious gift, though to some degree estranged, is assiduous and determined in trying to maintain a relationship with his father, persistent in striving to penetrate the impermeable wall of egoism and introversion circumscribing his parent's personality. Ralph has only two interests in life: his work, and his political commitment. His former wife had found him initially charismatic, brilliant, witty, committed: but sooner or later learned that he has no real interest in any other person, but lives for his profession, and for what he calls his part in the class struggle. His son had found him congenial, fascinating, often fun: but in person strangely remote and inaccessible, and deep-down incapable of any true openness or intimacy.

Now, as he walks towards the High Street, Ralph reflects on the motives underlying his son's provocative birthday gift. Recently Martin had developed an interest in genealogy, and begun to investigate his family history. He subscribed to a genealogical website, which for a hefty fee offers user-friendly access to social and family records of births, marriages and deaths, census reports, criminal and military records.

Martin was fully aware that his father, who likes to call himself a professional historian, though his academic background is really in literature, and most of his work spans literature and history, disapproved of the whole enterprise, on both scholarly and political grounds. Ralph's first degree was in English, his interest in History a later acquisition, driven more by political commitment and materialist philosophy than academic curiosity. He had managed to balance these loyalties by developing interdisciplinary work, and was a founding editor of the left-wing journal *Literature and History*. Much of his work came to focus on Shakespeare, a notoriously malleable resource which answered readily to historicist appropriations and Marxist theoretical readings. His first book was a Marxist study of *King Lear* that wrestled the play into a historicist framework demonstrating the collapse of feudalism and the inevitable rise of capitalism. In company with other like-minded young scholars, Ralph set about turning Shakespeare studies into a gladiatorial arena of bitter conflicts between old and new approaches, an arena of contestation that paralleled the fault-lines of contemporary politics. In the teeth of furious resistance from a centuries-old academic establishment, the young Marxists installed 'political Shakespeare' at the heart of Shakespeare studies.

As a historian Ralph acknowledged the value of collecting and digitising documents, and providing online tools for sorting them. But he saw genealogy as at best a lazy way of accessing historical evidence, its methods so crude and simplistic that the mere coincidence of names and places would inevitably lead the zealous researcher to false conclusions. Desperate to establish some antique pedigree, users would follow hints and prompts back into the past, tracing their imagined heritage via a narrow patronymic line – as if everyone were royalty, their heritage transmitted by primogeniture – failing meanwhile to grasp the bewildering proliferation of relationships that in practice renders any 'family tree' inevitably narrow and exclusive. Individuals exist synchronically in society, their lives defined by their social and economic relationships with others: not diachronically in a long, continuous line traced across generations from father to son. He took pleasure in explaining to Martin the absurd theological origins of popular genealogical research, established by the Mormons in order to find and baptise all those souls who, by accident of time, had missed the saving revelation of the Mormon gospel.

In addition, Ralph saw this modern enthusiasm for genealogy as symptomatic of a pervasive racism and xenophobia. Stories abounded of far-right groups and individuals plundering genealogy to prove their Aryan origins. The predominant teaching of modern genetic science, he would forcefully argue, is that all western societies are in reality far more diverse and cosmopolitan than previously thought, and every individual within such a society is a composite hybrid of remote ethnicities and racial characteristics, all derived from common African ancestors. We should be acknowledging our kinship with the diverse peoples of the world, not scrabbling to unearth merely local and parochial attachments to people we believe to be just like ourselves.

Reaching the south end of Putney Bridge, he stops for a moment, leans on the parapet of warm Cornish granite, and admires the Church of St Mary the Virgin, a landmark of great importance to him, though its significance has nothing to do with religion. In the 1960s Ralph went up to Oxford to read English, his first enthusiasm and his strongest academic subject. But as a postgraduate he switched for his doctoral research to History, and fell under the spell of the great Marxist historians, Eric Hobsbawm, Christopher Hill, E. P. Thomson. Inspired by Hill, he specialised in the 17th century, and began to see the Civil War, or the 'English Revolution' as he soon learned to call it, as a great rehearsal for the long, unfinished class struggle in which he had felt, ever since school, destined to play a part. He did his PhD on Leveller pamphlets. After university he landed a job at Blacksmith's College in Bloomsbury, and moved to Putney not just for the ease of the commute, but because it was here, in the hot August of 1647, when Charles I, defeated in the first Civil War, brooded and plotted at Hampton Court, and while the Long Parliament remained in session at Westminster, that Cromwell led the New Model Army to Putney, from where he could keep an eye on both, and established his headquarters. Ralph had chosen to rent his house partly because of its imagined associations with this history: tradition held that the redbrick wall at the bottom of his garden was a surviving fragment of the estate then occupied by General Fairfax. The young John Milton had lived just up the road in Hammersmith.

The 15th century church of St Mary, where the Army held its regular Council meetings, stands only a few minutes from his house, its squat, square yellow tower, with the sky-blue gilded clock, reflected on the rippling surface of the Thames. In October of the same year the church had seen the opening of the Putney Debates, where the army and the Levellers wrangled over a new constitution. In this very church Cromwell had chaired the opening session, and listened, as the soldier known only as 'Buff-Coat' read aloud that great manifesto of popular democracy, 'An Agreement of the People':

> … the power of this and all future representatives of this nation is inferior only to those who choose them …[2]

Incognito, ranked only by his buff leather jerkin, the anonymous soldier had had the courage to stand up in that assembly, and address the Lieutenant-General Cromwell himself, defying the Grandees of the army as vigorously as he had resisted the king. Confronted by those prescient arguments for the sovereignty of Parliament and the over-riding power of the people, Cromwell had pursed his lips and shook his head in negation: 'This paper doth contain in it very great alterations of the very government of this kingdom …'

It was here on that same October day, in this very building, that Commissary-general Henry Ireton had argued with the Levellers about the scope and limitations of the suffrage. Here the Leveller Colonel Rainborough had uttered that great plea for equality and universal suffrage that became a modern socialist manifesto:

> The poorest he that is in England hath a life to live, as the greatest he; and therefore truly, sir, I think it's clear, that every man that is to live under a government ought first by his own consent to put himself under

2 *The Levellers: The Putney Debates*, ed. Philip Raker (Verso, 2018), p. 52.

> that government; and I do think that the poorest man in England is not at all bound to that government that he has not had a voice to put himself under … (p. 69)

'No man has a right to this', retorted Ireton, defending the electoral property qualification, 'who has not a permanent fixed interest in this kingdom …' Cromwell, Fairfax, Ireton, Rainborough, had all ridden through these streets, tied their horses in this churchyard, paced in their high leather riding boots these worn old stones. Here in this modest, unassuming building by the Thames, through argument and counter-argument, protest and suppression, a version of English democracy was born. History, as he had come to realise at Oxford, is more about the future than the past. Today and tomorrow are pressing, urgent, imperatives: yesterday forgotten unless its memory is kept alive. The past is useful to us only insofar as we can use it to expose the roots of the present.

Ralph straightens up from the parapet of the bridge and resumes his journey. Pausing for a moment, he checks in his briefcase to ensure he has the notes for the article he is writing for *History Workshop Journal* on cultural memes in early 17th century political discourse, with specific reference to Shakespeare's *Coriolanus*. His fingers touch the box containing the DNA test, which he had already forgotten, and wonders again what his son might mean by sending it. Martin knows his father's opinions on genealogy. His gift must be some kind of practical joke. But also, a challenge, to which, for the moment, Ralph does not know how to respond.

He resumes his walk across the bridge, reflecting on the past. As for his own genealogical legacy, which seemed infinitesimally minor compared to the world-shaking historical events he has just been recalling, Ralph felt that he knew as much about that as he needed to know. He had been born into a working-class family in the northern industrial city of Leeds. His father remained all his life a manual labourer, his mother a housewife. Ralph had gone to Oxford from a provincial grammar school on the outskirts of Leeds, the first member of his family to attend university, indeed the first to remain in school beyond the age of fourteen.

His father, Eric, had left school at twelve, worked in factories, and joined the Army as soon as he could in 1944, only to find (to his immense frustration) that the war was more or less over. He never saw action. After demob he returned to find his family home reduced to dust and rubble by the Luftwaffe, and his widowed mother relocated to a stone cottage in a small industrial village with the modest name of Meanwood, on the northern fringes of Leeds. Now subsumed into the conurbation of Leeds, at the time Meanwood was still a 19th century village, with roots going deep into the past: the name derived from the 'common woods' between two mediaeval manors. Industries grew up around a big stream, Meanwood Beck, which provided water for corn and flax and paper mills, dyeworks and tanneries. An old village centre of black stone cottages around church and school survived intact, but in the 20th century, following both world wars, the city began to build large council estates around the hamlet's perimeter. Eric joined his mother in Old Meanwood, took a job in the local tannery, and within a few years was married to a girl who worked in the laundry, and settled in one of the new council houses further north.

Here Ralph was born in 1950. Used to slum conditions, his parents had been delighted to move into the substantial semi-detached council house, with its bright front door, sandy-coloured pebble-dashed walls, and private garden. His father grew roses and dahlias in the flowerbeds. The estate lay on the very edge of the city: you could walk across the street, cross a common, enter farmland, and hike uninterrupted, if you wanted to, through the open country of the Dales, all the way to the Lake District.

Right across the road was a high hill, one of the most elevated points in the city, with a bristling clump of tall birches, among which stood the ruins of an old castle. It was actually a Gothic folly, erected by a wealthy merchant in 1770. But no-one questioned the antiquity conferred by its name, which in turn transferred incongruously to the council estate: King Alfred's Castle; King Alfred's Estate. A plaque among the ruins commemorated the Anglo-Saxon king: 'To the memory of Alfred the Great, the pious and magnanimous, the friend of science, virtue, law and liberty'.

Though happy to live under the shadow of 'King Alfred's' castle, there was literally no concept of family history in this community. People loved to talk about the war, but the global conflict erected a wall between present and past, blocking the backward view of anything beyond it. His parents had shown little interest in the past, which had after all consisted largely of poverty, unemployment and war. The spirit of the times was progressive, a future of brightly coloured plastic and polished aluminium. Everything faced forward, like the big red trams that rattled past his grandparents' house. The village centre was familiarly known, to the perplexity of outsiders, as 't'Terminus', because the trams, when they reached the end of the track, would spin in a loop to turn round, never going into reverse.

His father's family, as far as Ralph knew, had for many

generations lived in Leeds. Ralph knew that his paternal grandfather had died very young, of tuberculosis, before he was born. His paternal grandmother had also died when Ralph was baby, and of her he had no memory.

His mother's people were from the south of the city, the oldest part and the most proletarian. For such people there was no family history, no ancestry, nothing to be proud of, or to bother to remember. His mother's family remained in Meanwood, taking a big 1920s council house when the central city slums were cleared, declining the opportunity to move further north into more modern accommodation. The big back gardens seemed like huge private spaces to people accustomed to tiny back yards with outside toilets. But they were treated as work and play areas, rather than as cultivated gardens: with no plants, bare earth with rubbed-off traces of grass, usually the carcass of a car or motorbike someone was slowly restoring. His grandad's house had a wartime Anderson shelter, its bowed corrugated iron roof covered over with thick layers of soil and turf, an ideal 'den' for the children. Much of Ralph's childhood was spent here, in the midst of a close-knit working-class community where kids played together in the street and on the bombsites, children grew up and lived across the street from their parents, and people were continually in and out of one another's houses. Neighbourhood was largely an extension of family: being in the open streets felt no different from being in the enclosed gardens. Family was neighbourhood, neighbourhood community.

It was here that Ralph, as a very young child, five years old or so, suffered a life-changing accident. Coal was delivered from a big truck that drove slowly from house to house. The neighbourhood kids would all pile onto the lorry to take these short journeys. One day Ralph perched himself perilously on the running board under the driver's cab. The truck seemed to pick up speed, and in a sudden panic he tried to jump off. He fell on his back, and one of his legs slipped under the big double wheel. He watched the lorry drive slowly over his leg, audibly snapping the bones like a twig. In a long nightmare of chloroform and plaster of Paris, the limb was badly set, so at the end of a painful six months, and despite numerous re-settings and the use of a calliper, Ralph's left foot stood at 45 degrees to his leg. But that six months of immobility and relative solitude was decisive in his education. It was occupied in reading, so that on his return to school, instead of losing time, he was moved up to the next class. Education became synonymous with solitude and introversion, and created a disengagement between his mind and the normal processes of life around him. After the accident little Ralph was changed, both physically and intellectually. He was cleverer, more knowledgeable, and more alone. He began to harbour his first closeted secret, never confided to anyone, which was that the fall from the lorry was no accident, but a loss of nerve, a shameful act of cowardice which made his life-changing injury self-inflicted, his own fault. He lacked the courage and insouciance of the other kids, who cheerfully clung on as the lorry jerked and swerved across the road. He limped and constantly tripped over nothing. But the path to his future of solitude and study, haunted by a nebulous shadow of guilt and shame, was already largely mapped out.

Much later in life Ralph found it difficult to describe this childhood, especially to younger listeners. There was a kind of disjuncture between his actual experience of a common social life, shared with his parents and their wider family and community, and the perspective he later developed on how such a life needed to be evaluated. His parents lived an existence that today would be thought of as one of poverty and deprivation. His father worked all his life as an unskilled manual labourer in heavy industries such as coal, steel and power, earning below average wages, working shifts, picking up piece-work to maximise his income. They never owned their own home, and never had a car before the 1970s. They had no television or telephone; no washing machine, or fridge, or any other modern home appliances. After the war nobody in their class travelled abroad: neither of his parents ever owned a passport. They travelled locally and regionally, by bus and by train.

And yet there was in this community very little social dissatisfaction, hardly any class resentment, certainly no inclination towards political militancy or activism. His mother took no interest in politics, but his father read the *Daily Express*, and though he always reluctantly paid his union sub, always voted Conservative. As a family they seemed satisfied with the way things were, so much better than the way things had been, before and during the war. They had no reason to dissent when Prime Minister Macmillan told them they had 'never had it so good'. It was true. They hadn't.

For Ralph all this changed with school. Going via the 11+ to an all-boys Grammar School, he was abruptly and disconcertingly hauled out of his social class. Most of his peers were now from the middle classes. Their parents owned their own homes, cars, televisions and telephones. They wore suits to work, took holidays abroad, went to restaurants and stayed in hotels. His world suddenly opened up, its horizons shifted visibly outwards, the possibilities of life exponentially increased. And he began to see his childhood and his family in a new perspective.

The school was academically elitist: the head prided himself on the number of pupils annually admitted to Oxbridge. But most of the teachers were zealously and confidently left wing, their politics shaped by the 1945-51 Labour government that founded the Welfare State. This was Ralph's first exposure to socialist ideas, since his working-class culture had been dominated by conservative values and virtues: hard work, family and social decency, patriotism, respect for the military, a stern endorsement of law and order, and a tough individualism that shunned collectivism, regarded state handouts as a badge of shame, and placed a high value on education as a means of social mobility.

At school, in a new environment of socialist thinking, detached from his cultural roots, he realised for the first time that he was, in terms of social identity, working class. He came to understand that the working class was exploited by the rich and powerful, and that the world needed radical change. His teachers singled him out for his proletarian credentials, and treated him as a nascent class warrior destined to make a mark on the movement. It was acutely embarrassing to him that their image of his parents as working-class heroes, probably derived from the Soviet posters depicting muscled Stakhanovite heroes and formidable head-scarved women that decorated the walls of their staff room, were so remote from what his parents were actually like. He revealed little about them to teachers and friends, and minimised the extent to which they would be invited onto the school premises.

A branch of CND was formed by some of the teachers, and everyone joined, pinned on their badges and marched to Ban the Bomb. One of the teachers even took them out canvassing for Labour at the 1964 election. By the time he went to university in 1970, he had signed up to a comprehensive catalogue of socialist views: he believed in public ownership of industry, trade union power and unilateral nuclear disarmament, wage and price control. He supported civil rights in the USA, marched against the Vietnam war, began to prefer internationalism to patriotism. He was predisposed to believe that socialist countries were better than capitalist ones, and people around him talked respectfully of Cuba, and Tito's Yugoslavia, and even (despite Hungary 1956) of the Soviet Union. In the coalescence of protest movements around the Vietnam war, he became anti-American, and so by corollary pro-Soviet. He even started learning Russian, though not for long. But his new-found political beliefs helped to inspire his lasting interest in History, and decisively shaped his perspectives on the past, the present and the future.

All these changes put him on a collision course with his father, of greater intensity than any normal coming-of-age process. He became increasingly impatient with his parents for their stoic acceptance of the existing social order. His father, a heavy drinker in his wild youth, had chosen temperance over domestic disharmony, so they rarely went out socially. Except when his father was on 2-10 shift, they would sit quietly together in the evenings, smoking the occasional cigarette, listening to the wireless and talking. At weekends they would ramble the neighbouring fields, as if pretending to be country squires surveying their lands. How could they remain so docile in the face of the rapacious capitalist exploitation which reduced them to wage-slavery? Why was his father not more involved at work in trade-union militancy, strikes and pickets? How could he bring himself to vote for his own oppressors? Could he not see that evil triumphs when good men do nothing?

He tried to explain to his father some of the Marxist concepts he had acquired, and tenuously understood: about surplus-value, capital and labour, the class-struggle. None of it seemed to have any impact. Gradually the distance between Ralph and his parents widened. He stopped trying to argue with his father, and instead began to spend more and more time away from the house, counting the days when he could be free. The school prepped him to read English at Oxford, and sent him for an interview at one of the smaller colleges with links to the North of England. A week later he came home from school to see a letter, postmarked Oxford, propped prominently on the mantelpiece, and both his parents staring at it, then from it to him, and then back again. He intuited immediately what an effort it must have been for them – especially his mother, who was notoriously nosy – to refrain from steaming it open and peeping inside.

It was the offer of a place, his passport to liberty. He could see nothing but unalloyed delight in their faces as they congratulated him. But for him the moment was conflicted between the elation of imminent escape, and a dislocating guilt he felt obliged to suppress.

Once he had moved to Oxford, the relationship on his side became one of duty and obligation rather than affection. His whole world expanded, enlarged, exploded into colour. Oxford was the gateway to London, and London was a portal to the world. Affluent university friends invited him to accompany them over the Channel to France to stay in a family villa in Normandy. He queued at the Post Office to buy a temporary paper passport. One trip took him to Paris. As he stood on the

Pont Neuf and gazed in wonder at the Ile de la Cite, his centre of gravity imperceptibly shifted from England to Europe. Thereafter the great wide world beckoned, and the road back to the North narrowed.

His visits home became rarer. When he settled in Putney, he intended to bring his parents down to visit, but since he shared the house with other tenants, accommodation was awkward. A couple of years passed by, and it became too late: his father died suddenly from a stroke, and his mother survived him by only a few months. After her funeral he refused invitations from his relatives to stay a while, and ran to catch the next train back to London.

He never returned to the North.

At Oxford, after an initial year of more or less compulsory dissipation, during which he learned that sherry cannot safely be drunk from a pint glass, Ralph knuckled down to study, and to his own surprise, if to nobody else's, graduated with a First Class Degree in English, excelling in Mediaeval Studies, and was invited by the Faculty to apply for a PhD. Having submitted his application, he suddenly found himself plunged into a dark psychological crisis with no apparent cause. He felt that he had spent three years in the past, and it was time to re-join the modern world. Determined to shake off this depression he declined the offer of a place in English, and applied for doctoral study in History.

This was the breakthrough he needed. History seemed relevant, concrete, addressed to the real world. The same impetus took him into student politics. He sampled most of the left-wing parties on offer: International Socialists, Workers' Revolutionary Party, Socialist Workers Party. All seemed to consist entirely of middle-class students with inflammatory ideas about direct action, permanent revolution, street violence. He suspected that these Trotskyist groups would generate noise and cause damage, but have no lasting impact, and that most of their members in the future would become bankers and stockbrokers rather than revolutionary leaders. The group that appealed most to him was the Communist Party of Great Britain, which managed at least to recruit a few working men from the car factories in Cowley, and which seemed to espouse an interpretation of Marxism-Leninism, culminating in the pamphlet *The British Road to Socialism*, that was both creative and pragmatic. The student organisers reminded him of his left-Labour schoolteachers, and the workers were like his father, but with the heightened political consciousness Eric had so signally lacked. So he joined the party, attended branch meetings, and began to identify and define himself as a Communist, a Marxist-Leninist, a 'Red'.

Politics and academia were in perfect harmony at this stage of his life. He was enormously encouraged to discover that his hero Christopher Hill, then Master of Balliol, the great historian of the Civil War and biographer of Cromwell, was a prominent party member, as were Hobsbawm and E.P. Thompson. He learned there was a Communist Party Historians' Group, and was able to attend some of their open meetings by showing his party card. He lacked the courage to approach any of those iconic figures, including Hill himself, who spoke so eloquently of the struggle, and showed how Britain's past pointed inevitably towards the need for revolution. These men were so much more than formidable teachers and world-class researchers: they were intellectual leaders of the people. Hill, he knew, had tried to join the International Brigades in Spain to fight for the Republic.

He had been blacklisted by MI5, and blocked from various high-profile academic posts. Already recognised as one of the great historians of his generation, he also stood at the forefront of a popular progressive movement that promised a workers' paradise. Like the Old Testament prophets – attacked, undermined and discredited by the establishment, persecuted by the state, betrayed by their colleagues – they had the courage to stand on the lofty mountains of their own intellectual eminence, and point out the long and hard way towards the Promised Land.

Gradually Ralph became aware of the ideological conflicts within the Communist Party that would lead to its eventual demise. The leaders of his own branch, especially the working-class members, were pro-Soviet, and fervent apologists (as was Christopher Hill) for Russian suppression of the revolt in Hungary in 1956. But Eurocommunism and the New Left were gathering force as the old guard of the party held on to their deep-rooted loyalty and affection towards the Soviet Union, motherland of the Bolshevik Revolution, architect of the Comintern, beacon of hope for the wretched of the earth in every country of the world. The impact of the Soviets' crushing of resistance in Czechoslovakia in 1968 emitted ripples that eventually sank the party in a sea of irreconcilable difference.

These wrangles became ever more bitter and destructive as Ralph began to build his academic career in London. Imperceptibly the party lost its hold over him, and his involvement diminished. In any case, the 'New Left' in the universities was now focused on advancing the revolution by ideological rather than political means. There were still plenty of opportunities for getting into trouble with the authorities

– joining in with student movements, supporting pickets and occupations – but these seemed more and more marginal to the great intellectual struggle. Ralph read Gramsci, and began to define himself as an 'organic intellectual' of the progressive movement, dedicated to changing the world by revealing the truths of history, and educating a new generation that would take the struggle forwards in their work and their personal lives. By the time the Communist Party of Great Britain was dissolved in 1991, he barely noticed the difference. He never joined another party.

And so we find him, in the twilight of his years, alone with his thoughts, as he often is, but contented, self-satisfied, at ease with his world. His academic career could only be described as mediocre in terms of achievement, since he had always been more concerned to follow his own interests, to plough his own furrow, rather than pursue goals, in management or research, that others identified with success. He had never become a professor, or Dean, or Head of Department. He had quite easily achieved prominence in a middle-ranking university, and never sought to move to a more high-profile institution. He was personally very proud of his research, which had subordinated his early interests in imaginative literature to a highly politicised view of history: though he was not in the front rank of his discipline, and his books sold only in hundreds. But the enthusiasm available from a small coterie of like-minded colleagues and students could be scaled up in his mind to match the adulation due to a best-selling author, the sound of a few people clapping amplified to the roar of a crowd. He was a big fish in a small pond: in his childhood people used to talk about such a person as 'a big bluebottle on a little midden'. He preferred the grandiose words Milton ascribed to Satan: 'better to reign in Hell, than serve in Heaven'.

He pauses and leans on the bankside railing for a last look at the tranquillity of the river. As he joins the crowds jostling to enter the tube station, he makes a decision. He will phone Martin and suggest they meet on Friday for a drink.

Chapter Two

Fight

'The trilling wire in the blood
Sings below inveterate scars'
– T.S. Eliot, *Four Quartets*

Jutland, 934

It was Ulf Erikson's first taste of battle, and his tongue clove to his palate from dryness of fear. Ulf was with the war-band of his father's lord, Hnaef, occupying one of the timber forts strung out along the Dannevirke, that great barrier against Frankish and Saxon invasion that stretched from sea to sea across the neck of the Jutland peninsula, built in distant days by the old kings of Denmark. Henry the Fowler, Saxon king of the Franks, feared as a conqueror throughout the Viking lands, was leading his troops north, before the winter began to close in. Ulf's father Erik was with the lord's house-carls around the door of the fort; Ulf had been placed by a window facing the eastern side. It was still very dark. Looking down he could just make out the bulky rampart of earthworks, and the undulating line of the tall wooden palisade. At the foot of the slope a deep trench was cut into the marshy soil, a treacherous ditch half full of black peaty water. The fort itself rested on stout, stubborn stone walls. From its protection the warriors would rain arrows and spears down onto the attacking forces as they slipped and slid into the boggy moat, and then sally forth to slaughter them as they clambered, wet and heavy, muddy and bedraggled, up the steep slope. This was the theory anyway. He had no idea how well it would all work in practice.

Fourteen-year old Ulf had known no life but that of a farmer, toiling daily on the long strip of lands his father held from their lord Hnaef. His days were spent tending to the animals in the compound, felling wood and fetching water, working the hard soil of his father's fields. Ulf had been trained in warfare, as were all young men, and could hold his own with axe, spear and sword. But he had never before seen action.

Erik, his father, was the younger son of a small landowner, so had acquired no wealth from his family. His father, Valter, it was said, had followed Viking custom by laying a sword in his son's crib and saying: 'This is all the wealth you will inherit from me'. So in his youth Erik had been a raider, plying the long oar down the coast of Francia, sacking Christian monasteries and plundering villages. Ulf was raised on stories of his father's exploits in battle, which in saga and song seemed as grand as the feats of Odin or Thor. But unlike the heroes of legend, Erik's courage had not translated into wealth. The expeditions he served in had found the coastal lands already devastated by previous raids. Though he had fought bravely, he had never raised enough plunder to reward followers or build mead-halls, and when he married settled perforce for the hard life of a small farmer. His wife and he were happy together, even more so when she gave him a son, and promised another. But then she died in childbirth, and his heart was broken.

Ever since, in her memory, he had resolved to be both father and mother to his only child. He had received from his lord, in return for his service, valuable weapons, a pattern-welded sword, and a painted linden board shield; a long broad-bladed ash spear and a short iron axe. But after his marriage these were carefully wrapped in cloth and stored in the roofbeams against some future call to arms.

Now as king Henry's forces prepared to throw themselves against the Dannevirke, the moment had arrived. Gripping his father's broad-bladed axe, Ulf stared out of the window, still seeing nothing but impenetrable darkness. The night was unusually, eerily silent. He listened hard for a clink of iron, the whinny of a horse, a whispered command. Nothing.

Suddenly he saw what looked like a light, shining in the darkness somewhere to the east.[3] It grew stronger and flickered like a windblown flame. What was it? Erik, glancing back at his son, saw his concentrated gaze and came over to join him at the window.

'There', said Ulf in a whisper. 'See it? What is it?'

His father peered over his head into the darkness.

'Is it daybreak?'

'No', said his father. 'Too early'.

'Lightning?'

Erik looked up at the sky, and shook his head. 'No thunder'.

'What then?' asked the boy. 'A dragon's breath?'

A wry smile creased Erik's face under the stiff black beard. 'It's fire. That's the next fort'.

The coppery taste of fear filled Ulf's mouth. Now he saw clearly the blaze catching and gusting in the night wind. He could imagine the flames roaring through the roof beams,

---

3 *The Finnesburh Fragment,* ed. D.K. Fry (London: Methuen, 1974).

rattling the rafters. He thought he could hear on the wind the screams of burning men. Worst of all was the realisation that this stout defensive barrier was, after all, vulnerable. If the Saxons were breaking through, they would be encircling them from the north, as well as facing them from the south. That great friendly obscurity behind them, protecting their backs, would become a menacing darkness hiding an implacable enemy.

Still there was nothing else to see or hear from his position, but he observed the older men tense into a roused alertness, hefting their weapons. His sweating fingers tightened around the haft of his axe. The Saxons were coming.

All around the darkness was coming alive. The beasts of battle were gathering. Nearby a raven coughed hoarsely. From the woods behind them came the howl of a wolf. Above in the blackness shrieked the eagle. And now the moon began to ascend through the cloud-wrack, gleaming fitfully on the helmets and weapons of men hidden in the fields below. The advancing line must be very long, for the eastern fort was on fire, and from the western fort he could hear the rhythmic drumming rattle of warriors preparing for battle, banging their weapons against their shields. The spear-shaft's song on the shield-face clattered.

Then with an immense roaring and shouting the Saxons came on. The moonlight was bright now, and from his window Ulf could see waves of men running towards the wall, stopping short at the moat, and turning to converge on the fort. Again his heart quelled with fear. These men were quite unlike a band of Danish warriors, randomly furnished with their own weapons, the spoils of previous battles, gifted or plundered, often without even a helmet: these were all well-equipped with the same conical helmet, the same bossed round shield, the same weapons, spear and sword. They moved together with discipline and purpose. For the first time Ulf wondered if courage and fighting spirit would be enough to withstand such an army.

Then there was no more time for thought, as with a resounding shock the first wave of Saxons flung themselves against the fort's entrance. The band's best fighters were grouped around the doorway. The tall figure of Hnaef stood behind them, spear weighed in his hand. Ulf could not see what was happening outside, but he could clearly hear the sounds of slaughter: the hacking of helmets, the shattering of shields. He could see bright swords rising and falling, blades stained with blood. The Saxons, who were no match for these warriors, momentarily paused their assault and waited for reinforcements. But Ulf saw men drag into the hall the mangled lifeless bodies of Garulf and Guthlaf, their first casualties. Enraged at the sight, men began to sally forth from the fort, taking the fight to the enemy.

The dawn was breaking. Through the window Ulf could see men meeting in the shock of battle. The shimmer of swordplay shone brighter than the sun. Again and again the Saxons were beaten back.

Daylight began to lighten the hall, and Ulf could see his father, close to the door, crouching now half in front of Hnaef, ready to defend his lord, shield raised and sword at the ready. Then with a sudden crunching, punching sound the broad blade of a thrown spear suddenly protruded between Hnaef's shoulder-blades. Ulf saw his father turn and stare with horror at the pierced body of his ring-giver. The boy knew that this was the end: Erik was sworn to protect his lord, so could not without ineradicable shame leave the field of battle alive. As Hnaef's knees crumpled and bent, his lifeless body slumping awkwardly, propped against the long shaft, the Saxons began to burst into the hall. Saxons dropped, but Danes too. Erik's sword rose and fell. The hall's hurt heroes finally began to fall back. The enemy kept on coming.

At last it was Ulf's turn. A big Saxon began to rush towards him, sword raised high. Ulf could see the man's broad, red face under the rim of his helmet. He tried to remember his training. 'Your man will come at you', his father had said. 'He will move fast, and there will be murder in his eyes. You will want to turn and run. Don't. You will want to duck and flinch. Don't. You will want to close your eyes. Don't. Whatever you do, not that. Keep your shield up, your weapon ready and your eyes open. You will fear him. But he will fear you. Not for who you are, but because you are a Dane. You have that power. You can kill him'.

This man did not look frightened, but Ulf forced his eyes wide open, watching the trajectory of the enemy's weapon, and took the blow of the sword on his lifted shield. From under the shield he could see the man's feet, and with a swing of his axe sliced at the legs. The Saxon fell, and Ulf stood up again to see another rushing towards him with the same fury in his face. But this man was struck by a spear thrown from behind, floundered forward and fell on his comrade. The dead were beginning to pile high. Ulf sensed for the first time the addictive joy of battle, and wanted to feel again the bite of his axe against bone.

Over the shield-rim he could see Erik laying about him, scattering Saxons left and right. But one big man broke past him, eluding his sword's swing, and began to run towards Ulf.

High he lifted his sword, wide his mouth opened in a wild war-cry. Ulf gripped his shield tight and stood his ground, but the man came on. He was big, and fast, and his sword shone with a blinding brightness. Through the window Ulf caught a glimpse of a raven, grim and greedy, threading its ring of darkness. Perhaps this was the end. This was his fate. If so, what could he do but accept it? The Saxon struck a huge blow against Ulf's shield, that crushed him down onto his back, his axe-arm trapped uselessly behind him. He could sense rather than see the man raise his weapon again for the death blow.

Then Ulf was overwhelmed by an emotion he never expected to feel, and would never confide to any other person as long as he lived. He felt a sense of blissful release at the thought of just giving up. A sweet wave of surrender washed through him, as he sensed the certainty of his own death. It was like a river of peace flowing around him, bearing him down some long dark stream. No more fear, no more pain, no more responsibility: just soft, dark oblivion. It had names, this feeling, and he knew what they were: cowardice; surrender; dishonour; shame. But in that moment no emotion had ever seemed more welcome.

But then, instead of the anticipated sword-thrust, he felt the Saxon's whole weight come crashing down onto his shield, and roll off sideways, leaving him clear. At the same time a rough hand seized his collar, dragging him up and back, away from the fight. It was Erik, who had killed the Saxon, and was pushing him forward to the back of the hall. Ulf found himself running with his father, out through the small rear entrance and towards the woods behind.

They ran into the fringes of woodland, among the spaced and slender birch trees, their feet scattering debris from the leaf-meal floor. They pushed on, soon reaching the forest, where the undergrowth grew thick and profusely, and the trees gathered closer and shed their dark, cool shadow. Erik stopped for a moment and listened. No sound of pursuit. The Saxons had attacked strategically, seeing no point in breaking through the line until the defenders had been eliminated, reluctant to find themselves cut off and confronting another war-band. Father and son were now crashing noisily through the undergrowth of the deep forest. Reaching a small clearing, through which clucked and trickled a small stream, they paused to catch their breath. The battle at the fort must be over, but there was still no sound from behind them.

Ulf found he had lost his shield, but the blood-stained axe was still bound to his wrist by a cord. Erik took it from him, and carefully wiped the blood away with a handful of leaves soaked in the cold water of the stream. Then he proceeded to clean his sword in the same way. Ulf said nothing, perplexed at the turn of events and his father's calm and deliberate manner. He had seen with his own eyes their lord Hnaef killed. He had seen his father crouching before him, ready to fight to the death to defend his lord. Yet Erik had left the field.

'Father', he began. 'I don't understand …'

Erik continued cleaning the weapons, his face pale and shut, and made no reply.

'I saw Hnaef', the boy persisted.

'Peace, boy', said his father irritably. 'Leave him be. He's gone. There will be time for all that. We have other work to do'.

Erik gave the boy back his axe, sheathed his sword and resumed their trek into the forest. Ulf followed him, still deeply troubled. Hnaef was his father's lord, his ring-giver, the benefactor whose generosity merited only loyalty and love. Erik was his man, his spear-bearer, sworn to him by oath, committed to die by his side in battle. To leave the field alive after the death of a lord: worse, to run away while his comrades were still fighting. And why? Ulf himself had been ready to die, in truth more than willing, even eager to welcome death's cold embrace. His father's conduct seemed inexplicable.

Everything in Ulf's world was divided into two categories: *innangeard* and *uttangeard.* Indoors and out. Inside was warmth, shelter, protection and security. Outside was danger, menace, threat. Inside was the house, the farmstead, the lord's lands. Outside was the beyond, the forest, the wild lands to the north, the pitiless sea. As a loyal thane Erik had dwelt *innangeard,* endowed with his lord's gifts: the use of his land, the companionship of the mead-hall, the strong hand of protection.

Now he had no lord, no place in society, no defender. Anyone could kill him with impunity, with no obligation to pay compensation, no fear of revenge. Ulf had been given to understand that a man could not live with himself under such conditions, so overwhelmed would he be by grief for the loss of his lord, shame at his own desertion and fear of the life of an outcast. He remembered hearing a poem sung in the mead-hall, that told the story of a king, killed in the course of slaying a great dragon.[4] Ten of his men, terrified at the sight of the armoured scales and flaming jaws, had run away and hidden in the woods. Returning to find their lord slipping away towards death, they faced a rebuke from the king's comrade: 'see here', he said, 'your ring-giver, wrapped in his death-throes. Now all sword-giving and ring-receiving for you

4 *Beowulf,* ed. C. L. Wrenn (London: Harrup, 1969), 2860-2890.

must cease, all the joy and delight you have lived for in the land. Nobles from afar will learn of your flight, deprive you of land. Death is better for all men than a life of dishonour'. Yet there was his father, clambering urgently onward through the undergrowth, harbouring some ulterior purpose the boy could not as yet fathom.

They pressed on through the forest until the sun was high in the sky, filtering down through the tall tree-tops, stippling and dappling with light the grey trunks, the clumped bushes and the brown leaf-strewn floor. They reached another stream, and stopped to refresh themselves in the icy brook-water. Erik squinted up at the sun, and examined the trees around them, as if taking his bearings. Satisfied, he signalled to Ulf that they would stop for a while and rest. Ulf lay back against a fallen trunk and closed his eyes.

He woke to find his father squatting down at the other side of the clearing, facing towards the west, his eyes closed and his hands lying open before him. He must be praying. Automatically Ulf touched the hammer of Thor he wore about his neck. Hearing the boy stir, he came over to sit beside him. Taking a piece of smoked fish from a bag on his belt, he handed it to Ulf and bade him eat.

His manner was changed: gentler now. He spoke, thoughtfully, confiding.

'There are things in this life', he said hesitantly, his words breaking under the strain of so long a speech: 'not easy to understand. Wisdom, we all want it. Galling to get, hard to hold on to. Age and experience bring it, they say. Not always. We find things out through pain. Think of Odin. Nine days and nine nights he hung from the branches of the tree, dangling over the abyss, blown to and fro by that mighty wind.[5] No food or water: staring down into the Well of Fate. Into the blackness … No god ever suffered so much indignity, so much humiliation. But he found what he sought. Afterwards, no god was wiser than Odin. Your pain is real. But it will pass. You will live, now …'

As he said this, he put his arm round the boy's thin shoulders, and there was a catch in his breath. 'You will live. To know that pain's place in your destiny'.

'Now', he said, glancing again at the sky. 'We have a journey to make. When darkness falls, we will make our way back home, grab what we can carry, and travel to the west. Our life will be elsewhere'.

His eyes downcast, Erik thought for a moment, and again spoke tenderly to his listening son. 'Hnaef will be avenged. Have no fear. Saxons will fall for what those Saxons did to us. But not now. And not here'.

He stood up and peered around him through the trees.

'Where then?', asked the boy.

'In another country'.

---

5 'Sayings of the High One', *The Poetic Edda*, ed. Carolyne Larrington (Oxford: Oxford University Press, 1996), p. 32.

Chapter Three

Meeting

'Humankind cannot bear very much reality'
– T.S. Eliot, *Four Quartets*

Bloomsbury, 2015

Ralph's tube journey to work takes him swiftly along the green serpent of the District Line to Earl's Court, where he switches to the blue vascular network of the Piccadilly Line, squashing himself into an already overfull carriage. Usually he remembers to keep his book or magazine in hand when switching trains, since once in, you are so compacted against other passengers that no movement of the arms is possible. Today he is slightly disoriented by Martin's message, and finds himself trapped, arms pinned to his sides, forced back disconcertingly onto his own unassisted thoughts. Alighting at his stop he queues for the lift and emerges into the colourful, crowded brightness of Russell Square.

Bloomsbury was the scene of his first arrival in London many years before, and the area still sheds a glow of the same remembered magic. He passes the elegance and affluence of the Hotel Russell, where attending for the job interview at Blacksmith's, he had spent his very first night in a London hotel. Innocent of London culture, though not in any other way, he had nervously smuggled his girlfriend into the single room. Accustomed to the strict protocols surrounding dirty weekends in Blackpool bed-and-breakfasts, and the Draconian surveillance of Oxford scouts, and fearing some penalty for double occupancy, he kept her hidden under the bedclothes when a waiter arrived with room service. The smirk on the man's face as he glanced at the improbably amorphous shapes under the quilt indicated to Ralph that to London hotel staff, this was something neither new nor strange.

He had marvelled at the busy crowds of people on the populous pavements around Russell Square, all focused on their destination, a continual motion of purpose and power. And just across the square, behind the fluted columns of the British Museum, underneath the great glass dome, he had discovered the British Library, where day after day, surrounded by piles of books, Karl Marx had scribbled the text of *Das Kapital*. There he had sat, the bearded, grey-haired revolutionary, day after day, surrounded by the edifice of empire, and wrote of the inevitability of its downfall. It had suddenly dawned on Ralph that underneath that arrogant dome, armed with nothing but pen and paper, it was possible to change the world.

Arriving in London back then, Ralph had felt like a mediaeval intellectual encountering Copernicus: his universe became for the first time heliocentric, metropolitan. The place he had always inhabited, the North, which had remained the centre of his world, undeflected by the weak gravitational pull of Oxford, suddenly took its place as a great lumbering planet, obediently tracking its distant orbit around the bright metropolitan sun. The discovery that his favourite Commonwealth poet, Andrew Marvell, had lived in Great Russell Street, was for him one of the decisive moments of illumination that began to connect past and present, then and now, history and the modern world that was still, after four centuries, crying out for change.

The college is just across the square, accessible by cutting through, with a momentary glimpse of glittering art deco, the white tower of Senate House, leading to the ugly brutalist building of Blacksmith's College. At the gates Hari Krishna devotees with shaven heads are dishing out trays of curry to the students, who set aside their dislike of religion to take advantage of the free food. He enters through the severe geometrical doors in the red-brick façade of the old building, formerly the library. Blacksmith's was originally a Mechanics' Institute, founded for adult working-class education, but became a specialist centre for humanities and social science teaching in the University of London. Ralph had never considered moving away: the college is congenial to him in every respect. Blacksmith's is run by the staff and student unions, both led by militant activists. The titular leaders of the college management try ineffectively to govern what is in reality a chaotic anarcho-syndicalist collective. Academic staff prioritise their research, do as little teaching as possible, display no corporate loyalty and spent much of their time moonlighting as paid consultants. The curriculum is determined by the students, and changes continually with the vagaries of intellectual fashion. Every Rector is appointed with an agenda of reform, is strongly backed by the Board of Governors to implement change, and after a short interval leaves in despair, having achieved nothing. The previous Rector, a tough operator from the former polytechnic sector, had arrived with a mission to make all research strategic, commercial or income-generating. Patient and persuasive, he had effected extensive structural alterations to support this agenda. But after a year he had been plucked out to save some Northern university from bankruptcy, and within a few months his reforms had been obliterated, and his place knew him no more. The new Rector, Professor Davies, an educationalist with a background in teacher training, has been in post for about six months, during which he has tried to impose a new culture in which staff see their primary activity as teaching rather than research; in which no research is permitted unless it supports teaching or makes money; and in which research-only posts are banned. This agenda constituted a serious threat to Ralph's peace of mind.

It is not easy to understand how the institution can continue so impervious to change, since no-one ever explicitly objects to the various strategic plans and manifestos senior managers bring to the committee table. Instead, staff and students conspire to ensure that not one single detail of any reform plan is ever put into practice. Using tactics of obstruction, passive resistance and interminable arguments over trivial details, every current of change is diverted and dammed until it finally dries up. Individual cases are wrangled over with exhausting thoroughness; new regulations are simply ignored; 'best practice' is honoured in the breach rather than the observance. Once progress is stalled in one area, management turn their attention to another, allowing any achieved improvements to be quietly reversed.

Over the years Ralph's workload has gradually and imperceptibly reduced. For years he taught half-time in recognition of his union work, and after relinquishing this role never really became full-time again. He has managed to shed all his undergraduate teaching, keeping only a few graduate students, and concentrates solely on his research. Occasionally he is forced to offer a taught postgraduate course, an unwelcome intrusion into his privacy; but he simply insists on controlling admissions and ensures that not enough students are recruited to make the course viable.

He walks through the crowded and noisy entrance hall. The peeling walls are covered in political posters promoting a bewildering variety of left-wing causes and movements: *Support Venezuela, Hands Off Palestine, Black Lives Matter.* Students thrust leaflets aggressively into every passing hand. He stops at one trestle table to sign a petition demanding the cancellation of an event organised to debate the question of Brexit, the controversy over whether Britain should leave or remain in the European Union. The Conservative Association had issued an invitation to a speaker from the UK Independence Party, or UKIP, which was campaigning to withdraw the UK from the European Union. Ralph was slightly embarrassed by this debate, which was gaining momentum after UKIP's success in the 2009 European Elections, since as a young Communist he had campaigned, like many on the left, against Britain's membership of the Common Market, and was even involved with a colleague from the LSE in the founding of the Anti-Federalist League, formed to oppose the Maastricht Treaty, the organisation which in turn went on to spawn UKIP. Today however support for the EU and opposition to Brexit had become a mandatory item on the tick-list of left-wing causes to which every right-thinking person should display affiliation. He scribbles his name on the petition demanding that no UKIP speaker should ever be permitted to enter the premises.

He takes the stairs to his office on the first floor. The passages are dimly lit like the corridors of a hotel, devoid of any natural light. Attempts had been made to introduce glass panels to the office doors so managers could see if staff were there, and if so, what they were up to. But this had provoked furious rows about privacy and individual rights, which escalated to a strike, and was as quickly abandoned.

The agenda for today's meeting lies on his desk, unread, untouched. He places it on top of his own notes for the article he is working on. This simple expedient enables him to appear involved in the business of the meeting, while in reality being absorbed in his own work. He thinks of it as multi-tasking. Ralph likes to arrive slightly late for the meeting, which is held in the Boardroom, newly decorated after the most recent student occupation, so there are no chairs left around the table, and he has to assume a seat by the wall. In this position no-one can overlook his papers.

The Rector takes the Chair and opens the business of the day: the Board is asked to approve the new strategic plan, which promises to prioritise teaching over research, compel staff to accept minimum teaching loads, and restrict contractual time for research. 'Good luck with that' whispers Ralph under his breath. He has seen it all before, in different forms. The committee will argue over a few details, invoke innumerable potential difficulties, and then accept the plan. Implementation will begin with the next academic session, and the guerrilla war of resistance, starting with protracted negotiations over contracts of employment, will begin all over again. The Rector glances up at Ralph with barely concealed dislike as he enters the room. He has been trying to get rid of him ever since he arrived, but so far Ralph has successfully defended his position with the weapons of human rights legislation and employment law. The Rector has not given up.

The strategic plan is accepted, *Nem. Con.*, and the meeting moves to what is usually the real business of the day, always set by the student representatives. 'Decolonising the Curriculum' is a standing item. For the first time Ralph glances around the table to check on who is present, in case he needs to get involved in any kind of argument. The usual suspects. There are young historians who had adopted a smart appearance, wearing suits and ties, emulating the small number of historians who had managed to establish successful media careers. The Literature staff tend to be older, grey-haired and bearded, but still sporting the denim jeans and jumpers of a bygone age. The Philosophers dress as if responding to an invitation to a country-house shooting-party, one even wearing a bowtie. The Sociologists are pale and saturnine, favouring thick horn-rimmed glasses, and wherever possible European accents.

Three student representatives are elected annually. In the past, when Ralph had been much more active in institutional politics, the student body had routinely elected reps. from ethnic minorities. But this diversity had gradually eroded as the politics of the elected reps. were found to be insufficiently extreme. Today the three reps. – Toby, Hugo and Ophelia – are all white, middle-class and most likely privately-educated. The three had become a cause celebre as a consequence of their role in a climate change protest in which the production facility of a conservative media group was blocked, and production of right-wing newspapers halted. All three were arrested and charged, but acquitted at trial by a liberal judge who prioritised climate change zealotry over the freedom of the press, and who was reminded by the protestors of his own children.

Today the students are proposing that the name of the Literature programme should be changed. Initially the course had been called 'English', but that word was attacked as imperialist and racist, nationalist and xenophobic, and replaced by 'Literature'. Chunks of the traditional curriculum were expunged, including Chaucer and the rest of mediaeval literature, and all Renaissance literature other than Shakespeare. The curriculum had to begin in the 17th century with the East India Company and the history of the slave trade, and feature a majority of works by colonial authors.

Today students have become convinced that 'Literature' is also a tool of oppression, and needs to be abandoned in favour of 'White Discourse'. 'Literature' includes 'literacy', they argued, and 'literacy' means rules of grammar, spelling and punctuation that discriminate against those lacking a colonialist education.

'You're, like, trying to make everyone talk with the same accent, you know', argued Hugo, who spoke distinctly with the accent of private education. 'The accent of white privilege. These rules – they're arbitrary and divisive. They're destructive of diversity and inclusion. They're a barrier to progress'.

Requiring good written English, so their argument ran, disadvantages ethnic minorities and students from underperforming schools. To demand a technical proficiency in English is to reinforce a homogenous North European, white, male, elite mode of expression. This is unfair to some students, notably those for whom English is not their first language. It would be fairer to focus marking on ideas, and how well the student has communicated their understanding of the subject, rather than on spelling, grammar and punctuation. The students go on to demand that all assessment penalising students for breaching rules of correctness in grammar, punctuation and spelling must be abandoned. Assessment must allow for true diversity and difference in approaches to language, and not force universal conformity to an imperialist code.

In the past, Ralph had always supported the students in their radical demands on reforming the curriculum, indeed taking the lead from the staff side in the decolonisation movement. In the teeth of bitter opposition and resentment from some of his colleagues, he had been instrumental in cutting great swathes of literature and history from the programme. Mandatory courses in Anglo-Saxon and Mediaeval literature had been the first to go, followed by much Renaissance literature except for Shakespeare. Jobs were threatened, but through his trade union influence Ralph ensured that the staff were protected, redeployed, or more commonly offered lucrative redundancy terms and emeritus posts. The curriculum was reconstructed to begin with the early modern, so that European culture could become clearly visible as a great project of oppression and subjugation. Ralph's own research, which had increasingly come to focus on Shakespeare, the stable rock that continued to survive the raging currents of obliteration that swept so much else away, remained therefore secure.

Increasingly, with the passage of time, Ralph had been affected by a growing realisation that student radicalism was an unstoppable force that would ultimately destroy everything in its path. He was also concerned about the exponential growth of the intolerance on the extreme left that had long been his ideological home. He knew such bigotry was endemic to the movement: it had been the hall-mark of the Trotskyites he had worked with in the 1970s and 1980s. To them ideological purity was far more important than popular class power. The

Communist Party had focused on building class solidarity, for example in anti-fascist organisations, across a broad range of opinions, from Labour left to militant ultra-left. 'We must take people as they are', he used to quote from the Stalinist Dimitrov, 'not as we would wish them to be'. Now it was more a matter of taking or leaving them. The class-politics of the 20th century had been replaced by a curious blend of critical race theory, identity politics and environmentalism. Practical progress in class struggle was now subordinated to virtue-signalling and gesture politics. The aspirations for democratic freedom set by Marxism were now reduced to assaults on symbols and the policing of language and behaviour. A statue of Christopher Columbus, salvaged from some demolished Victorian town hall, which had stood quietly in a hidden quadrangle of the college, unnoticed by anyone, became a symbol of racism since, in the course of colonising the Americas, Columbus had ordered massacres of indigenous communities, and violently enslaved thousands of innocent native inhabitants. The statue itself was not oppressing anyone, but a student mob, whipped up into hysterical fervour, had pulled it down and smashed its head off as if it were a statue of Saddam Hussein. Nothing had changed, except that there was an empty space where the statue had been, a collective emotion of self-satisfaction among the student organisers, and a new gap in the historical record.

During his own maturity, student demands had seemed politically sound and entirely rational. Today the campaigns seemed to be verging on the absurd and surreal. His generation had set the axe to the root of the tree; but today's students were sawing off the very branch they were perched on. Without the ability to write good, intelligible English none of them would be able to do any serious work of any kind; certainly none would be employable. Instinctively he would have argued against such ridiculous demands: but he is reluctant to switch his position from one of support to one of opposition to the long march of progress.

So he stays out of the conversation, listening with only half his mind. Instead he is focused on his article, which aims to devise a new way of connecting 17th century literary and political discourse. He is using influential ideas promoted by evolutionary biologist Richard Dawkins in his book *The Selfish Gene*.[6] Dawkins argued that 'memes' are units of cultural transmission analogous to genes, structured by a kind of DNA and capable of independent power of action, and which 'propagate themselves by leaping from brain to brain via a process of imitation'. Strong ideas, like genes, possess a selfish momentum which propels them to survive in human minds if the conditions are favourable, and mutate and lose their power if they are not. The meme is likened to a virus that parasitically infects human hosts and competes with other memes in the competitive contagion of the memosphere.

Ralph's idea is to apply this theory to Shakespeare's *Coriolanus,* by arguing that the civil unrest around food shortages that opens and precipitates the action of the play can be defined as a 'more equitable food distribution meme', which spreads from mind to mind in the processes of replication. Correspondingly the state is shown generating a 'counter-meme' of authority and trust in response to the insurrection. Versions of the 'more equitable food distribution meme' being active in the minds of his audience, Shakespeare was able to re-activate them in his depiction of a parallel

6 Richard Dawkins, *The Selfish Gene* (Oxford University Press, 1976).

infection among the plebeians of ancient Rome, and to demonstrate how the patricians produce counter-memes with the same adaptive tendencies. The play becomes here a kind of scientific thought-experiment: Shakespeare is more interested in staging the mechanics of memetic contention – the parasitic power of the meme to find supportive hosts – than in the potentially dangerous ideological charge that the memes hold.

Suddenly Ralph feels the impact of a prolonged silence that rouses him his self-absorption. Looking up, he sees the student reps. appearing self-satisfied, some members of staff looking decidedly discontented, and the Rector staring at him with an expression that can only be described as one of triumph. Careful to maintain an air of studious detachment, Ralph does not betray his temporary absence from the immediate. But his present attention is firmly grabbed, when the Rector announces what has just been agreed: the abolition of all 17th century history and literature, including Shakespeare, from the curriculum.

The Rector looks at Ralph, his face garlanded in victorious smiles. In an instant Ralph's research has become redundant, no longer justified by any element of teaching. Taken off-guard, he has been trapped by the very forces he has always endorsed and supported, hoist with his own petard. They have got him.

Chapter Four

Departure

‘Home is where one starts from’
– T.S. Eliot, *Four Quartets*

North Sea. 934

Ulf woke from a deep sleep, and at first did not know where he was. It was pitch dark and bitter cold. Then the sound of water lapping against the prow and the flapping of sailcloth told him they were at sea. As the moon broke intermittently through clouds, he looked around the deck of the boat. Aft he could see the tall figure of his father, bundled in his sheepskin, standing in the stern, one hand in the rigging, looking back at the image of a coastline that had already disappeared into the darkness. Along the sides of the vessel he could make out the hunched shapes of men, leaning forward against their oars, then strongly pulling back as they pushed the prow forward through the ocean’s emptiness, heaved with their hands at the foam-flecked oars.[7] The only other passenger, aside from the oarsmen, was a man he did not know, though he had seen him at the harbour before they embarked, sitting in the prow and looking seawards. Ulf could see his bald head and bunched back, but not his face. This was the man who had

---

7 *The Wanderer*, ed. R.F. Leslie (Manchester: Manchester University Press, 1966).

ushered them aboard, nervously looking landwards beyond the harbour, anxious to cast off. Erik had spoken to this man in whispers, and Ulf thought he had seen something pass to him from his father's hand, but he could not see what it was.

They had boarded the vessel from a small fishing village on Denmark's west coast. After escaping the battle at the fort, Ulf and Erik had travelled back towards their farm, taking a long meandering route in order to stay concealed in the woods. From time to time they heard the noise of armed men moving on the roads, and hid themselves among the trees until they passed. At least one such group was a troop of Saxons, riding purposefully north. They were the enemy to be avoided at all costs: but Erik had no inclination to meet his own countrymen either. No-one could be trusted in such a time of foreign invasion, switching loyalties, widespread treachery and betrayal. The man who had betrayed his own lord, leaving him alone in death, could expect no hospitality from his friends, and from his foes no mercy.

Eventually, as night fell, they reached the farm, and for a time watched the buildings from a hiding place. Satisfied there were no interlopers, they crept around the back of the house, and peered in through the window. Reassured by the sight of an empty interior, Erik felt it safe to enter. Without comment, he began to gather a few belongings. Then he beckoned Ulf outside into the yard. Leading the way, he went over to the pen where the pigs were kept. The rich, acrid smell of pig-shit crinkled his nostrils. Erik opened a little wicker gate in the fence, and they entered the pen to join the pigs. Ulf could see bulky shapes coming towards them in the expectation of food. He felt the warm, sharp-bristled hide of the big sow as, snorting and snuffling, she shoved her wet snout against his leg. In a corner of the pen a heap of pig-shit lay piled up against the fence. Erik took the broad wooden shovel Ulf used to muck the pigs out, and cleared a space by the fence-post; then signalled to Ulf to dig there with his axe. The soil was soft, well-manured, broke easily under his blows. Soon the axe-blade clinked against something metal, and his father tapped his shoulder to move out of the way. Erik knelt down and extracted from the hole a leather bag that jangled with what sounded like coins. Silver maybe. His father's hoard. Without speaking, Erik removed his helmet, cheek-hinged, and his mail shirt, hard and hand-linked, laid them in the hole, and gestured to Ulf to bury them.[8]

Soon they were leaving the farm, without looking back, his father carrying their few belongings. Erik had disposed of his armour, retaining only his sword. It was but a few miles to the port, but the journey took them most of the night, avoiding the roads, working their way through fields and over ditches. At last they reached the edge of a hilltop from which they could see the sea, a dark moving mass fringed with white foam, and below them the little harbour with its cluster of wooden buildings, with fishing boats riding gently at anchor.

They rested under a hedge until daybreak, then walked down to the port. Leaving Ulf by the water's edge, Erik went off on his own to find someone he knew. Ulf saw him enter a low building from which a smudge of smoke was emerging against the growing daylight, and re-emerge soon after with a stocky, bald man. This was where Ulf thought he saw his father give the man something. But he was not sure. Erik told Ulf he had secured passage in a boat to another country, where their new life could begin.

---

8 *Beowulf*, ed. C. L. Wrenn (London: Harrup, 1969), 2242-2269.

'What country', asked his son. 'England?'

'No', said Erik.

'Ireland?' asked Ulf.

'No', said Erik, 'further away. You'll know it when you see it'.

They took their positions on the deck, the bald man released a rope and jumped on board, and the ship began to move, away from the land where the sun was rising over a conquered country, and out towards the wild surging waters of the west.

Chapter Five

Legacies

'In my beginning is my end'
– T.S. Eliot, *Four Quartets*

Putney, 2015

Martin and Ralph had agreed to meet at 7 pm that Friday evening, in the bar of the Arab Boy in Upper Richmond Road. It's 7.30. Martin, who had taken a train from the City to Putney Mainline, sits flicking through the *Evening Standard* and waiting for his father. There's no reason for him to be late, as he lives a quarter of a mile from the pub. Perhaps he's delayed at the university.

&

Martin's feelings about his father are complicated. He was only ten years old when his parents divorced. He remembers him as genial, often indulgent, expansively tolerant, sometimes fun. But that was when he was there. Most of the time he was not. He was at work, or at a political meeting, on a picket line, at a demonstration.

Martin never thought of his childhood as exactly unhappy: but it was certainly unusual. When his father was there, and sometimes in his absence, the house was completely full of people. Mostly men, but some women too, all talking, sometimes shouting at one another. They filled the sofa, the armchairs, perched on the arms of the chairs, sat on the floor. They smoked, and drank, and argued incessantly. All of them seemed peculiarly intense, excitable, passionately indignant about something or other. None of them seemed to have children, and if he wandered into the living room they would look at him as if not quite sure what exactly he was.

Much later Martin and his mother Hannah were able to talk with relative freedom about the past. She admitted that initially she had been as much a member of this academic and political culture as his father: she was a mature student taking extra-mural classes, and they had met at an Anti-Nazi League meeting. She was a schoolteacher, not much younger than him, but she was dazzled by the charisma of his status as a lecturer and intoxicated by the utopian excitability of his ultra-left views. She fell pregnant, and Ralph retained enough of his inherited working-class respectability to feel obliged to get married.

Marriage did not immediately change them. But having a child set her apart, imposed on her responsibilities to the immediate and everyday that others in their circle simply didn't share. Ralph and his comrades were too busy saving the world to be concerned about the trivial details of domesticity. Why bother to clean up after yourself, when your greater goal is impose the dictatorship of the proletariat? She found that the dutifulness she had admired in Ralph went along with equally old-fashioned ideas about marriage. He was expert in all the new critical theories – post-structuralism, deconstruction, post-colonialism – but apparently untouched by feminism. It did not seem to occur to him that responsibility for childcare and domestic work should be shared equally. When challenged he protested that such preoccupations were bourgeois constructs: clothes didn't have to be washed all that often, children were fully capable of looking after themselves. There were people in the world with no clothes to wash. Millions of children in developing countries didn't even survive to adulthood. There were more important things to be thinking about.

As a baby Martin kept his mother preoccupied in the early years of the marriage. She shrank into herself, and formed a close-knit bond with the boy that detached her from the noisy floating population filling the house. Later she started to go out when the house was occupied by Ralph's comrades, just to get away, thinking the boy could come to no harm when baby-sat by an entire Communist Party cell. This left him to his own devices and remarkably free, as no-one took any notice of him at all. He could feed himself, put himself to bed, and then lie there waiting for the incessant raised voices to die down. Eventually the guests would all leave. He would hear his mother come home, and sometimes the sounds of arguing between her and Ralph. The next day there would be a brittle silence between them. Then his father would be even more absent, if that was possible, which was actually better: the little duo of mother and son could have the house to themselves. When Martin was ten years old his mother simply decided she had had enough, took the boy and moved to her parents' home in Surrey. They agreed an informal arrangement where Ralph would take the boy for weekends, but this commitment was broken as often as it was fulfilled. Martin became accustomed to his father's indifference, and saw less and less of him.

Martin had enormous admiration for his father's academic

expertise, but felt that he himself was of a more practical bent. He avoided the more academic disciplines and took a semi-vocational degree in Business Studies at Bristol. When Martin left home to go to university he made the effort to build bridges, and managed to reach a kind of accommodation with Ralph where they would meet up occasionally when convenient.

He badly wanted to understand his father. His mother wanted them to have a relationship, and tried her best to be impartial, though she could barely disguise her resentment against the man, and her disappointment in their failed marriage. When Martin started again to visit Ralph in Putney, the atmosphere of the house was certainly different, but still more like a public meeting-house than a home. The conversations were more abstract, rarefied and theoretical, difficult for a non-specialist to follow. The raucous oppositional dissent of the Thatcher years had dissipated with the election of the new Labour government under Tony Blair, and replaced by a more conspiratorial atmosphere of secrecy and plotting. Living with his mother and among her circle of friends, Martin had become used to a more moderate left-wing atmosphere: after leaving Ralph, Martin's mother had shed her ultra-left views and reverted to voting Labour, in itself something of a revolutionary gesture in Conservative Surrey. Her parents were regarded as radicals in the neighbourhood simply by voting Liberal Democrat. So the achievement of Blair's huge majority generated genuine rejoicing for his mother and her friends. Ralph's associates on the other hand seemed to find little joy in the victory of what they saw as Labour's right-wing, and were busy trying to build a left-wing alternative within the party, salvaging the remnants of the Militant Tendency and shaping what would eventually become Momentum.

The floating population of the house was more diverse than he remembered, with more women and more foreigners. He was particularly intrigued by a small group of young men of Middle Eastern appearance, who sat very quietly listening to the discussions, and who all seemed to be known by the same name, 'Ali'. They would occasionally disappear upstairs with Ralph for some kind of private conference. This set-up mystified Martin, so he set out to find out who they were. Later he learned that they were student members of the Iraqi Communist Party who had organised a highly secretive solidarity campaign in Britain, of which his father was a prominent leader. For these young men, he realised, politics was no game. They lived and worked in genuine fear of their lives from the merciless Baathist regime of Saddam Hussein. The secrecy was no mere gesture or pose, but a serious strategy of survival: if intelligence of their political activities leaked back to the Iraqi authorities they would simply, on their return, disappear into Saddam's prisons and never be seen again.

Martin realised, as he learned more about this context, that his father was doing genuinely important work in conditions of imperative secrecy. This knowledge elevated Ralph in Martin's estimation: he seemed to be genuinely helping people who were risking their lives for a cause. Martin started to attend more carefully to his father's views, and even began to be persuaded by some of the arguments against the reformist agenda of New Labour.

But this compromise did not last. The exact point in time where Ralph and Martin violently diverged on politics, and indeed on virtually everything else, was 11 September 2001.

Everyone remembers where they were on 9/11, just as all people old enough to remember the assassination of JFK know their exact whereabouts on hearing that earth-shaking news. Martin had just graduated in Bristol and was in London, meeting some friends in a pub in Mayfair. He was walking down Oxford Street, and fancied cutting through the elegant enclave of South Molton Street, with its designer shops and pavement cafes. He liked the street, which seemed to him quintessentially metropolitan, and enjoyed particularly walking past the house in Brook Street where G. F. Handel had anachronistically lived next door to Jimi Hendrix. Passing the wedge-shaped obstacle of the Pig in the Pound he looked through the windows and could see a TV screen on a bracket above the bar. On the screen he glimpsed the blurry image of two buildings, tall against a vivid blue sky, easily recognisable as New York's World Trade Centre, and suddenly from the left the impossible image of a plane heading straight towards one of the towers, nearing it and finally colliding into its side in a huge explosion. The tower began to stream white vapour from its top like an erupting volcano.

He knew instinctively that something dreadful had happened, and went into the pub to get a closer look. The punters inside were grouped around the screen, staring up at it in a stunned silence. Again and again the same image was presented of the plane hitting the building, each impact as shocking as the last. An accident? He stood there, saying nothing, staring at the screen, long enough to see, impossibly, the second plane hit the South Tower in a ball of flame. The on-screen newsreaders were talking about hijackings. An hour later he watched in shock as the South Tower collapsed. In the meantime conversation started up again round the bar.

People were guessing how many occupants of the building must have already been killed – 2000, 3000 – and who would be responsible. No-one doubted that this atrocity was the work of Islamic terrorists who had clearly hijacked a number of passenger planes and forced them on suicide missions. He had seen enough. He felt a sudden impulse to phone his father, and went to find a payphone. Ralph answered the phone straight away and was obviously glued to his TV screen. Martin thought that of all people, his father might be able to offer some words of explanation.

'What do you think, Dad?' Martin asked helplessly.

The response was immediate and self-assured. 'Chickens coming home to roost', said Ralph. 'America gets a taste of her own medicine'.

Martin put the phone down. The images of 9/11 long haunted his imagination: the streets of New York filled with billowing grey dust, a kind of sandstorm or snowstorm of dust, and people moving through the clouds like wraiths. Car alarms ringing unattended, ghostly figures shambling through the debris-strewn streets, an eerie silence everywhere. The sheer scale of death and destruction gave the event a kind of sublimity, like a great natural disaster, an earthquake or volcanic eruption.

But what troubled him most, and still does, was the reaction of his father. Almost as shocking as the event itself was this glib dismissal of so much suffering, so many innocent lives lost and ruined, such unthinkable cruelty visited by human beings upon their fellows as merely collateral damage, the casualties of war. Martin had heard this type of argument before from his father, this implication of a moral equivalence between terrorism and the capitalist state. Confronted in this immediate way by the atrocity of 9/11, Martin found this viewpoint repulsive. Later he tried to follow the subtleties and nuances of the oppositional narrative, even read some Derrida and Baudrillard, struggled to follow the argument that violence is endemic to capitalist society, and terrorist violence nothing more than blowback from the long history of imperialism, capitalist violence exploding in the face of the privileged and entitled. But for him nothing could dissipate that initial response to the tragedy of 9/11, or equate the suffering he shared with its victims with the twisted motives of their attackers. He heard a lot in the years that followed about 9/11 as an instance of a 'clash of civilisations'. But he could see nothing civilised in mass murder, or anything good in the religious pretensions of men who attempted a short cut to heaven by making this world a hell on earth.

Eventually Martin found it necessary to set aside this difference, and attempt again to relate to his father, albeit across a yawning ideological crevasse. They simply tried to avoid talking about politics at all.

At last Ralph enters the pub. He is of the extended-arm, firm-handshake generation; his son likes to embrace his father, in what is perhaps too effusive an attempt at bonding. Ralph gingerly pats his son's back, and extricates himself from the unaccustomed bear-hug. Ralph sits down at a small table in the window, and Martin goes to the bar to fetch two pints of Greene King.

Ralph seems pleased to see his son, though he has the usual air of a man painfully dragging himself up from the mental mineshaft where he has spent most of the day, thinking about his research. He asks after Martin's wife and son. Martin updates him on some details of family life, though he doubts his father is really very much interested.

Ralph takes a swig from his beer, and gets straight to the point of the meeting.

'So, what's this all about then? The DNA test? Your idea of a joke?'

Martin grinned. 'Partly. I'll explain later. In any case I wanted the opportunity to talk to you. About some – work I'm doing'.

'Oh? Ralph looks mildly interested. 'Genealogy, I suppose?'

'Yes. Look – I know you disapprove – but I don't think you realise how little I know about my own past. Our past. Even your parents. Mum didn't know them, it seems'.

'Yes, they died before I met her. They were nothing out of the ordinary. Common working folk. They wouldn't have shared your interest in the past, I can tell you that. They lived in the present, and focused on a brighter future ahead. I don't think they knew anything at all about their family history. Paid no attention'.

'Any clues? Anything I can pursue?'

Ralph deliberated. 'My mother's family were poor, I know that. They'd always lived in south Leeds, the rough end of the city, and washed up in north Leeds when the slums were cleared after the war. My dad's mother disapproved of my dad's choice of bride. Thought she wasn't good enough for him. She worked in a laundry'.

'But your dad's parents were workers too?'

'Well they worked in printing, so they felt that bit superior. They were more literate, put greater store on education. And they had a piano. My dad had music lessons as a boy. But his father died, and he left school at fourteen and went out to work'.

'What about family traditions? Any assumptions they made about their – origins?'

'I've always thought there might have been some Jewish connection, on my mother's side. My maternal grandmother used to go to a lunch club for older Jewish ladies. They all liked the food from a Jewish delicatessen: my mother used to send me to buy bagels and *kuchen*. My gran did look very Jewish, very dark hair and eyes. As did my mother. And all the men were called Samuel … of course that could be just Biblical. But all the same …'

'Very interesting. What about your father?'

'His family used to talk about having come from East Yorkshire, generations before, from the country. Migrated to Leeds for work. Agricultural labourers, I suppose. No land or money, so free to drift to the cities for work. They were the proletariat: never owned anything, least of all the fruits of their labour'. The narrative tailed off, as if Ralph realised how inconclusive this all was. 'But as I say it's not something he talked about'.

'Right. That gives me something to work on, at least. What about previous generations? Beyond your parents? I can find some records, gather a few documents, fill in the family tree with names and places. But there are no – memories. You were there, at least as a nipper. You must remember stuff. Stuff you've never told me'.

'What I can remember is all pretty uninformative, really', Ralph replied guardedly. 'Personal recollections. Anecdotes. I'm not sure how it would stand up as evidence. What specifically do you want to know?'

'On your father's side, I've got some lines of inquiry going. Promising. I'll fill you in when it's firmed up a bit. But on your mum's side I'm drawing something of a blank. So to start with, tell me about your maternal grandfather. Samuel. Of course, I never knew him. I've got some of his records: birth, marriage, military service, death. I know he was born in 1892, married your gran in 1914, just before he went off to war. And died in 1956, so naturally I never knew him. But you must have. I want to know what he was like. Do you remember him?'

'Of course I do', Ralph replies. 'Grandparents looked after the kids back then. I spent most of my time at his house'. A slight but wry smile momentarily creases Martin's features. His grandparents died before he was born. Ralph had never volunteered to babysit his own grandson.

But Ralph is staring into his beer and thinking. He takes a long, slow draught of his pint, and remains silent.

'Well' he began lamely. 'My Grandad was – an old man. Obviously he was, I mean, in his sixties, which was old then, but he seemed – well, by comparison with others, perhaps, particularly old. I remember him sitting on a wooden bench in the garden, on a warm summer day, with his flat cap and black coat on. He always looked – cold. His face was thin, and very pale. He had this – puffer – sort of metal thing with a rubber bulb …'

'An inhaler?'

'Yes, of course. And he kept sucking on it. His breath was short. Harsh. Laboured'.

'So he had what – asthma?' asked Martin.

'No, no. His lungs were buggered. By gas, of course'.

'Gas? Oh you mean in the war? I know he served'.

'Yes, didn't you know? They probably kept it out of the

Army records. He fought at Ypres. In 1915. Chlorine. He was never the same afterwards'.

'Bloody hell. Ypres. A real veteran. So that's why he was – well, old. And ill'.

'Yes. Undoubtedly'.

There was a pause between them. Martin looked at his father. Then sat back in his chair and asked, out of the blue: 'Was he kind to you?'

Ralph seemed taken unawares by the sudden shift of emphasis, and replied with the first thing that came into his head. 'Kind? He gave me the belt once'.

'The belt?'

'Yes. Oh, that was just normal then. Criminal today. Put me over his knee and lashed my arse with this broad leather belt. But I deserved it. A little terror I must have been. Must have led him a hell of dance. And he not a well man. But was he kind? I don't know. I can't remember'.

Suddenly, perhaps as a distraction, he fixes on a random recollection of life in the old house. 'They had a record player'.

'A what? An old gramophone?'

'Yes, a wind-up. Steel needles. But small, portable, in a case. Very modern, at the time, I think'.

'Wouldn't that have been expensive?'

'Well yes, I think so. But my uncle seemed to – come by stuff like that. I'm not sure how. Never really thought about it. Anyway, they only had two records. I remember one of them: Harry Lauder singing "Stop Your Tickling Jock". I remember the scratching and hissing. And that tinny voice'.

Martin laughs. 'Really? What was on the flip side? "Donald Where's Yer Troosers?"'

Ralph laughs and shakes his head, still in his reverie.

'That's what they called it, isn't it', asked Martin, fearful being caught in a historical inaccuracy. 'The flip side?'

'You know what', says Ralph, suddenly looking up at him, his face unusually frank and open. 'There was no flip side. The records were one-sided. They hadn't yet worked out you could put another song on the reverse!'

And both men sat back in silence to reflect on the remoteness of that immeasurably distant world of the 1950s, where old men bore the scars of the Western Front, where kids played in the Anderson shelter, and where gramophone records had no flip side.

&

As they rise to leave, Martin notices the name of the pub in red lettering prominently displayed on the mirror behind the bar, and notwithstanding the embargo on political topics of discussion, cannot resist goading his father about it. When Martin was a youngster Ralph had joined a local protest by students and left-wing activists against the name of the pub, *The Arab Boy*, as a symbol of colonial condescension. Their cause blew up in their faces when a local historian revealed to them the real origin of the name, which derived from an actual Arab boy, Yusef Sirrie, servant to Henry Scarth, the original publican, a property developer who had the pub built for himself in 1849. Master and servant ran the pub together. On his death Scarth left his entire estate, including the pub, to the servant, who then became the eponymous landlord. The two lie buried together in Putney cemetery.

History turned out to be more complex than the polarised binaries of postcolonial interpretation. The object of their protest, far from an instance of colonial oppression, was in fact a touching bromance, a tale of love transcending barriers of race, class, gender norms and sexual legislation. The protesters had quietly drifted off and moved on to their next symbolic target.

'Name's still the same, then', Martin joked to his father, nodding at the lettering on the mirror.

Ralph raises his glass towards the name. 'To Yusef and Henry. Still together. Somewhere'.

As they file through the door onto the street, Martin suddenly recalls the DNA test, somehow neglected among his father's inconclusive recollections.

'Just do it', he pleads with Ralph. 'It can't do you any harm. Get the results, and we'll talk about it. Compare notes'.

'All right', Ralph agrees. As Martin walks off towards the main line station, Ralph calls after him, with incongruous formality: 'Goodbye'. Martin turns, waves, and walks away.

Chapter Six

Wanderer

'To make an end is to make a beginning'
– T.S. Eliot, *Four Quartets*

North Sea, 934

Erik stood in the stern and watched his homeland recede into distance and darkness. As the boat plunged forward into cold but calm seas, so the low flat line of land slipped imperceptibly below the horizon. Deep down he knew that he would never look upon his home again.

He glanced over his shoulder to where Ulf sat cross-legged in the boat's centre, flanked on either side by the ranks of rowers. The boat was a *knarr*, one of the heavy pine vessels merchants used to transport goods, not the *drakkar*, the dragon-beaked longship familiar from his youthful expeditions. The *knarr* relied on the sail rather than the oar, so there were fewer oarsmen, though now both oar and sail were being employed to maximise the speed of their departure from the coast. In the prow he could dimly make out the bunched form of the man he had paid to take them, a criminal he knew would transport people abroad, no questions asked. Erik had heard of this practice, and knew the smuggler's name and his usual haunts, knew where in such an emergency he could be found.

He had never before had dealings with anyone involved in such a barbarous trade.

But Erik knew that he himself was now an outlaw. Back at the fort a sudden decision had been made for him, imposed upon him almost, when he saw his loved lord Hnaef fall at his feet, and in the same instant, his cherished son Ulf about to be cut down by a Saxon sword. All the bonds that had governed his life suddenly snapped, and one thought alone seized him: to save his son. In that split second of reckless self-surrender he acted, though he knew he would lose everything, place and protection, status and safety; that thereafter his own life would be worthless, and the son he saved would always wear a badge of inherited shame, unless he could make a new life for him, find him a new home.

As long as there had been work to do, the impact of his decision had hardly hit home. He and Ulf had to get clear, hide in the forest and evade pursuit or detection, make it back to the farm before the invaders arrived. There was no choice; and action was his element. Almost without hesitation he handed over the greater part of his wealth, a lifetime's savings, to the trafficker who in return would give them safe passage.

Now the work is done, the action completed, and the full force of his predicament begins to darken his spirit. What moves through his mind now is not a matter of words, or thoughts; but of feelings, emotions which have their own rhythm and cadence, their own way of softly falling and settling on the heart, like snow. He would not be able to form these words himself. But he had often heard them, sung in the mead-hall, voiced in the harp's clear harmony, echoed in the poet's sweet song. He had never himself experienced exile, but the language of banishment was familiar to him from the old elegies, songs of heartache and homesickness, of anguish and loss. He had never been a wanderer, but he knew what it felt like to be one.

&

The outcast man must always mourn alone, telling himself the tale of his griefs.[9] There's no man alive to whom he may talk freely of his fate, or confess his cares. A man is wise to trap his thoughts tight in his head, fasten his feelings firm in his breast. A secret is only safe if you keep the key secure in your skull.

So he, sorrow's servant, forlorn of his fatherland, fetters his feelings deep in his heart. Gone to the ground is his giver of gold, enveloped in earth. Woeful as winter, he leaves his land, commits his keel to the water's waste. Through the world he must search, sick for a home, hungry for a hall, wanting only one to befriend him, friendless, one wistful to wind him in welcoming arms.

He has not slept since the fight at the fort. Now sleep and sorrow, subtly linked, lull the loner in deception of dreams. His fantasy fills with voiceless visions of the love he's lost. He kens that he kisses his loved liege-lord, with head and with hands caresses his knee, remembers the rites of gift and service, the endless exchanges of loyalty for love. Cruel memory calls then to mind, in the milling mead-hall, the granting of gifts from the gold-giver's grace; how in years of his youth his loving lord embraced his loyalty, joyed him with gems.

Then he awakes to the yellow waves, and glimpses the gulls fanning their feathers in baths of brine. The glee's all gone, and the harm he harbours hits him hard. Sorer then still is the heart's hurt, when musing memory calls to mind kind

9 *The Wanderer*, ed. R.F. Leslie (Manchester: Manchester University Press, 1966).

company, the sweetness of speech from loyal lips. Deluding dreams all, that melt into mist, and sink without trace, leaving no sign on the sea's surface.

Surges of sadness constantly assail he who must steer on the icy ocean his cold and aching heart.

So why in the world should he not despair, and his heart grow dark with the northern night sky's annunciation of snow, when he has seen such peerless princes and royal retainers, valiant men, so suddenly vanished, the homesteads vacated, voided the halls? His homeland was now under foreign occupation, and he himself was a traitor to his people, every door closed to him, every man's hand against him. Dawn was breaking, and as he looked around at the featureless ocean he understood the meaning of those ancient elegies, and saw, as in a vision, the world's ultimate destiny.

What a dreadful place this world will be when all of its wealth stands waste! All the old sagas and songs spoke of that grim future when the whole middle-earth would moult and moulder, wither and wane. He had witnessed the signs in other lands: vast buildings, said to have been built by giants, now lying in ruins. He remembered seeing in Francia the windswept wall of a broken building, tattered with tempests, fringed with frost. As well-wrought as it had been, this wall, fate had fractured it, smashed this stronghold. Toppled towers and ruptured rafters rotted in rubble.[10] Hail-hammered gateways crumbled with cold. Daring defenders had stood by that wall, vaunting in valour, protecting their prince: but still in their pride they had perished, and fell at its foot. Deprived of delight, they lie with their liege-lord, while the mead-hall quietly moulders in the rubble of its ruin.

10 'The Ruin', *Three Old English Elegies*, ed. R.F. Leslie (Manchester: Manchester University Press, 1961).

He turns to face the boat's prow, faces his back to the past, looks to the future. Somehow he must find wisdom. You have to have had your fair share of winters in this whitening world, he had been told, before you can call yourself worldly wise. He was still far from attaining that goal. What is wisdom? He did not know what it was, though he knew its properties. Wisdom is patient, long-suffering; keeps control of its speech; bears and believes and endures all things. Wisdom is neither recklessly rash, not faltering in the fight; not avid for glory, nor greedy for gold. Wisdom is neither too careless, nor too concerned. Wisdom will wait, before voicing a vow, till the mind's crystal clear in purpose of action. With wisdom the wise see the world as it is.

Was it wise of him to place the life of his son before everything? At this moment, he had to admit, it did not seem so. The son he had saved had no future as an exile: he must find a lord to serve, a host community to join. Otherwise he would share his father's fate, and become a wanderer on the face of the earth, nowhere to lay his head, nowhere to call home.

He observed that the boat was turning to starboard. The square-rigged sail bellied and loudly flapped as a strong southerly caught it and began to drive the vessel northwards. The rowers shipped their oars and lay down on their benches to sleep. Only one man remained alert to steer the vessel by the big steering oar on the starboard side. To his left Erik could see land, a flat, marshy strip of shoreline that looked much like the land he had left. Perhaps this was the kingdom of the East Angles, though he himself had never journeyed this far north.

There were Danes here, he knew, who had ruled these lands, but were now under the rule of the Saxon king Aethelstan.

Soon the shoreline seemed to swerve westwards, but the boat stuck to its northerly course, and made no attempt to hug the coast. Shortly the reason became clear: they were passing an estuary, some five miles across, a great inbite chewed deeply into the land. Then they passed a long thin promontory trailing out into the sea, ending in a teardrop shape, a flat green spit fringed by beaches of white sand that seemed to form the northern tip of the estuary. The trafficker, whose name was Rune, a cryptic soubriquet that suited his secretive profession, had moved to the stern of the boat to take a turn on the steering oar. Reluctant as he was to communicate with him, Erik asked the man where they were.

'That's *Hrafns eyr*', was the reply. 'The raven's tongue. Northumbria. The English rule there now. There's a port, tucked behind the headland. *Ravenser Oddi.* Named after the point, you see? And curved, like a bird's tongue'. His hand swept the air in a cursive motion.

Then miles and miles of coast, fronted by beaches or low brown cliffs rising slowly to a shallow green plateau, good farming land. In some places there were hills and higher levels that looked like moorland. Further north a great headland jutted out to sea, mounted on stark white cliffs and guarded by treacherous black rocks. Erik could see smoke rising from a settlement inland.

'*Fleineborg*',[11] said Rune laconically. 'Norsemen hold it'.

'Are they friendly?' asked Erik.

Rune uttered a sharp barking laugh. 'Not particularly. They hate everyone, even one another. But most of all the

11 Flamborough Head.

English who rule them now. There's peace there, for now. Not for long'.

The wind was with them, and the boat continued unerringly on its northerly course. England was not their final destination. The boat pressed on, into the sallow swell of the northern sea, the white waves and whelming waters at the end of the world. Their goal lay ahead, still further north, where Erik hoped to find friends and a place to live. And there also, even more elusive in the sea-mist and sea-spray, that phantom of wisdom that preceded him like a ghost, always beckoning, always out of reach.

Chapter Seven

Memories

'Time future contained in time past'
– T.S. Eliot, *Four Quartets*

Putney, 2015

Walking home from the *Arab Boy*, Ralph finds himself oddly disconcerted by his meeting with Martin. His unconscious has been shedding recovered memories he had forgotten, or ignored for years, like concealed letters tumbling from between the pages of an old book.

Instead of going straight home he walks down to the bridge and leans on the parapet, staring at the lights on the water. There are very few people about. A chill breeze gusts up from the river.

He can't help but feel that Martin must be disappointed in him. His son had come to him, a teacher, in the persona of a student, a seeker after knowledge. He wanted to learn things only Ralph could know, which is after all the perfect rapprochement of mentor and disciple. Professionally Ralph would have been able to respond to such an inquiry without hesitation: he loved answering questions. But the request for personal information unmanned him, threw him off balance, rendered him defensive and evasive. Or perhaps, when he claimed that there were things he could not remember, he was just being inadvertently dishonest, since there were aspects of his life he was unwilling to share or even disclose.

At least Ralph is being honest about his dishonesty. There are many things he couldn't, or wouldn't, remember.

He stands now on the old bridge, under the gentle light of the Victorian streetlamps, watching on the water wavering reflections from the softly illuminated buildings opposite, and begins to remember. Other recollections flood in on him now, with the strange surreal precision and vividness of a dream. He remembers his grandfather's garden at the back of the big 1920s council house: the muddy, trodden grass; the overgrown privet hedges; the Anderson shelter, half buried in soil; the old BSA motorbike rusting against the shed.

He remembers his grandfather's elderly weakness and disability, his slowness and shortness of breath. He remembers the old man's sickness, as he struggled to draw air into those phlegmatic, congested lungs.

And suddenly he remembers his grandfather's death. Particularly vivid and exact, this memory. Taken by the hand into the darkened front room, the curtains closed against the strong sunlight outside, the long pine coffin resting on the table. He remembers that same sallow face, now lying in the box, still and cold, the pale eyelids closed. The oddest thing, he is reminded, was the cotton wool stuffed up his nostrils. What was that for? To stop his nose running? Did he have a cold? Was that what he died from?

He remembers the fear, the strange darkness, the hush, the sharp chemical smell. But he can't remember crying, or even feeling upset, only over-awed. But he does remember, though, his uncle, saying, in a low, quiet voice, 'Time to say goodbye to him, now, son'. And then he can't remember anything else.

Ralph's memories of that time are like the gramophone record he described to Martin: one-sided. They tell only half the story. They're one-dimensional, filtered, censored by a controlling ego that selects and rejects whatever fits or disturbs its own grand narrative. Of his grandfather, for example, he remembers only distance and remoteness. But how much care must have been entailed, for a frail elderly man, in the work of looking after a small kid all day long, so everyone else in the family could work? 'He gave me the belt once'. He remembers an exceptional moment of violent punishment, picked out from a long continuum of indulgent tenderness. And he remembers his first experience of death and bereavement as something that happened to him, was there for him to observe, something merely interesting and curious.

But why does he remember this now? Why does he retain, with such precision, his uncle's tenderly spoken injunction, 'Time to say goodbye to him now, son'? What makes that stand out? It must have been some emotion that crystallised the memory, fossilised it so it's now so sharp and vivid under the microscope of recollection. But he can't access any experience of bereavement or separation: the feeling, if it was ever there, is lost in time. He remembers the facts and has forgotten the reason why he remembered them in the first place.

Martin had asked Ralph about his parents. Turning towards home, he starts to think about them, and again taps into a lost well of forgotten memories.

It is his eleventh birthday. His mother has woken him very early and brought him downstairs. He has already passed the 11+ one year early and is due to start grammar school in a month or so. It is still dark, the curtains still closed. His father is on 6-2 shift and wants to see him before he leaves for work.

There on the table stands a cardboard bookcase containing ten volumes, cased in bright primary colours, red, green, blue. Ten classics of English literature, whose titles Ralph would always recall by heart: *Gulliver's Travels*, Charles Kingsley's *The Heroes*, *Alice in Wonderland*, Anderson's *Fairy Tales*, *Black Beauty*, *Children of the New Forest*, *Robinson Crusoe*, *A Christmas Carol*, Palgrave's *Golden Treasury*, and Charles and Mary Lamb's *Tales from Shakespeare*. Each book is marked with the logo 'Presentation Library', published by Beaverbrook, and has been acquired from the family's daily newspaper, the *Daily Express*.

This gift was easily the most influential of Ralph's life. It introduced him to the principal kinds of literature, novel, drama and poetry, to history, to classical civilisation and to major authors. The books covered all literary forms, and filled him with an insatiable appetite for adventure, and fantasy, and tragedy, and satire, and lyric, and history, and fairy-tale, and for the richness and beauty of poetic and fictional language. From *Children of the New Forest* he derived a fascination with the Civil War, and from the Lambs an abiding interest in Shakespeare.

But the most seminal text for him was undoubtedly the *Golden Treasury of English Verse*. The text was based on Palgrave's 1861 edition, covering verse from the 16th century to Tennyson. But it was the poetry of the Romantics that changed his world and shaped his youthful imagination.

Though he liked to speak of himself as having grown up

among the dark satanic mills of the industrial North, in truth his environment was largely rural and agricultural. Meanwood was built around the Victorian tannery, an industrialised rural facility built on the site of a mediaeval corn-mill, that stood by the beck, disgorging vivid purple dye into the fast-flowing stream. The acrid, pungent smells of leather processing permeated the whole village. The heavy industries, the textile mills and engineering foundries where his father's generation worked, lined the long, tram-lined road into the city. But the village was surrounded by fields, mostly pasture for cows and sheep.

Many of the men of his father's generation would rent small patches of land, what they called 'yards', to keep animals. His uncle held such a yard, at the end of an old disused quarry. Here, hunched beneath rough sandstone cliffs, there were sties for pigs, and sheds for chickens. Together with his cousin, Tony, Ralph would be sent down to feed and muck out the pigs. In a shed over a brick stove stood a big set-pot, into which were thrown remnants of household food, leftovers and vegetable peelings. These were stirred together with pig-meal and water, and the whole mess cooked over the heat into a thick, pungent swill. The boys had to drop a bucket into the set-pot, draw it out, carry it down to the pigsty and slop it into the pig-troughs. The beasts would ram their faces deep into the trough, snorting and snuffling as they gobbled up the swill.

The more difficult task was to muck the pigs out, which of course entailed entering the pigsty. Ralph, who was at best a fair-weather farmer, was unnerved by the immense weight and bulk of the pigs as they pushed against him, rubbing their rough pink skin with its grey bristles against his leg, occasionally attempting a bite with amazingly strong jaws. A steaming pile of dung mixed with straw had to be shovelled up and loaded into a wheelbarrow. Ralph was always glad to be out of the pigsty once the task was complete.

An easier job was feeding and cleaning out the chickens, collecting eggs, giving them clean straw. Until that is his uncle acquired a cockerel, a big white bird with a vivid red comb and a sharp beak. He was particularly aggressive, and fiercely attacked anyone who came near the hens, flying at your legs with beak and claws. Tony would hit him with a bucket. Ralph just tried to keep his distance, but occasionally fell victim to those long, scaly talons.

Other animals appeared from time to time on this miniature farm: a young sheep rustled from the fields around Otley; even a couple of ponies bought from gipsies at the Weatherby Horse Fair. On this little patch of land was recreated in miniature a whole agricultural economy: the rearing of beasts, slaughtering for food, the processing of skins, animal dung fertilising the soil, the circle of life.

King Alfred's estate was similarly positioned on the edge of the country, flanked by fields of waving yellow wheat. His daily walk to and from grammar school passed through woodland, or he could take the ring road which bisected fields of farms. On one occasion a farmer called him into a field to help with an awkward lambing. Ralph had to grip the wiry wool of the ewe while the farmer rammed his arm into her uterus, dragging out the reluctant lamb, which gingerly stood up and immediately took the udder. The old man was dressed archaically in a shiny old suit jacket, flat cap and muffler, clearly on his way home from the *Myrtle* or the *Bay Horse*, which in those days closed at 3 pm. The smell of sheep on his clothes mingled with the hoppy odour of beer, warm on his breath. He seemed to Ralph a creature of the earth, a character from one of Wordsworth's poems.

The language of Wordsworth and Coleridge, Shelley and Keats began to invest this bucolic world with a veil of enchantment, heightened by the waking emotions of puberty. Walking home through the woods at twilight he could feel the livingness of nature all around him, his senses provoked by the sights and sounds and smells: the ripple and plop of trout rising to flies on the surface of the beck; the maddening, repetitive cooing of ringdoves in the tall branches; the frenzied buzzing of a wasp's nest he unwittingly exposed at the foot of a tree. Even the grim industrial city began to wear an aura of the same glamour: thick white cow-parsley lining the banks of the canal, the hot dust of a summer's day merging with hazy sunlight on cast iron and red brick.

The A-level English course he took in the early 1960s was dominated by poetry and drama, and by fiction of a highly poetic kind: *Lord of the Flies, The Great Gatsby, The Rainbow*. Every book he opened seemed to deliver Gatsby's 'heightened sense of the promises of life'. He devoured Milton and Shakespeare and Donne and Herbert, Gerard Manly Hopkins and T.S Eliot. As preparation for reading *Paradise Lost* his English teacher had them reading classical epics, Homer and Virgil, and even Dante.

Inflamed by this intoxicating diet of heightened language and intensified emotion, he unwittingly encountered spirituality. His soul twisted and tormented by some unremembered teenage tragedy of passion, he asked the universe for help, and to his astonishment received it. In an immaculate blue sky, a spiral circle of clouds suddenly formed around the sun, which pierced through the spindle of the cloud-wheel and struck his face with the force of a blow. It was like something out of Dante's *Paradiso*, or the writing of some mediaeval mystic, except that it was really happening to him, here at the foot of the hill below King Alfred's castle.

Thinking of this as a summons of some kind, he felt he should try attending the parish church. The mid-Victorian Gothic Revival building, with its tall slender spire blackened with smoke and soot, was a familiar local landmark. He had often paused by the lych-gate and stared up at the crucifix in its wooden housing, a thin, twisted Christ, blackened like everything else in the locality, but with streaks of gold showing like wounds through the coating of soot. There was no religion at all in his family: church was a curious place where people went to be christened, married and buried. Clergymen were all ridiculous, particularly bishops in their big funny hats. So he had no idea how to negotiate an Anglican service. He rummaged among the foxed pages of the mildewed prayer book and could find nothing to match the muttered imprecations and responses that seemed so familiar to everyone else. When the congregation rose to file forward and take communion, he legged it to the door, and it was many years before he entered a church again.

Outside in the woods and fields it was different: nature spoke to him in a language he had learned from the poets, a language he understood. Everything important, vivid and exciting seemed to happen outside, particularly in those strait-laced days before the sexual revolution. But there seemed to be nothing in the church that resembled what he had learned of religion from poetry, Donne's sexual torment or Hopkins' spiritual struggles or Dante's anguished passion. Revelation had come to him from the sky, so spirituality, like sex, was an outdoor experience. He remained content with the kind of pantheistic spirituality expressed so well by Wordsworth:

> … something far more deeply interfused,
> Whose dwelling is the light of setting suns,
> And the round ocean and the living air,
> And the blue sky, and in the mind of man.[12]

Literature inducted Ralph into a world of enchantment where all his experience seemed to coalesce into an undifferentiated unity. Everything in this world seemed to be literally interfused: the poetry he read, the schoolwork he undertook, the natural environment he inhabited, his sexual awakenings, even his first and premature glimmerings of a spiritual life, faint intimations of immortality. The whole infinitely rich and beautiful universe was centred for him in this little spot of ground, among these particular people.

This strange spell, woven all around and through him out of the magic of words, he carried with him to Oxford, where he formed an intense love-hate relationship with what was to him a most unfamiliar and disconcerting place. The first term was a cold nightmare of dark autumn skies, gloomy decaying buildings and bitter home-sickness, rendered only more depressing by bouts of drunken dissipation and promiscuous

12 Wordsworth and Coleridge, *Lyrical Ballads and Other Poems* (Wordsworth Editions, 2003), p. 63.

sex. When he later read Hardy's *Jude the Obscure*, he felt that he had already lived it. Today students think of university, like 'travelling', as primarily a lifestyle choice, concerned with building an expansive social circle and partying from dusk till dawn. He initially found no companionship at all in this alien class environment, and what prevented him, against all his instincts, from leaving and returning home was the work. The first two terms of the English degree consisted of Latin, Anglo-Saxon and Milton: 'three dead languages' as one colleague dryly observed. He had a head start from school with Virgil and with Milton, and he took to Old English like a duck to water. 'It's easy for you', a fellow undergraduate wryly remarked, 'you talk like that anyway'. And indeed it was exciting for him to discover in the Anglo-Saxon texts words familiar from his own dialect, still in daily use after a thousand years. He was thrilled to come across his own surname in the text of *Beowulf*: *Hrefnwudu*, Ravens Wood, where the grim Geats launched their assault against the savage Scylfings, and where Ongentheow slaughtered Haethcyn, Hrethel's son.[13]

The course, based on an old-fashioned version of literary history, selected authors in a chronological timeline, so Ralph found himself immersed in medieval poetry. Chaucer he knew, but *Sir Gawain and the Green Knight*, with its northern provenance, and Langland's *Piers the Plowman*, with its revolutionary politics, seized and compelled his imagination. The summer term revealed to him all the traditional delights Oxford had to offer: the melancholy greyness of *Jude the Obscure* gave way to the sunlit brilliance of *Brideshead Revisited*. He woke every morning to sunshine and birdsong in a world that seemed continuous with that of Chaucer's Oxenford. He strolled in the Botanical

13 *Beowulf*, ed. C. L. Wrenn (London: Harrup, 1969), 2925.

gardens, punted on the Isis, was driven out to riverside pubs to watch the sunset. He made more friends, met more girls and luxuriated in the wonderland of poetry.

He saw the world through a veil that rippled with magic and pleasure. It was the same holistic, heightened world he had brought with him from school, but people played little part in it, appearing more like actors in his own private theatre, and his socialist politics were a long forgotten dream. The world beyond was convulsed with mutiny and rebellion, and Oxford students tried to emulate the *evenements* of Paris 1968. But it felt like none of his business. He sat in the Bodleian Library until closing time at 9 pm, while drifting through the tall windows came the sounds of shouting and crashing, police sirens and car horns, as the students staged another demonstration or sit-in. He could not take their gestural hippy politics seriously. He had work to do.

When his Finals Results came through he was surprised not only to get a First, but to find his best marks were in Anglo-Saxon and Mediaeval Studies. His tutor, a high-profile mediaevalist, earnestly counselled him to stay on at Oxford and stick with the Dark and Middle Ages. The offer was flattering, and the prospect of a future spent studying mediaeval culture in what was basically a mediaeval town seemed irresistible. The past exerted a magnetic pull over his feelings and his imagination.

But then mentally everything seemed to collapse about him. He woke up one morning to the bleakest depression he had ever encountered, suddenly seeing in a harsh psychological light the pointlessness of all his plans, and the littleness of life itself. His soul seemed afflicted with some mediaeval *accidie*, the dark melancholy inseparable from that 14th century world where death waited around every corner, or under a nearby tree as in *The Pardoner's Tale*. Everything seemed hopeless, like the despairing vision of the Old English elegies, a whitening world evacuated of brightness and meaning. Walking across Magdalene Bridge towards an angry red sunset, he felt that if he continued in the same path he would enter a kind of living death. He began to see himself grown old in Oxford, still sitting in that dark panelled library, still poring over the same foxed and mildewed pages, like one of the bald respectable old heads in Yeats's poem, shuffling and coughing in ink. He had to get out.

It was this crisis that compelled him to change direction. He began to feel it was time he grew up. He realised that the life he had inhabited thus far was nothing more than an infantile playground, and that as a man he should put away childish things. He turned his back on English and applied to do doctoral work on the English Civil War. He chose to pursue what he came to understand as reality, rather than that half-created, half-perceived landscape of fantasy. He chose History over Literature. The books that had nourished his imagination became reduced to historical source-material. He came to believe that he had been playing around in the cloud-castles of the superstructure, not confronting the tough and solid demands of the economic base. He became immersed in politics, and began to look for ways of representing his class in a synthesis of academic and political campaigning.

&

Ralph reaches home and lets himself into the empty house. He is aware of its echoing vacancy, contrasted now with the memory of a warm, noisy solidarity, the domestic life in which he grew up, where there was constant social interaction, and little privacy. Absent-mindedly he makes a cup of tea and takes it upstairs to the bedroom. Standing at the window to close the curtains, he looks out at the quiet desertion of the street, the parked cars and the bunched hedges, distinct under the harsh orange sodium of the streetlamps. But his mind is elsewhere, hovering over the landscapes of the past.

It would be an exaggeration to claim that at this point in time Ralph experiences some kind of sudden illumination. But we see him at the beginning of a process of revelation that will change his understanding of his past. At present he is simply troubled by a shadow of anxiety, the usual clarity of his mind clouded by unwelcome recollections. He has always been robustly confident about the decisions he has taken in life, serenely self-assured about the directions he has taken, secure in the grasp of his manifest destiny. But now a niggling doubt starts to disturb his tranquillity, an elusive uncertainty that begins to suggest that somewhere he might have taken a wrong turning.

He has always thought of himself as a self-made man, gifted with unusual talents that set him apart from his family and social background. This difference enabled him to seize the educational opportunities that took him out of his social class and away from his family. But such distance and alienation were necessary conditions that allowed him to gain the necessary perspective, to reach an understanding of class-struggle that his parents never had. His role in life, he came to believe, was to speak and act on behalf of that exploited class, and to change the world to improve the lot of the toiling masses.

He had never of course asked them if they wanted him

to speak and act on their behalf, convinced as he was that they laboured under the illusions of false consciousness, and had no voice with which to articulate the real struggles of their existence. In truth the people he grew up with had become merely instrumental in a professional programme of detachment and alienation. But now his memories start to tell a different story.

As he lies alone in bed, staring at the white ceiling, another memory comes to him. He is very young, only four or five. He is sitting on a heap of untreated sheepskins against the wall of a great, cavernous workshop. The air is resonant with the sound of machinery, and sharp with the acrid, pungent smells of tanning. He is reading some little picture-book, probably by Enid Blyton, *Noddy* or *Mary Mouse*. In the middle of the room there stands a huge glass screen, stretching from floor to ceiling, dripping with a sticky white liquid that runs down and coats the surface with a viscous glue. Between himself and the screen stands his father, stripped to the waist, his body sweating in the close warmth. He picks up a big cowhide from a pile of skins at his feet, lifts it bodily above his head and slaps it onto the glass screen. Then he picks up a blade, broad with a wooden handle, holds it in both hands and begins to scrape the hide to remove the bristles, starting at the top and working carefully downwards. He works quickly since he is on piecework, paid by the number of hides he can strip in one shift. He looks round to check that the little lad is all right, and nods at him before turning again to his work.

That image of the small boy reading his book while his father works disturbs and arouses him. He associates it in his mind with the gift of the Beaverbrook Classics, and begins to appreciate the extent to which his parents shaped his future for him. They provided him with the learning materials. But they must also have furnished him with the motivation to make full use of them. In what way was such investment in their interest, rather than in his? He remembers the shopping list of clothes and equipment provided by the grammar school, and the anxious look on his father's face as he perused it. He remembers his mother taking him down to Leeds to buy his uniform, and football kit, and cricket clothes, and running shoes, from the recommended outfitter, the kind of swanky shop he had never previously set foot in. The cost of all this must have been the equivalent of a modest-income middle-class family sending a kid to Eton. Why did they do it? Virtually all his peers, friends and relatives, were attending secondary school, and would leave at sixteen to work, contributing to the family exchequer. His parents were sponsoring him on an open-ended journey of incalculable expense and no hope of profit. What induced them to make such self-denying sacrifice?

Simply, he is obliged to accept, because they wanted him to get on in life, have a better life than they had, become a complete and contented human being.

He lies in bed, alone with his thoughts, waiting for sleep. Eventually a dark current takes him, sweeping his unresisting body into a submarine world of wavering shadows and undulating green weeds. Over the sandy bottom, through the glassy swell, he dimly perceives buildings, rough stone cottages with thatched roofs, some bigger half-timbered houses with tiles, and larger buildings of wood, barns and warehouses. A whole mediaeval town, sunk deep beneath the pull and swell of the sea. Fish flicker and waver in and out of the open doors and windows. A sound reverberates through the water, visible in bubbling waves like a strong current: the pealing of a church bell. He has no idea where this place is. But he feels that he has been here before.

Chapter Eight

Arrival

'The end is where we start from'
– T.S. Eliot, *Four Quartets*

North Sea, 934

Ulf had been on the boat for days now, tormented with restlessness and desperate to feel land beneath his feet. They were fortunate in that wind and tide stood for rather than against them, so their progress was swift. But the boredom of sitting on that wet deck, day after day, night after night, was beginning to tell on him. His father regarded the voyage with much more stoicism and patience, and grew more relaxed as the distance from his homeland increased. Ulf tried to sleep, whether it was day or night, just to escape from the tedious heave and slap of the oars, the furling and flapping of the sail, the scream of the gulls that followed the boat's wake.

The boat had hugged the Northumbrian coast to its northernmost point, rounded Scotland, skirted the Orkneys, then steered across the straits to the Faroes. It was an unfamiliar world, shaped by increasingly strange contours, that came floating towards him out of the sea mists. Flat, treeless islands; rugged, towering cliffs thick with nesting white seabirds; a promontory where two great chunks of rock were broken off from the point of land, one hooped and arched as the sea surged through it, the other polished like a piece of wood hacked from a tree-trunk. The same bright green vegetation topped all three, homogenous and smooth as moss on a barn roof, but the white waves whelmed between, and sundered them inexorably one from another. The boat threaded the islands and they made their final exit into the narrow sound of the Atlantic, leaving astern a huge wall of rock that continued to loom behind them in a shadowless midnight twilight.

But it was his first glimpse of the unknown land that was their ultimate goal, that seemed to him like nothing else in the world for its fierce and forlorn beauty. It was a dark morning of storm and rain, with a solid blackness behind them out to sea, and ahead the sun riding very bright, under a black canopy of cloud, over the land. They began to follow the coast towards the west, and the boy gazed in astonishment at an immense glacier, from which rivers of ice seemed to run right down into the sea, their grey translucence beginning to sparkle in the early sunlight. Between them lay desolate beaches of volcanic rock and sand, and beyond the glacier sharp peaks, some black and snow-flecked, others sheathed in a skin of pure ice, now beginning, as the clouds dispersed, to stand out in distinct relief in the pure air, hard and beautiful against the vivid and intense cobalt blue of the Arctic sky. He saw a towering cone of mountain, with a faint drift of smoke hinting at the volcanic turbulence and power that lay at its heart. In the evening, over these heart-rending sights, the sun set with a watery, copper-and-green splendour; but then did not, as he expected, disappear beneath the rim of the world, but clung to the horizon, continuing the night long to emit a weird and unearthly twilight.

At last, as dawn broke on the final day of their voyage, the boat touched the shore at their destination. The crew jumped with alacrity into the shallows, and dragged the boat up onto the black basalt beach. Ulf marvelled at the landscape: to the east great towering pillars of stone standing up from the sea like the fingers of a submerged giant; to the west high brown cliffs with vegetation growing half way up their slopes; at their feet a broad green meadow. Ulf was one of the first to leap from the boat and splash into the surf. Erik followed, carrying their few belongings. With a curt nod Erik bade farewell to Rune, and then led the way up the beach and towards the little town. The crew climbed back into the boat as if they were anxious to remain unseen, and rowed off towards the west.

Ulf looked around as they walked up the beach, to survey what appeared to be his new home. The sand of the beach was black, now dull and lifeless, now glinting in the rays of the rising sun. There were black rocks that seemed as if chiselled into geometric patterns out of the cliffs, eroded by the savage ferocity and tenaciousness of wind and wave, but to his young imagination suggesting the sculpting handiwork of giants. The town was a huddle of low buildings, crouching beneath the cliffs as if to shelter from the weather, and bunched tightly around the little harbour. Most of them were made of wood, but in the centre stood a big longhouse built from stone, with an earthen roof lined with moss, windows along the wall and a timber-framed door. From the chimney emerged a blur of blue smoke, and through the doorway the sound of voices. Erik told Ulf to stay by the door while he went inside.

After a while Erik emerged with another man who bore a distinct family resemblance. This was his cousin Arne, who had left Denmark some years earlier after killing a man over some disagreement about money or land. His victim served a wealthy lord, so Arne was faced with an extortionate man-price he could never afford to pay. He had grabbed his belongings, much as Erik had done, and fled from the blood-feud, trying out various settlements along the way, and finally finding the security he needed here. He had sent word to Erik indicating that shelter and a livelihood would be available also to him should he ever need to quit Denmark. Ulf had a vague memory of him from when he was a child.

Arne resembled Erik in appearance, with the same balding head and stiff black beard. But he was smaller than his cousin, thinner and paler. In the extended family Arne was always known as 'the clever one'. He would talk his way out of trouble where Erik would stand and fight. Arne seemed genuinely pleased to see them, and gave them an expansive welcome. He clapped the boy on the shoulder and led them into the longhouse. The place was full of smoke and the smells of cooking. They were welcomed by a woman named Gretta, who seemed to be in charge of the kitchen, giving orders to slaves, and who seemed to be some kind of consort to Arne, though they were not married, and had no children. She urged them to sit and eat, as they must be hungry after the long voyage. Mead was provided for them, and delicious, greasy lumps of charred lamb from the spitting and crackling fire. After spending so long on the boat their appetites were insatiable, so they ate and drank ravenously.

After a while Erik asked where they were to sleep, and took their belongings to settle in. Ulf remained at the table, voraciously curious to know more about the life they were to lead, and the place they were to live in. He did not even know its name.

'This is *Vik*', Arne told him. 'Named after some place in Norway. The country has been known by various names. We know it now as Iceland'.

Ulf had heard of it, and was eager to know more. Arne was only too glad to oblige the boy's curiosity, and began to tell him stories and legends of his new home.

He told first of a man named Naddodd, from Norway, who was making a voyage to the Faeroe Islands, and found himself lost in an impenetrable sea-fog, unable to navigate by sun or by stars. He missed his destination by 400 miles, and this country was the first land he came across. The crew went ashore and combed the land in search of human settlement, but could find no trace. So Naddodd climbed a mountain and surveyed the land as far as the eye could see. But there was nothing to see, save an immense plain of glaciers and hard, frosted fields. He could see none of the smoke that should be issuing from the fires of settlers' hearths. He returned disconsolately to his ship, and quit the shore just as snow began to fall. It was Naddodd who gave the place its first name: 'Snowland'.

When Naddodd returned to Norway the news soon circulated of an empty, unclaimed land to the northwest. A Swedish merchant named Garthar followed with a little fleet in Naddodd's wake, and found his way to Snowland. Instead of going ashore he continued to sail round the coast, eager to know if the land was an island or part of some main. Winter overtook him, so they beached their ships on the northern coast and survived a bitter season, living off the eggs of seabirds and the harvest of the sea. Having circumvented the land and found it to be indeed an island, and uninhabited, Garhtar named it after himself. So the country acquired its second name: 'Gartharsholmi'. But Garthar could see no prospect on this hostile, snowbound land of the prosperous life he had dreamed of, and left his name and the island behind.

Hearing of Garhtar's story, bolder travellers began to attempt more ambitious expeditions. A man named Floki left Norway with his family, other settlers and a cargo of animals. He took the precaution of bringing three ravens, which he released one at a time. Only when one of the birds failed to return was he sure of the direction in which the land lay. He was given the name 'Raven Floki'. Taking advantage of the summer months, and the long daylight hours under the midnight sun, these settlers felled birch trees and built a farmstead, grazed their animals and settled to a pleasant life. But the harsh winter undid them: their fodder ran out, their animals died. When they tried to leave they found the fjords blocked by icebergs, and had to wait for the warm unlocking of the spring. Floki returned to Norway disillusioned, and reported that the famed land to the northwest was uninhabitable. Nothing there but frost and snow, icebergs and glaciers. 'Iceland', he called it.

But others were determined to succeed where he had failed. A Norwegian named Ingolfur Arneson, involved in a deadly blood-feud, with his family and household set sail for Iceland. Ingolfur left it to Thor to decide where he should land, so he cast two wooden poles into the sea, promising to settle wherever they landed. They went ashore and searched for the poles, which they found washed into the bay of a fjord on the south coast. There he built his hall, and flanked his own seat at the head of the table with the two posts. He called the place Smoky Bay, or Reykjavik.

ᘐ

So absorbed was the boy in Arne's narrative that he had not noticed his father, quietly returned and sitting beside him with a cup of mead. Ulf thought he detected a pattern in Arne's account of Iceland's founders.

'Are all the men here outlaws, then?' he asked.

Arne laughed at the innocence of his question. 'Not any more', was the reply. 'Many are exiles, wanderers, people who've left their homes in a hurry. Like me, escaping a blood-feud. Like your father. People who've got into trouble of some kind. Others fell foul of ambitious lords and kings imposing their wills on the people. Lots of people couldn't stand Harald Fairhair. He became too powerful, keeping a close watch on any farmer or landholder he suspected of disloyalty. Anyone who disagreed with him got a choice: enter my service, or face death, torture or exile. Many gave in, became his retainers, pay his tributes. Others left. And his son Eric Bloodaxe is even worse. Some came here from Denmark and Sweden because they just wanted a place of their own – a bit of land, a place to call home. They came here to farm, grow crops, raise beasts, to live quietly. They came here for – freedom'.

'So is it – dangerous here, then?' asked the boy, 'with so many living outside the law?'

'Have no fear, son', put in Erik. 'We left home with nothing, so we can't be robbed. And I still have this' – touching the hilt of his sword – 'to defend us from harm'.

Arne laughed. 'That's the one thing you won't need here. We have our own law, and no-one is above it. We keep it, and respect it, because its ours, voluntary, not imposed by someone else. Here there are no wars, no strife, no challenges, no rebellions. We all have a common cause. The law gives us that security. Being able to live without looking over your shoulder'.

'Do raiders not visit these shores?', asked Ulf.

Arne laughed again. 'Nothing here for them. No monasteries, no churches. No palaces, no wealth to plunder'.

'And no-one comes here to seize the land from you?', asked Erik.

Arne shook his head, and turned to his mead, giving no reply. Ulf felt a certain evasiveness in his manner, as if he were hiding something. After a pause he gave a sort of answer. 'This island is full of – spirits. Land spirits, you know: *landvaettir*. They protect the country. It's important not to upset them. Our law says that ships must remove their dragon-heads before approaching the shore, so as not to upset the spirits. And they hate bloodshed. There's a place where a man was murdered. Good grazing land. But no-one will go there. The spirits are still angry. Once the king of Denmark sent a wizard to spy on the Icelanders. He took the form of a whale, and swam around the coast. But everywhere he went, he felt that he too was watched. The spirits saw through his disguise. He tried to swim up a fjord: but a spirit took the form of a great cliff-ghost, and he fled in terror. So keep on their right side, whatever you do. Keep the peace, protect the land, and you'll be rewarded with good fortune'.

Ulf found this discourse fascinating, but he could see that his father was sceptical, and growing restive. 'Who is your king?' asked Erik, changing the subject. 'I would like to offer him service'.

Arne turned to look at Erik, and spoke softly. 'That's the strangest thing about this place. We have no king. No lords.

No-one stands in authority over any one else. So many came here to escape from tyranny, nobody wants to reproduce it. We just live together. Each family has its own place, its own house, its own bit of land. We help one another when times are hard. There's no government here, no army, no taxes. Just families, getting by'.

'There is no chieftain here, then, in this place?', asked Erik, showing some disappointment. He had planned to put his military experience to use in the service of the island's authority. 'But there must be disputes?'

'We have leaders, yes. They are called *Gothi*. Wise men. We can consult him if we disagree. They know the law, and give advice. We accept their rulings. They get no benefit from their position – no wealth, no land. They live much as we do, simple farmers. When one of them dies, we elect another'.

'Elect?' asked Ulf. 'What's that?'

'You'll see', Arne replied. 'But that's enough politics for one day. I've got to settle the beasts before nightfall. You two must rest and prepare yourselves. You'll be up early tomorrow'.

Erik led the boy to Arne's house on the edge of the village, on a green slope that rose towards the high brown cliffs. It was a big barn-like structure, with a separate outhouse to shelter the animals in the winter. Around the house Arne's livestock, cattle and sheep, roamed the fields. From here you could see the sea, and the strange fingers of rock that reached out from the white waves.

'Father', Ulf asked him, 'what are we to do here?'

The answer was short and decisive. 'Work'.

They had been given living quarters at the end of Arne's roomy house. Here they had everything they needed: straw mattresses and bed clothes for the chilly nights.

That night Ulf went to bed with his head spinning from the mead, the smoke and Arne's conversation. Though physically exhausted from the journey, he found that his mind could not rest, and he lay awake long after his father had sunk into sleep.

Silence descended as the village slept. He lay listening to the sleepers' snores. From outside he could hear the whinny of a horse, the grunting of pigs, the swishing of a cow's tail.

Gradually he became aware that the quietness of the night beyond was permeated and fractured by unfamiliar sounds. On the breeze he could hear a kind of crackling noise, punctuated by sounds of grinding and splitting, followed by a subdued distant booming as of some great mass falling. Then a kind of groaning sound. The island seemed alive. He even felt some kind of movement, a flutter or tremor of the floor beneath, as if the land itself was shifting its ground. He thought of Arne's stories of the land spirits, and wondered if here they had come closer to the dwelling places of the gods. Perhaps the strange sounds came from dwarves, working at metal in their echoing caves. Perhaps the booming noise was the thudding of Thor's hammer as, in one of his many rages, the irascible god smashed it down onto the earth.

He stared through the window at a great crowd of unfamiliar stars, clustering and tumbling through the night sky. Then a faint glow of orange and green trembled, on the edges of the sky, or on the border of his vision, he could not be sure. The aurora seemed to emanate strange sounds, fizzing and crackling, as if his ears were full of water. Surely that is the *Bifrost*, he thought, as he drifted into sleep: the rainbow bridge that leads to Asgard?

Chapter Nine
Fountain

'I am here, or there, or elsewhere'
– T.S. Eliot, *Four Quartets*

Bloomsbury, 2015

The 'Reception' area outside the Rector's office is nothing more than an alcove in a corridor, furnished with a couple of cheap armchairs and a low coffee table bearing empty Styrofoam cups and the previous week's *Times Higher Education Supplement.* Against the wall is a glass-fronted cabinet full of Annual Reports. No-one ever takes them out. Their spines are routinely studied by occupants with no interest at all in their contents: absorbed rather in in the apprehension or excitement they bring to a feared or anticipated meeting.

Ralph is waiting for his Annual Appraisal with the Rector. So far as he knows there is nothing for him to be apprehensive about. The unions and staff organisations have negotiated an appraisal system that focuses entirely on the individual employee's own definition of goals and objectives, making it impossible for managers to measure people against any real performance indicators, or against the institution's own strategic objectives. Instead the employee sets out his or her own aspirations, measures his or her own success and presents a shopping list of resources required if such success is to be repeated in the subsequent year. In short, appraisal is a tool designed to permit the employee to do exactly what he or she wants, with as little interference from management as possible.

As usual Ralph has completed his appraisal form in the most cursory way, stating generic research objectives, impossible to measure, and appending a list of his recent publications and conference papers. In the previous year he has had no teaching at all, as his two PhD students are both writing up their theses. He has listed the few committees he sits on under 'Management and Administration'.

Above the Rector's door there are two lights, one red and one green, as if the office belonged to a chief of the intelligence services in a spy thriller. The lights have not long been installed, so some plaster and paintwork still needs finishing. The workmen have been called elsewhere to paint a seminar room in preparation for a teaching inspection. The red light goes out, and the green light flicks on. Nobody comes out. Ralph taps on the door and enters.

The furniture has been rearranged since he was last in this room. Professor Davies sits behind a big desk with the window behind him, so any bright light falls directly on the person opposite. Another trick borrowed from spy fiction, thought Ralph: he must be a devotee of Graham Greene and John le Carré. The black leather desktop is completely empty apart from Ralph's Appraisal form, conspicuous – and looking even more desultory – by virtue of its solitude. Davies is looking down at it with a carefully controlled expression somewhere between amusement and contempt, which he quickly clears to present a face of impenetrable blankness. He waves for Ralph to sit down.

'Research going well, then, I see?', he begins. His manner is polite, even genial. Only the voice betrays the deeper currents of boredom and frustration that will eventually propel him out of the institution altogether. Ralph hopes to outlast him, as he has outlasted so many of his predecessors.

'Yes, as usual,' replies Ralph confidently, and embarks on a long exposition of what he regards as his performance successes, following this up with a statement of what he will need in the following year: research funds for conference attendance, money for casual research assistance, more and better equipment, more books for the library. The Rector swivels his office chair sideways, and seems to find the handles of a filing cabinet marginally more interesting than the appraisee's elongated discourse.

'And teaching?', the Rector asks dryly, bringing his chair to face forward again, as the long exposition comes to an end.

'Well as you see, as it happens, I haven't had any this year. So there's nothing to measure'.

There is a long pause. This time the Rector swivels his chair round 180 degrees, with his back to Ralph, and for a while stares at the window. Then he pirouettes back again, leans forward, and puts his hands together.

'Look, Ralph', he begins quietly. 'Let's level with each other, shall we? I'd like us to be able to talk not just about last year, but the next. And the one after that. And – the future. Your future. How it fits into the future direction of the University'.

Ralph is immediately on guard. 'That's not on the agenda', he observes, immediately assuming his barrack-room lawyer manner. 'No previous notice. If you want to talk to me about contractual matters, employment terms and conditions, then I need to be pre-informed and given the opportunity to bring a representative'.

'All right, all right' sighs the Rector. 'There's no need for all that. All I'm asking is that you hear what I have to say. Without prejudice. There's only the two of us here: no unions, no HR. Complete confidentiality. Total deniability. For both of us. If you want to make it formal, fine. Get yourself lawyered up, we'll set up a formal meeting, I'll bring the Director of Personnel. We can play the game. Or', and again he paused. 'We can just have a conversation. No strings. It's up to you'.

Ostentatiously Ralph takes a notebook out of his briefcase, opens it and prepares to write things down. The Rector proceeds to set out his personal strategic vision for the University. The institution has been haemorrhaging money for decades. Its primary income is the funding council grant for teaching, and student fees. The disciplinary profile of the university, oriented towards humanities and social sciences, results in a low and increasingly reduced block grant. Research funding is minimal, and staff persistently refuse to apply for research grants. Staff energy and application are focused on research that produces no results, with the consquence that the university receives poor ratings for teaching. This leads to reputational damage, and to problems with recruitment. Some subject areas hardly recruit enough students to remain viable.

The only solution, Davies argues, is to harness staff time and motivation into teaching; to enhance teaching ratings and student satisfaction; to improve recruitment; and to maximise student income. Once these goals have been achieved, there would be surplus money to invest in research.

'Now', he explains, 'what that means is that posts dedicated primarily to research – like yours – become unaffordable. If you calculate your income-generation, it's less than your salary costs. And you're not the only one, of course. So what we're going to do is to require all staff to teach a minimum of two undergraduate courses. If research time is squeezed, so be it. Scholars who bring in research income to cover their costs can keep up the research: we'll appoint temporary teaching staff to cover them. Teaching mustn't suffer. Now I can imagine none of that particularly appeals to you'.

Ralph gave no answer, but thoughtfully made jottings in his notebook. The Rector changes tack slightly.

'You've just had a birthday, haven't you? Many happy returns. Mandatory retirement age doesn't mean anything anymore, of course. Which is good: 65's an arbitrary age. You've got plenty left to give. But there's a consequence to that. The system becomes – sclerotic. Less opportunity for us to bring on younger staff. Less scope for us to diversify the workforce. Even here, our profile needs work. We need to recruit more ethnic minority staff, as well as younger people. If the system had been like this in – 1970, was it? – when you started; well, you wouldn't have been appointed at all. Isn't it reasonable for us, when we reach that certain age, to want to make room for early career academics? "Shake all cares and business from our age, conferring them on younger strengths?"'

He's planned to drop that in, thought Ralph. *King Lear.* Look what happened to him.

The Rector pauses here. Ralph's silence is unnerving. Davies had expected more active resistance. He shrugs slightly, and decides to continue anyway.

'Now I have a proposal that might interest you. You're 65, been in service for over 40 years, so you would be on a full pension if you retired. That's over half your current income.

What about this: you retire. Three months notice. Take your pension. Then, we re-employ you, offer you a temporary three-year contract, research only, on half your current salary. You can do what you like. Go abroad. No strings attached. Pension plus salary, your income remains the same. Half from us, half from the pension scheme. Then you go. We'll make you Emeritus. Keep your library membership. You can still apply for research grants. You'll get invites to the degree ceremonies, and so on. It's a great opportunity for you. Become what you really want to be: an independent scholar. For three years we'll pay you for reading books in the sun. It's win-win. Mutually beneficial'.

He pauses and looks hard at Ralph, who still remains disconcertingly silent.

'Any thoughts?' asked Davies.

Ralph continues to make notes in the exercise book. He puts back his pen top, and gathers his papers. Then he stands up, says 'Thank you, Rector', and walks out.

&

As he walks down the corridor Ralph begins to prepare his defence. Automatically he marshals all the arguments supporting the existence of research posts. His research is high-profile, as measured by citations, and brings reputational benefit to the university. Experienced senior researchers act as research leaders, setting an example and mentoring younger researchers. The top-rated universities are always the research universities: there's no such thing as an excellent teaching-only institution.

Next, he wonders if his notes will be acceptable as evidence of age discrimination. The Rector had unwisely mentioned his birthday, which made it personal. The argument about making room for younger researchers was bullshit: you can't discriminate against one protected group in order to discriminate on behalf of another.

He would go straight back to his office and call an influential friend at union headquarters. Then a contact at the *Times Higher* to leak news of a compulsory redundancy programme being prepared at Blacksmith's. Then set up a meeting with the local union branch officers to get the ball rolling. Maybe he would go see his doctor and get a sick note: work-related stress. Medical evidence is always useful.

Some of the old excitement he used feel when embarking on a political campaign begins to resurge. There is the frisson of personal risk, usually exaggerated or imagined: he had never really put himself in any serious danger. There is the thrill of involvement in a fight, in itself perhaps small and inconsequential, but part of the progressive movement of history: a parochial squabble over teaching hours could be made to feel like a chapter in the world-historical revolution. Above all, there is an overwhelming conviction of the probability of victory. The Rector could say what he liked: university staff are virtually impossible to get rid of.

Then suddenly, in the middle of the corridor, he stops. Before him is a glass-fronted display case full of official notices and pictures of graduation ceremonies. Prominent among them, and already familiar to him, since it's been there for a few years, is a detached page from the college alumni magazine, with the image of a black woman in graduation cap and gown, under the banner headline: 'You don't have to be male, pale and stale to become an MP'.

One of the university's alumna had become a Labour MP, and the PR department had capitalised on her success to push a drive for diversity in recruitment. Unfortunately the gesture had backfired, when the MP had lost her seat following a criminal conviction for perverting the course of justice: she had tried to duck a speeding fine by passing it on to her brother. But the image remained powerful despite the undermining of its factual basis, and the poster had stayed in place.

Ralph had known the future MP when she was a student, a prominent member of the student Labour branch, and was very proud of her achievements. Indeed he had himself suggested using her as a role model in the advertising campaign. He had thought nothing of the slogan, finding it punchy and effective. When her reputation came under challenge, he had proselytised on her behalf, arguing that the charges must be slurs deriving from a right-wing plot.

But suddenly he sees those words again – 'male, pale, stale' – and realises, for the first time, that they apply to him. That's exactly how the Rector has portrayed him: the relic of an old, superseded epoch of white privilege, selfishly blocking the system and preventing the cleansing irrigation of new blood, an old imperial trophy preserving the colonial domination of white homogeneity. An old man, an emblem of white fragility, long past his shelf-life. A slow-burning fuse of anger, long dormant in his breast, suddenly flames into life, demanding action. He walks quickly back to his office, and picks up the phone.

Then something causes him to pause. The sun is streaming through the window. Outside it's a beautiful July day. He looks out of the window at the green tops of the London plane trees in Russell Square. He decides, quite against his character, to go outside and sit in the park to think.

&

Ralph sits on a bench and watches the bustle of activity around the park. He can't remember when he last did such a thing, and everyday normality seems new and strange. Young students sit around in groups, talking, laughing, chugging cans of cider and beer. Mothers push their kids past in giant pushchairs; he wonders when baby buggies became so big. And he sits there, with his grey hair and pale face, feeling like a white ghost, ignored, perhaps even unseen. The feeling of spectrality is so strong he imagines someone might come along and sit in his lap. No country for old men, perhaps. Male, pale and stale.

The meeting with the Rector has disturbed him more than he cares to admit. The bald, unashamed declaration that in the view of management Ralph is surplus to requirements has taken him by surprise. He has never thought of himself in this way, and here outside his comfort zone of tenure and protected status he begins to feel a sense of derealization, an almost physical perception of himself as dissolving, the molecules of his existence drifting apart and evaporating into the sunlit air. A droll colleague had once said, in a heated discussion about what constitutes a person, 'Ralph is not a person, he's a random collection of atoms being driven forward by history'. For the first time Ralph began to feel, enclosed within the witticism, a kernel of potential truth.

In the centre of the park is a network of fountains, concealed jets countersunk into the paving. The fountains are often, perversely, switched off by the council during hot weather to conserve water, just at the time when a cooling stream of water is most needed. Today however they are operating, and a bunch of children, already soaking wet, stands above the jets and wait for the sudden rush. When it comes, startling though expected, they scream and jump around, delighting in the deluge. The water literally bursts from the pavement, like the gush of a geyser from the grey ground, spurting and lancing and dancing in the air, rising and falling and thrusting up again.

Ralph watches the interplay of cascade and children, the screaming and the splashing, as the fountains seem to play themselves out, their flow diminishing, then sinking down till there is nothing but water running off into the drains, trundling and trickling and pooling in ponds. Again the children are still, standing there shivering in their wet clothes, silent but for the occasional shaken giggle, waiting for the water to renew.

Ralph thinks about the pipes, buried deep under the ground, resisting with closed valves that irrepressible pumping force. Then with a turning motion the invisible valves open, the water gushes forth, rushes up the pipes and breaks with a great spume of spray into the empty air. He can almost feel, beneath the surface of the earth, the pumping pressure of a fretful force, chafing to channel its passage to the light.

Something like that is happening within him, too; the growing pressure of some repressed power, held in check by tightly screwed valves. But he is not sure what it is. It ought to be a current of righteous indignant anger at the way he has been treated, a resolute political will to defend his rights and liberties, the taste for another battle with authority. But he feels nothing of this. In its place there is a sudden realisation that what he really wants, here and now, is personal freedom. Not political liberty, freedom of organisation, the right to protest: but the freedom to go somewhere else, to do something else, to be someone else.

Three years of getting paid for doing nothing? The fact that it's a bribe, an inducement designed to get rid of him, a longer-term financial saving for the university, makes no difference: it looks like an offer he can't refuse. He feels slightly ashamed of himself: surely he should fight this battle to the death? Confer with colleagues, make a formal complaint, seek redress, take the college to an industrial tribunal? Or at least play hard-ball, and negotiate for an even better settlement?

But he doesn't want to do any of this. He has already surrendered, given in to the sweet promise of deliverance. Again the fountains burst up from the pavement, and their rivulets run through his mind with the foam and the flurry of a surging stream. Again the children rush and splash through the jets of water, screaming and laughing and slapping their sides.

People say they retire to spend more time with their family. He looks forward to spending less time with his employer. He gets up from the bench, his decision made. He will accept the Rector's offer, apply for retirement and wait for re-employment. Then he can embark on the rest of his life.

Chapter Ten

Katla

'A vortex that shall bring
The world to that destructive fire
Which burns before the ice-cap reigns'
– T.S. Eliot, *Four Quartets*

Iceland, 935

Ulf had been working on Arne's farm for a year since their arrival. The work was hard, the hours long, but it was no more than he was accustomed to. After a few months he was used to both the routines and the laborious graft.

The longhouse stood at the centre of Arne's landholding on the upper edge of *Vik*. The building was timber-framed, with the weight of the roof resting on beams supported by pillars. The thick outer walls were constructed from a mixture of stone and turf, which served as insulation. At one end was the fire-room, which served as kitchen and source of heating. An enclosed bed-closet afforded private sleeping accommodation for Arne and his consort: the rest of the household bedded down in the main hall, sleeping on benches or on the floor. The house was always warm, but also filled with choking smoke, not all of which cleared through the vent in the roof. Two wings jutted out northwards from the main building, one housing the latrines, the other big storage barrels for preserving food through the winter. A smaller separate building housed the smithy.

To the south was the hayfield, surrounded by a rough dry-stone wall. The harvesting and storage of hay was a top priority, he had been instructed: the early settlers in Iceland had not stored enough to get them through the harsh winter, and all their animals had died. Arne had prudently extended his grass meadow as far as he could, maximising the crop.

Ulf had had to learn new skills in handling sickle and scythe. The longer tool was much harder to manage, and he never did succeed in mastering the effortless long round sweep of the blade, and the soft wet crunch of mown grass, accomplished by the older workers. The sickle was much easier, but the repetitive chopping motion inflicted blisters on his hands that would not heal, and stung with acute soreness in the biting winds. One old man, another of Arne's cousins, told him to piss on them, and though Ulf was sceptical that this was nothing more than a prank, he tried it, and the remedy seemed to work.

To the north of the longhouse were the animal sheds, built in the shelter of the sloping hills. The sheep were kept next to the meadow so they could be let out to graze in the spring and summer months. The cowshed adjoined it, and the cattle enjoyed their own enclosure. To the east was the pigsty; to the west a barn in which Arne stabled a few of the island's small horses, bred from the steeds imported by early settlers from Norway.

Every member of the farm community worked, and there was no specialization. Everyone was expected to turn his or her hand to anything. Hence on their first arrival Ulf was given a wooden shovel and instructed to turn over an area of soil close to the house for a vegetable patch. Accustomed to the soft wet soil of Denmark, he found he could make no impression at all on the obdurate dark dirt of Iceland, which seemed to be not only hard, but riddled with flinty stones and black volcanic ash. He chipped and hacked away, but to no avail, especially once the frosts began to take hold. Erik observed the boy's difficulties, and had a word with Arne. Ulf was put on the less arduous duty of mucking out the pigs. This was work he was used to, and here it had its upsides, since the pigsty was always warm, and the massive heap of composting shit he piled up in a corner of the yard also radiated its own heat. Far less pleasant was the associated job of shovelling up the household shit from the latrines and burying it beyond the wall. At times he would retch and gag over the stench, but he was a punctilious worker, and never failed at his task.

One day his father called him over from the milking-shed where Ulf was tugging persistently on the teats of a reluctant, refractory cow that kept trying to stamp its heavy hoof onto his foot, and told him to fetch his sheepskin from the house. Erik had expressed to Arne his interest in seeing the interior of the island, and they were to go on a trek some miles inland. Arne had said that he wanted to take a closer look at a nearby mountain, which he called by a strange name: 'Katla'.

Three horses were provided for them. These seemed to Ulf to be small in stature, but they were very strong, and coarse-haired to defend against the cold. Each was fitted out with a wood and leather saddle, with tall stirrups slung from long leather straps, and a rope bridle attached to an iron snaffle bit. The style of riding was unfamiliar to Ulf, and it took him some time to get used to it. The saddle, with its high pommel and cantle, was set far back on the horse, so the legs could be stretched out forwards in the stirrups. But his horse was patient and obedient, and soon he was confidently trotting behind Erik and Arne.

They followed a well-worn track across the foothills, passing by a lake that Arne said was called *Heidarvatn*, and began to climb upwards. Pressing up the steepness, they soon left the green lower slopes behind, and reached the edge of the ice-cap. Here they entered a track that threaded between the successive ice-waves of the glacier. As they ascended, they found themselves travelling across a bleak landscape of black gravel and dust. Ulf marvelled at the contrasts they had encountered in a mere half-day's travel, from fertile green lowlands, to the great grey glacier, and here at last this dark swarthy realm of black dust and ash.

'Surt's land', said Arne. Surt was the Fire-Giant, destined to lead his army against the Aesir at Ragnarok, the final battle between giants and gods.

At the summit Arne led them to the edge of a jagged crater. Currents of hot air wafted up towards them, bearing clouds of sulphurous gas. The interior was a great darkness, with the occasional fissure opening to emit bubbles of gas and puffs of black smoke. As his eyes grew used to the blackness Ulf began to perceive flashes of dull heat, as the bubbling lava turned and twisted into momentary visibility through the fracturing and re-forming crusts of cooling rock.

'What is it?' asked Erik, who had never seen anything like it.

'Heat. Gas. Melting rock'. Arne shrugged. 'The restless earth. You see why we call her Katla. She bubbles and boils'. He laughed. 'Like a kettle'.

The humour was not reflected in Arne's face. He seemed preoccupied as he gazed fixedly down into the crater. I'm sure he's hiding something, thought Ulf. He knows something he doesn't want us to know.

Arne roused himself from his reverie, and assumed his favourite role of story-teller. 'This is where it all began.[14] In the beginning. There', he said, pointing down the crater: '*Muspelheim*. And there'. Gesturing towards the glacier. '*Nifelheim*. And over there' – indicating the immense plain of black rock and ash – 'they say, is where it will happen, in the last days. *Ragnarok*. The final conflict. The twilight of the gods. Here the enmity between gods and giants will burst forth, like the fire you see below you.

'You know the tales. First, the *Fimbulwinter*, everlasting winter, without a spring. Darkness, ice, cold will grip the ground. All bonds will fail: fathers, brothers, sons, killing one another. The axe-age, the sword-age. No shield will remain unbroken. The great wolves, Fenrir and Garm, will catch up with the sun and the moon. Mountains will shake and crumble, valleys sink and fill. The great ash-tree Yggdrasill will be torn from its roots.

'Then here, right here, the fire-giants will come from *Muspelheim* and congregate. Surt, singed and charred, will lead them. The Frost Giants from *Nifelheim* will come sledding across the ice. Jormungand will rise from the sea, and unfurl his coils onto the land. Fenrir, his jaws stretched wide from earth to sky, will devour the sun. Then darkness. Endless night. And over the bridge of *Bifrost* they will go, the giants and the monsters, right to the doors of Asgard'.

Arne stopped himself, as if waking from a vision. 'Stories',

14 'The Seeress's Prophecy', *The Poetic Edda*, ed. Carolyne Larrington (Oxford: Oxford University Press, 1996).

he said, dismissively, disclaiming the intensity of his narrative. 'Old tales. Will it really happen?' He shrugged. 'Who knows. We won't live to see it. Come on, I'll show you one last thing before we go'.

Arne preceded them, leading his horse by the bridle, away from the rim and down the slope of the fire-mountain. When they reached the glacier he took a track leading around the mountain, and bade them follow. The track dived sharply downwards, on a steep slope where Ulf had trouble keeping his footing, and ended in a declivity, where Arne stopped, turned to them and stretched his arms demonstratively outwards towards the mountain.

The sight he revealed was astonishing. Beneath the fire-mountain, sculpted out of the glacier, was an immense cave, its interior fashioned entirely from ice. Over the entrance long sharp fingers of ice dribbled downwards, like the eyebrows of the giant Ymir, who lived in the grassless void of *Ginungagap*. Ulf could see, through the entrance framed by icicles, flowing curved walls that billowed inwards, studded with embossed ridges. The ice shone blue and green, a glassy cavern, shaped almost like the rib-cage of a whale. Through a big round hole in the cave's roof bright sunlight dropped directly down from above, illuminating the chamber with the light of a thousand torches.

'You see', said Arne, nodding approvingly. 'Hot rock, melted in the cauldron, flowed down and cut this cavern'.

As they rode back down the mountain, across the black lava fields, Ulf's mind revolved obsessively around the extraordinary things he had seen. The fiery crater, Katla, simmering and bubbling like a kettle, but a kettle full of molten rock, fed by fire from the earth's belly. Then the realms of thick-ribbed ice, and the vast ice-cavern beneath the mountain of fire. The barren, hopeless lava fields, covered in black dust and grey ash.

And he was utterly convinced that *Ragnarok* would truly be fought, as Arne had picturesquely described, out here. He had looked into the flaming heart of the mountain, and seen. Beneath the mountain was the portal to *Muspelheim*, the realm of Surte of the flaming sword, home of the Fire-Giants. Surrounding it was the glacier, *Jotunheim*, domain of the Frost Giants. And the great cave of ice, that hollow space beneath the mountain, seemed to him like *Ginungagap*, the abyss, the primordial void, lying between *Muspelheim* and *Nifelheim*, between the elements of fire and frost. From here everything came, in the beginning; and to here everything will return at the end.

All this explained the strange sounds that had at first startled him from sleep, and later formed the soundtrack of his dreams; and the hot springs and geysers he had seen bursting from the ground. Deep in the earth, dwarves were forging weapons for the last battle. Iron was being heated to incandescence from the fire of the earth, then hammered with a sonorous clanging on huge stone anvils, then thrust hissing white-hot into the waters of the mountain. Meanwhile the gods were quarrelling amongst themselves, and their anger shook the ground with tremors. All those noises of creaking and groaning, splitting and cracking, were caused by supernatural beings, active above and below the world of men. The island was alive.

And somewhere, among the far black mountains, streaked with white ice and snow, was Valhalla, whence Odin would lead his hosts of the dead. And there, on that flat green slope between the fire and the ice, was Vigrid, before Valhalla, the field of surging battle.

He saw it, like a living event, as clear as if it were happening. He saw Vigrid darken in the sun's almost extinguished rays, as the great wolf Fenrir gradually but inevitably devoured the sun. He saw Odin, resplendent as the sun, in his gold helmet plumed with eagles' wings, brandishing the great spear Gungnir, fearlessly confronting the foe. He saw the jaws of Fenrir gape, blasting fire like a furnace; and he saw Odin swallowed easily and whole, his brightness suddenly extinct, as the night devours the day. Frigg, Odin's consort, fainting helplessly from grief and terror, begged the gods to avenge her lord. Then Vidar, son of Odin, flung himself on Fenrir and prised open the huge jaws, holding down the wolf's fangs with his enchanted sandal that no flame could devour, and stabbed downwards into the fiery throat, in revenge for his father piercing the great creature's heart.

They quickened their pace down the slopes, as over the western sea the red sun touched the rim of the world. Darkness was falling quickly over Iceland, just as, in the end, darkness would bury the Aesir. And the world he knew would come to an end.

Chapter Eleven

Dover

'There are other places
Which also are the world's end'
– T.S. Eliot, *Four Quartets*

Putney, May 2016

Ralph is driving his old diesel Mercedes E-class southwards along Putney High Street. The car is ten years old, but having been barely used is still a smooth and energetic ride. He bought it when diesel was confidently proclaimed, by scientists advising government, as the saviour of air quality, a clean fuel that would mollify the adverse effects of climate change. Though his political education pre-dated climate change activism, and thus had not included the Green zealotry now an essential element of leftist ideology, so he had half-heartedly signed up to it, disposing of his old petrol-driven Jaguar in favour of 'Blue Efficiency'. In the interim the wheel had come full circle, and a diesel car is now regarded by the same scientists as a virulently toxic death machine capable of killing children as it passes. He wondered if the experts had ever admitted their error. In any case, the days of diesel were now coming to an end: within a few years London's Ultra-low Emission Zone would be extended to include his house, rendering the car liable to a daily charge if it moved an inch. He would have to invest in an electric car. In the meantime, polluting menace or not, he loved the Mercedes, and had used it much more since his semi-retirement.

He had accepted the Rector's offer, not without misgivings, and taken the deal. He found himself ostracised by some of his hard-left colleagues, who felt that he was a turncoat, selling out, caving in too easily to the Rector's pressure, giving up without a fight, accepting thirty pieces of silver in a mean transaction that would only make it easier for management to move on to the next target. He found it refreshingly possible to live without their approval. He is still enjoying the temporary sinecure of life with a salary but no conditions, paid to do whatever he wants. He had always imagined that retirement would provide the space he had always yearned for to complete some larger academic projects. He discovered that he had in fact had that space all along, and that it must have been for some other reasons, perhaps merely professional, that he had neglected these more ambitious tasks, in favour of frequent small-scale projects and commissioned works. Now he felt no further need to keep up the regular flow of peer-reviewed articles to feed the research assessment machine. But neither was he strongly motivated to write the big books he had always dreamed of writing: the books that would definitely resolve all key controversies about the Civil War, or for ever settle the vexed question of Shakespeare's political and religious affiliations.

Instead he threw himself more vigorously into politics.

Once outside the university, he found the political atmosphere of the whole country in turmoil, principally around the question of Britain's relationship with the European Union. The Conservative-Liberal Democrat Coalition Government, effective only in tarnishing both parties with the taint of compromise, had come to an ignominious end. In the 2015 General Election the UK Independence Party established its position as the third largest party, the Conservatives won a majority, and David Cameron promised a referendum on membership of the European Union.

The single issue that above all others was generating a toxically divided political scene was immigration. Ralph saw the popular appetite for severance from the EU largely as a manifestation of anti-immigrant prejudice. True, in his youth he had campaigned on the left to block Britain's entry into the Common Market. But things had moved on, the issue of immigration had risen up the political agenda, and he felt obligated to play his part.

So he had joined the grass-roots organisation Open Borders, which combined campaigning for continued membership of the EU, and its attendant freedom of movement, with activist involvement in the efforts of migrants from outside the bloc to cross the Channel and enter Britain to claim asylum. Ralph's involvement was more on the ideological front, agitating for the benefits of immigration, and exposing the UK independence movement as a right-wing conspiracy rooted in racism and xenophobia. Other sections of the organisation took the struggle onto the front line, and worked in the infamous Calais Jungle, where thousands of migrants from Africa and the Middle East and Asia congregated in squalid conditions to smuggle themselves onto lorries, or

Eurostar trains, or even attempt the perilous Channel crossing in flimsy dinghies. Open Borders staff embedded themselves into the Jungle, offering general advice to migrants on Human Rights, and more covertly making suggestions about the best ways of getting across. Migrants, most of whom had destroyed any papers they may have had, were schooled in the most effective ways of making an asylum case, by claiming for instance to be under eighteen, or from a country officially at war, or fearing persecution as a consequence of their religion or sexual orientation. They were advised to join a local church and publicly convert to Christianity; or to acquire tattoos of a religious or atheist character, indelible marks that would inevitably compromise their safety in the Muslim countries they hailed from.

It was a messy business, Ralph had to admit. Migrants were only able to reach northern France by paying people smugglers to traffic them across borders. So in this respect Open Borders was assisting in a criminal enterprise. The Dublin Declaration stipulated that migrants should claim asylum in the first safe country they reached. But these people had travelled through Greece, Italy, France, without any attempt to legitimise their status. Their gaol was Britain, where they hoped to find much better conditions, financial support, housing, the absence of any identity verification system, and in Britain's cities large ethnic minority areas where their language was spoken, work was available and they could easily disappear. Failed asylum claims were rarely acted on, and any attempts to deport illegal stayers were blocked by Open Borders lawyers invoking the European Declaration of Human Rights. Successful deportation of illegal immigrants was virtually unheard of, and the migrants massing on the other side of the Channel knew this. But to Ralph the end justifies the means. Whatever their motivations, people fleeing from war, persecution, economic privation, should be given the opportunity of a safe haven, and a better life.

&

Traffic is heavy through the High Street and past the station, but eases as he began to coast up the hill. The green spaces of common begin to appear on either side, Putney on the left, Wimbledon on the right. He reaches the A3 roundabout, and filters onto the dual carriageway heading south. Soon to his left he passes Putney Vale Cemetery, where a few months before he attended the funeral of a friend and colleague, Robert, with whom he had worked closely for many years, but in recent times had barely seen. Robert was on the Literature staff, but was as historically minded as Ralph was literary. The two had many interests and beliefs in common: Robert too came from a working-class background, and was an ardent socialist. The two were kindred spirits, politically aligned and with complementary academic skills. Robert was a brilliant innovator and enthusiast who sparked bright new ideas as readily as a dynamo generates power. But he was too restlessly energetic to follow through on ideas, and needed a partner who could apply and consolidate them into projects and publications. They exerted a deep and abiding influence on one another: Ralph found he was able to factor some of the Renaissance literature he had loved into his historicist outlook, and Robert's work benefited from the application of historical methods of research. Indeed, Robert was one of the first scholars to propose treating literary works as historical documents that should always be studied in their earliest format and context, not modernised and annotated as in modern editions. In the College Arms, or the Museum Tavern, they would drink craft ale, and hatch radical schemes, such as the notorious 'Real Shakespeare' series, which produced the texts of Shakespeare's plays in all the variant textual versions, including the so-called 'Bad Quartos', alongside plays controversially ascribed to Shakespeare, thus breaking the link between author and works, and returning the texts to their historical context.

Ralph and Robert remained close collaborators, even when the latter took another job at UCL. But a breach between them occurred, effected by the same catalyst that divided Ralph from his son Martin: the catastrophe of 9/11. Robert was horrified by the event, and severed his relations with friends and colleagues who took the anti-American view, some of them coming close, in Robert's eyes, to defending the terrorists. In that great tectonic shift of political opinion, they found themselves on separate plates, sliding inexorably away from one another. The rift with Robert affected Ralph more than the disagreement with his son. For many years they barely spoke, and never worked together again. Ralph was aware, through mutual friends, that Robert had become plagued by various health problems, and sent him the occasional 'Get Well Soon' message. But when Robert was taken into hospital following a stroke, Ralph made no attempt to see him. The next thing he knew, he was standing beside a deep grave in Putney Vale, looking down at a wicker coffin that held the remains of his friend, trying to hear a weak-voiced priest shouting inaudible words of consolation into a cold east wind.

After the funeral Ralph dreamed about Robert. The two

were Arctic explorers, bundled in furs and carrying heavy packs, treading side by side across a great ice-floe. Glancing aside, Ralph can see only the outline of the bristling fur hood, and cannot see his companion's face. A sudden flurry of snow temporarily blinds him, and as suddenly clears. Looking sideways, he can see Robert in the distance, slowly moving away from him. A section of ice has broken off, and is floating into the distance. Robert raises a hand in valediction, and is gone.

&

Ralph concentrates on his driving as the traffic speeds up after the Kingston Roundabout. He takes the Hook Road, passing the monstrous Chessington World of Adventures, and joins the M25 around Leatherhead. Martin lives over to the west in Weybridge, but would be on his way to work now in the City, taking the South Western suburban commuter train to Waterloo. Ralph's destination lies to the south, into Kent, via the M26 and the M20; past Sevenoaks, and Maidstone, and Ashford; down to the very edge of the land: the Western Heights of Dover.

Chapter Twelve

Eruption

'Dust in the air suspended
Marks the place where a story ended'
– T.S. Eliot, *Four Quartets*

Iceland, 936

A mere two years after his arrival in Iceland, Ulf found himself once again on the wet deck of a boat, facing the grey-green swell of the sea, looking back at the white surf breaking against a fast-receding shoreline, compelled yet again to leave the place he had grown accustomed, even in so short a time, to call home.

It all began one morning in the previous year, when Ulf woke and looked through the window to find the sky black, and the sun turned to the colour of blood. He hurried outside, to find the entire household, family and workers, standing in the yard, staring up at the sky. Towards the sea the darkness was clearing a little, and light filtering weakly through, so they could just about see one another. Every face bore the same expression of anxiety and perturbation. Landwards everything was adumbrated by an impenetrable obscurity.

'What's happening?' he asked Erik, who gave no answer but shrugged towards Arne. Keeping his eyes fixed inland, Arne gave a one-word answer. 'Katla'.

Yielding no explanation, Arne set off briskly walking up the hill that rose above the village. Erik and Ulf followed him. Quickly they ascended the slope, and soon reached the edge of the cliffs that tower over *Vik.* From there they had a clear view right across the landscape towards the volcano. The sight was astonishing, and Ulf knew he would never forget what he saw that day.

The mountain was on fire. A pillar of flame surged up from Katla's cone, high enough to reach the top of the sky. Around the mountain the air was blood-red. The thick darkness of early morning had thinned to a grey haze, like a storm of dust, and the sun seemed to have no strength. The sky seemed viscous, almost solid, as if covered by a membrane, or a film of connective tissue. The air stank, replete with the sulphurous rotten-egg smell Ulf had encountered before, near geysers and hot springs. The everyday noises of cracking and splitting, fracturing and fissuring, creaking and groaning, were vastly amplified to a roaring cacophony of sound.

The men and the boy stood and stared. After a while the pillar of flame diminished, and was replaced by an immense mushroom cloud of dust and ash, that belched and burst, with a tremendous roar, from the crater, opened wide like a screaming mouth, or a gaping wound. The dust of the eruption was like a cloud, but solid, standing high above the mountain, buoyed up by its own strength. Flashes of lightning flickered and played within it, followed by crashings of thunder.

For days afterwards the twilight never really lifted, so there was little distinction between day and night. The sun remained blood-red, and all day long peered through the horizontal hazy air, stripped of its beams. At night the moon and stars were invisible. The air was full of dust, that fell continuously like rain, coating the earth's surface with a thick detritus of grey ash and black lava. After a time, as the heat of the eruption began to melt the ice of the glacier, the dust was replaced by rain, incessantly falling in thick curtains, blackened by ash, tasting of sulphur and toxic gas.

Erik had sent some men up to Katla with orders to approach as close as possible to the eruption, and to report back on what was happening. They returned hollow-eyed with dread. They had traversed the glacier and found the crossing perilous, since great crevasses were appearing without warning, huge lumps of ice breaking off and sliding down the slopes, rivers of ice suddenly gushing into green torrents. The lower slopes of the mountain were hot beneath the feet, and everywhere appeared, in the black soil, red gashes like wounds, gushing not blood, but fire. Big sink-holes appeared without warning, venting forth a hissing spray of steam. Then they could go no further, they said, since on the eastern side the mountain itself seemed to be melting, with a stream of molten rock cascading down the slopes, a great tide of hot lava, moving slowly but with an inexorable motion, carrying everything before it, destroying everything in its path.

Labour was impossible under this shadow of daytime darkness, so work was suspended. The household retreated to the longhouse, and the workers to the outbuildings where they slept. These people, whose lives were conducted almost entirely outdoors, found themselves seeking shelter within, as if the walls of a dwelling could protect them against the cataclysm outside. Arne ordered the fire to be built up, and they sat around the blaze in a circle. The light from the flames flickered and played over their white, scared features.

Then Arne spoke up, proposing that everyone there who had an opinion about what was happening, and how the community could deal with it, should say his, or her, piece. Had anyone seen anything like it before? Some had witnessed small eruptions in other parts of Iceland, but nothing like this. What could be the cause? Why, said some, the gods must be angry. We should make sacrifice to Thor, said one. No, said another, we should sacrifice to Loki: he rules the fire. Then, said another, to both gods: a ram for each.

One man, a relative newcomer who sat on the outside of the circle, his face downcast, suggested, in an almost inaudible voice, that they should sacrifice to Surte. The others looked shocked. Sacrifice to a *Jotunn*? They exclaimed. A giant: an enemy of the gods? Who ever heard of such a thing?

The man shrugged. 'His is the power', he said. 'He of the flaming sword. He dwells inside the mountain. And if the last battle is near', he went on, gathering confidence: 'who knows to whom the victory will fall?'

For a while there was silence. Then an elderly woman, a widowed aunt of Arne's whose name was Gudrun, moved to the front ring of the circle and stared into the fire. Framed by long white hair, her lined and sun-beaten face spoke of experience and wisdom. Gudrun knew all the songs and sagas, and often sang them to the assembled company. She averred that the old prophecies were coming true.

'All this has been foretold', she said, 'by the prophetess, when she was questioned by the All-Father himself.[15] The seeress told of the beginnings, the birth of the giants, in a time when there was no earth or sky and no grass, only a yawning chaos. She told of the origins of the sun and the moon, and the making of Midgard, when the ground was grown over with grass, and the sun shone bright on the stone-hall. And she told of the origins of the Aesir, the beautiful and powerful race of gods. They created the dwarves, and named them. Then came the birth of humanity, the man and the woman, Ash and Elm, born in weakness, destiny as yet unshaped. Yggdrassil came into being, the giant ash-tree, its roots stretching down to the earth's core, its branches brushing the heavens. From the tree's branches fell the dews of the valley.

'Then the Fates came into the world, three girls who knew and understood everything, laid down the law, determined destiny. She told, the prophetess, of the first war, when Odin hurled a spear into the host of the Vanir, and Thor struck the blow that burst all bonds, ruptured all promises and pledges.

'Then Odin demanded that the prophetess tell him of the future, for he knew that she was supremely wise, saw widely around the world, and possessed the spirit of divination. On her he bestowed gifts, necklaces and rings, to persuade her to speak. So she told him everything. She told of the death of Balder, slain with a branch of mistletoe by the blind god Hod, of the vengeance of Thor and the grief of Frigg. She told how the offspring of Fenrir, father of wolves, would be born to the old woman who sat in the Iron Wood, and that one of them, Garm, was destined to be the snatcher of the moon. She told of a fearful river, deadly as knives and swords, that

15 'The Seeress's Prophecy', *The Poetic Edda*, ed. Carolyne Larrington (Oxford: Oxford University Press, 1996).

would flow through a poisoned valley. She told of a darkness that would fall over the hall, and of poisoned rain that would drip through the roof-vents. She saw traitors and murderers wading through torrents, the serpent Nidhogg sucking on the corpses of men, the wolf devouring the bodies of the slain.

Gradually the old woman came to seem indistinguishable from the seeress whose story she told, possessed by her narrative, rapt in a poetic ecstasy. 'It is all there in the prophecy of the seeress, which I learned from my mother, and she from hers. It is wisdom as old as time, and it foretells of time's end. Of how the wolf Garm will snatch the moon, devour the lives of men, redden the gods' dwellings with crimson blood. The sun will become black, summer after summer, and cold so bitter that men cannot breathe the freezing air.

'And then will come the doom of the gods, the mighty gods, the victory-gods. *Ragnarok.* Brother will fight against brother, and sisters' sons will violate the kinship-bond. Then will come the axe-age, the sword-age, the wolf-age, and the world will plunge headlong into darkness.

'Yggdrasil shudders. Garm bays loudly before the Gnipa-cave. The great serpent will break free from the waves. A ship will bear the troops of Muspelheim, and Loki will steer them.

'See, she cried, pointing through the window to the darkness outside. 'Surt comes from the north, destroyer of Yggdrasil, the flames of the mountain gleaming from his sword. Odin will fight against Fenrir, and the wolf will devour the god. Vidar will kill the wolf, and Thor will kill *Jormungand,* and the god will die from the serpent's poisoned bite. The sun will turn black, the land will sink into the sea, steam will rise up in conflagration, and hot flame will burn heaven itself. It is the end', she cried, exhausted from her narration. 'It has come, exactly as it was foretold. And no man can stop it'.

In the days that followed, the community made their sacrifices, and said their prayers to Thor, and Odin, and Loki, and even, in desperation, to Surt. But the eruption continued. The ash-cloud continued to surge from the volcano's yawning crater, the foul-smelling ash continued to disperse and to fall from the sky, coating everything with a grey film. The acid rain continued to fall. After a while the animals, ingesting toxic sulphides from the contaminated fields, began to die. Ulf was one of the first to come across such a victim: searching the hillside for wandering sheep, he stumbled over the corpse of a ewe who had fallen among the thick tussocks of grass, and lay on her side, black lips stretched wide open, glassy eyes bulging from her head, white fleece maculated by black lava dust. Soon entire herds were succumbing to the poison of the mountain. Ulf watched his father grow increasingly worried. Without livestock they would not be able to survive another winter.

As the weeks and months wore on, the people of the community began to realise that their ordeal was not going to end any time soon. Something must be done, but no-one could agree on a course of action. Then word came from the west, where most of the other settlers lived, calling a gathering of the *Althing* at *Thingvellir,* which lay to the north-east of *Vik*.

Ulf had attended the *Althing* earlier that year at midsummer. This annual assembly had been established only a few years before their arrival, and had no equivalent back home in

Denmark. Every year the chief leaders or representatives, the *gothar*, of the different settlements met together at the summer solstice to hear the law recited by the law speaker, the wisest man of the commonwealth, to agree on legislation to govern the community of the island, and to arbitrate on disputes. All free men could attend the assembly, and many did, bringing their families with them. Anyone who had a complaint or a grievance or a disagreement would attend and seek redress or resolution. The *gothar* judged such matters, and their decisions were final and binding.

Ulf was fascinated by the proceedings, even though he only partially understood what was going on. The system he was used to was much simpler: the supreme authority was the king, or the lord. There were laws, certainly, but it was never clear who made them, or where they came from. Justice was dispensed by the proper authority, and people either submitted or rebelled. Here in Iceland the people gathered together in a kind of political community or congregation, and made or interpreted the laws for themselves. Their leaders did not assume position by virtue of rank, or wealth, or status, but earned it by their wisdom and their capacity to pacify disagreements. And the system, though still in its infancy, clearly worked. Here in Iceland there were no blood-feuds, no strife between families or clans. Crime was rare, and malefactors severely punished by execution or banishment, which invariably meant quitting the island, since there was no place to live, and no means of living, for one who had placed himself outside the community.

A small group of the men and women of *Vik* were chosen by the people to travel to *Thingvellir* and represent the community. Arne was chosen, and Erik, so Ulf accompanied them. The journey would take several days. As they rode north-west, the devastation caused by Katla was painfully in evidence. The pervading stench of sulphur hung over everything, making the world seem like an outpost of Hell. They rode across miles and miles of lava desert, grey and gravelled, strewn with misshapen lumps of rock. Not a single tree broke the monotony of the plain that seemed like a piece of the underworld flung by deep geological trauma to the earth's surface. Craters and domes displayed the wounds of cracks and fissures. Everywhere the same barren landscape, on which nothing grew except scrubby moss and lichens, struggling to find life among the black lava.

At last they entered the valley of *Thingvellir*. Between the tall cliff of the *Logberg*, the Stone of Law, and the broken lava ramparts that sloped down to the lake-shore, an immense square platform of dark volcanic rock was thrust up from the earth to form a natural rostrum. Above, the craggy pinnacle of the *Logberg* towered into the sky. Across the blue waters of the lake, black peaks were humped under dark grey clouds.

When all were arrived, the meeting was called to order and the Law-speaker mounted the platform to recite the law. The assembly listened in silence, their faces downcast and hopeless. They seemed to find no comfort or reassurance in the lengthy exposition of a legal code.

Eventually the Law-speaker invited the *gothar* to advise the assembly. Man after man climbed onto the platform and said his piece. One counselled the islanders to stay put. The eruption could not last much longer: there was not that much smoke and fire left in the bowels of the earth. Everyone in Iceland has suffered hardship and privation, just to reach the island's shores. Work here is hard, the winters cruel. But we have survived. Many of us came here fleeing from vengeance, or persecution, and no longer had a home to return to. Could we contemplate starting again, roaming the seas once more, ready to colonise another, perhaps even less hospitable place? Let every man stand fast, with his family, and wait it out. Sacrifice to the gods, and they will help us.

Another man stood up and proposed a mass migration to the north-west of the island. The prevailing northerly winds would carry the ash-cloud to the south, leaving the upper reaches of the island clear. Everyone knew that it was colder up there, and so harder to winter over. But cold was better than poisonous air; snow better than toxic smoke; ice better than fire.

Another argued that the whole population of Iceland should gather their armour and weapons, fit out their ships and form themselves into a great army. We are a warlike people, he said, and here we have become idle through years of peace. Let us sail back to Norway or Denmark in force, and challenge Harald Fairhair, or Henry the Fowler, or any other king. Let us do what our fathers did, fight for land and treasure. Take back our homes, take back our lands.

Lastly rose one who advised that the islanders should indeed convene a fleet, but sail to the west, in search of another land. Stories abounded of voyagers such as Erik the Red, who had found another island to the north-west, bigger than Iceland, free from inhabitants, swarming with whales and seals, foxes and hares, walrus and bears, ripe for colonisation and settlement. Some told of Erik's son, named Lief Erikson, who it was said sailed even further to the west, and came across a fertile country, of white beaches and rolling wooded hills, a land of forests and lakes, of rivers heaving with running salmon, where berries grew fat in the warm sunshine. They called it '*Vinland*', the wine country. He for his part would wish to take his family and his ships, and travel there.

The talk went on and on, reaching no conclusion. There was no unanimity among the *gothar*, and no supreme leader to decide on behalf of the people. The result was difference, disagreement, irresolution. In the end the Law-speaker returned to the *Logberg* and advised every man there to make his own decision, and to act accordingly. Inconclusively the Assembly broke up, and everyone prepared to return home.

As they rode back to *Vik*, Arne and Erik spoke earnestly together. Ulf stayed close to his father so he could hear what they were saying. At last Ulf realised the true significance of Arne's reticence when confronted with questions about the land: the possibility of such a disaster had clearly always lain at the back of his mind. The two men seemed with great reluctance to be rejecting the idea of staying in Iceland, and reconciled to leaving behind everything they had built. Neither could contemplate returning to Denmark. The fabled lands spoken of were clearly not calling out to them: Arne had heard of the big island to the west, which some called Greenland, but that it was uninhabitable. He had also heard the stories of Vinland, but did not believe them. They spoke of Ireland, and Scotland. But Arne knew of Danes who had settled in England, and believed they might find a welcome there. Erik concurred: at least they would be safe from the environmental disaster that was turning Iceland into a land fit only for giants.

Let them keep it. We will make our homes elsewhere.

Chapter Thirteen

White Cliffs

'Between the hither and the farther shore'
– T.S. Eliot, *Four Quartets*

Dover, 2016

A winking sequence of red brake lights heralds a slowing, backing up and eventual stoppage of the traffic, as Ralph reaches the final stretch of the A2 leading into Dover. There must be some kind of hold-up ahead, probably an accident. He opens the window, reclines in his seat, and rests his elbow on the sill. There is no hurry. Over the green chalk downland he can see the caerulean blue of the sea. A breeze through the window bears the salt smell of the ocean.

After a brief pause the cars in front start to inch slowly forward. He can see the blinking blue lights of a police car about half a mile ahead. There is a lane closure. He nears the point of obstruction and steers the car into a contra-flow. The left-hand side of the carriageway is completely blocked. He can see a dozen or so police officers in yellow high-viz jackets, standing in the roadway, and at their feet a similar number of people sitting on the ground, also wearing high-viz jackets, but coloured orange. Some are handcuffed. A man is sitting in the middle of the road, his hands touching the floor, his fingers spreadeagled, while police officers bend down in an apparent attempt to loosen his grip. As the car slowly passes, Ralph looks across to the left and is surprised to see that the group of protestors is characterised by one common feature: old age. He notices a preponderance of white hair; creased, sunburnt faces; a stiffness of gait as they attempt to sit down or get up from the road. Good God, he thinks. They're all my age.

He realises he is lucky to have come in at the end of this incident. Recently a splinter organisation from the millenarian climate activist group Extinction Rebellion, with the bizarre title of 'Insulate Britain', had embarked on a campaign of obstructive road-blocks, targeting the main motorways and traffic hubs. This detachment had clearly decided to blockade the Port of Dover. Their tactic was to glue themselves to the road, making it as difficult as possible for the police to remove them. Their objective was to force the government to pay immediately for the insulation of all Britain's dwelling-places.

Ralph regarded the group and their activities with scepticism. They seemed to consist entirely of middle-class zealots possessed by an apocalyptic conviction of imminent global disaster, but single-mindedly dedicated to a parochial preoccupation with something as trivial as domestic insulation. There was not a cat in hell's chance of their demands being met, and their tactics were guaranteed to alienate public sympathy, since the very people they appeal to are ordinary folk, going about their business, sitting fuming in their cars, or waiting for delayed deliveries, or anxiously looking out for the ambulance that is stuck somewhere out on the road. The protesters managed to waste a lot of police time, but that was about it. This was not serious politics, but rather virtue-signalling middle-class protest. He reached the end of the contra-flow and pulled back onto the carriageway. Was his rented house insulated? He wasn't sure. Certainly he was no more concerned with the matter now than he had been before.

Nearing the town, he takes a right and joins the A256 for the Ferry Terminal. His destination lies above the harbour, among the old fortifications that top the Western Heights. But he is early, and it is not a place you want to hang around for too long before your appointed time. So he overshoots his goal, and heads down South Military Road towards the sea, passing the ruins of the old Knights Templar church on the right, and parking up above a shingle beach separated from the road by a railway line.

Leaving the car, he walks across an iron pedestrian bridge and onto a narrow strip of sand. This is Shakespeare Beach, lying at the foot of Shakespeare Cliff. He always tries to spend a little time here when in this part of the world: it is one of his favourite places. He is particularly fond of the cliff because of its spurious association with Shakespeare's *King Lear*. By tradition this is the cliff to which Edgar leads the blind Gloster, and from which the old Duke believes he has tumbled. He glances up at the clifftop, and imagines an old man, kneeling in the grass, his son standing over him, leaning down to whisper in his ear the compassionate lies that will both delude and save him. Then stretching out his arms, Gloster pitches forward into imagined space, tumbling down those terrifying imaginary cliffs of fall, those steep mind-mountains, landing where he started from, and knowing the place for the first time. His blind eyes stare wildly at a place he can suddenly see, and a son he suddenly recognises as his.

Ralph stands under the tall buttress of chalk cliff and gazes across the Channel. This is the closest point to the continent, the shortest crossing. Channel swimmers starting from Calais land up here. He shields his eyes from the sun and squints across at the coastline of France. He enjoys the liminal sensation of standing on a border, that contested space between the United Kingdom and the rest of the world. For him it represents primarily a point of exit, the portal to Europe, gateway to the world, the embarkation point for the ferries that had often taken him from the terminal away to his left, shipping him from suffocating insularity to cosmopolitanism, internationalism, liberty.

It is also the primary point of entry, not only for the returning traveller, but for the immigrant. Here, thanks to the free movement of labour entailed in membership of the European Union, incessant flows of people from all European nations come into Britain, bringing a diversity of culture, importing new ideas, other languages, new and different experience, enriching and strengthening both the local economy and the national culture. And here other immigrants arrive from much greater distances, clutching their visas, from the continents of Asia and Africa and Latin America, to work in British industries and services, to join established families, bringing gaiety and colour and vibrancy to a stilted and stultifying national life.

And here also is the point of arrival for those seeking to enter the country illegally, smuggled onto trains and lorries, or risking the perilous Channel crossing in flimsy rubber craft, driven from their homes by war or famine or persecution, seeking a better life for themselves and their children. A few miles out to sea, Ralph can glimpse the small red speck of a migrant boat, crowded with yellow life-jackets and dark heads, drifting on the shining water, while a Border Force vessel slides slowly alongside, ready to take them on board and bring them safely to shore. Further away a French patrol boat, which has shadowed the migrants into British waters, making no attempt to detain and arrest them, is turning back towards home. He glances again across the Channel towards Calais, where his comrades from Open Borders would be working patiently in the Jungle to help other asylum seekers prepare for their voyage. A second migrant vessel is making its way towards Britain from the direction of Calais. The French patrol boat glides past on its way home, red white and blue pennon fluttering insouciantly from its mast, apparently indifferent to the illegal traffic flourishing alongside its smooth passage.

Ralph reflects for a moment on the mindset of the protestors who had delayed his journey. Insulate Britain? God knows Britain was insular enough, and needed no further attenuation of its island status. He didn't suppose any of the elderly do-gooders he had seen would be aware of the pun in their chosen title, or fully cognisant of the symbolic significance of their efforts to block the circulation of goods and people that was the life-blood of a global nation. He was familiar enough from his own political history with their methods and their tactics. The only way to compel people to understand a system is to foul the system up, stop it from doing its job. Strike to withhold labour, forcing people to reflect on what labour really is. Picket a factory to stop its goods and materials getting out and in, to highlight the structure of exploitation on which it depends.

But an attempt to blockade the Port of Dover, to throttle the conduit that permits free movement of people in and out of the country, seemed a benighted objective, and of a piece with that Luddite obsession with reversing industrial progress that seemed characteristic of climate change activism. This is what many of them stood for: restore clean air, decarbonise, reduce global temperatures, by stopping people from travelling. No more driving, no more flying. Less production, less consumption. They were anti-capitalist, but their whole campaign seemed based on a misunderstanding of Marxist teleology, in which the arc of history moves from primitive accumulation to capitalism to the dictatorship of the proletariat. If Extinction Rebellion had their way, the nation would slide back centuries to a peasant economy in which the workers, deprived of the organisation rendered possible by urbanisation and industrialisation, would have even less power than they do now.

He sits down on a rock and swivels to conduct a panoramic gaze around the seascape before him, from the long promontory of the ferry terminal to the left, around the blue horizon, to the undulating line of cliffs that weaves towards Folkestone. The white cliffs of Dover. He first heard of them, as did every kid of his generation, in the husky voice of Vera Lynn, voicing that poignant fantasy of an unchanged utopia to which Britons, leaving home to fight for their country, could always return. In fact there never had been, and never would be, bluebirds over the white cliffs of Dover, since bluebirds are native to North America, and Utopia remains nowhere. He first saw the cliffs in war films about the Battle of Britain, brightly-coloured images of camouflage-green Spitfires, badged with the bright RAF roundel, chasing Swastika-branded Messerschmits backwards and forwards over that long candid escarpment.

And here lay the huge symbolic significance of the white cliffs in traditional British culture: as a line of defence, a bulwark. He thinks of John of Gaunt's image of England as a precious stone, set in a silver sea, the cliffs like a wall defensive to a house, the sea a moat protecting the dwelling against the envy of less happier lands. 'This blessed plot, this earth, this realm, this England'. But instead of providing a reliable symbol of defence, the white cliffs have instead served as a collection point for national anxieties around invasion, occupation, conquest.

In Shakespeare's time, the age of the Armada, and in 1940, the age of Hitler, the symbolism of Dover cliffs was inseparable from fear of the invader. This rump of land, exposed and protruding out into the sea, has always represented an exposure to the dangers of incursion: from the Counter-Reformation troops of Spain, from Napoleon's troops, or from German-occupied France. The insular British mind, gazing across the narrow straits towards that threatening point of Europe that pokes aggressively towards the soft underbelly of Britain – so close, narrow enough to swim across or transit in a fragile rubber dinghy – easily accessible, wide open, undefended – cannot but apprehend the coastal neighbour as something to be feared and mistrusted. These south coast cliffs provided British culture with its most characteristic national image of vulnerability, exposure, openness to foreign invasion.

But, as he knew from his research, the mythological status of the white cliffs of Dover is far more ancient than 1940. Before modern historiography, Dover represented what anthropologists call a 'spot of origins', a geographical location regarded by legend and tradition as the point of a nation's inception. Such places engender 'myths of origin', narratives that seek to explain a country's evolution and place in history. The medieval historians traced the ancestry of their national populations and their monarchies to the fall of Troy, and the dispersal of the Trojan princes. Geoffrey of Monmouth claimed that Britain was founded by Brutus, a descendant of Aeneas. Holinshed's *Chronicles* describe this incursion as a conquest, since Brutus' friend Corineus had to overthrow the island's aboriginal inhabitant, the giant Gogmagog: *by reason whereof the place was named long after the Fall of Gogmagog, but afterwards it was called the Fall of Dover.*

Always the same pattern in these mythical charters: invasion, conquest, colonisation. A nation begins when a stronger force, a superior civilisation, proves sufficiently powerful to subjugate the native population and possess the island. Dover has always been the point of entry through which the invader enters in a violent incursion that entails a supersession, a transplanting and renewal. The legendary Brutus brought a classical civilisation, *Nova Troia*, the New Troy, to an island occupied only by a primitive giant, just as the Romans brought their language, their writing, their technology and their democracy to Dark Age Britain.

Successive waves of immigrants continued to arrive, and to shape the nation by the influence of their diverse cultures. The Anglo-Saxons came from the Germanic territories; the Vikings from Scandinavia; the Normans, displaced Northmen, from Northern France. That point of entry around Dover, source of the nation's identity, may seem simply the weakest point of the territory's physical defences. But it is also a source of strength, the point of entry for the immigrant who comes to these shores bearing the inestimable gifts of ideas, culture, knowledge, experience. Think of the Europeans who imported the spirit of the Renaissance: the Italians, who gave England its poetry and architecture and art; the Huguenot Flemings who brought their advanced technologies and crafts. And later came the Indians, the Irish, the Africans, the Germans, the Russian Jews. Enriching culture, broadening experiential horizons, opening minds. Some of the greatest ideas of the modern age – socialism and psychoanalysis for example – flourished in the work of Jewish emigrees like Marx and Freud.

He recalls how these ideas came to a head in the 1980s over the Channel Tunnel. Europhiles welcomed the link; xenophobes ranted about the dangers from rabies, terrorism, illegal immigration. Indeed it took a century from its first proposal for the tunnel to be built. It was here, right beneath his feet, that the first attempt was made to drill a tunnel between England and France, with pilot shafts bored on both sides of the Channel. Under the shingle beach, in 1881, a seven-foot boring machine dug some 2000 meters under the sea towards Calais. But Britain was not ready for her precious virgin white cliffs to be penetrated by a foreign invader, and a political clamour around national security killed the project stone dead for a hundred years. It was not until the 1980s that agreement to build the Channel Tunnel was finally reached.

Invasion and defence are the signature themes of Dover's landscape. Ralph recrosses the iron bridge, returns to the car, and drives a little way back up Military Road, towards the old fortifications that sit atop the Western Heights. He pulls into a left turn, following the juxtaposed and incongruous signs for 'English Heritage Western Heights Trail' and 'Immigration Removal Centre', and drives up the steep hill. Here he approaches the pentagonal complex of forts that date back to the American War of Independence, and assumed particular significance during the Napoleonic Wars. This rhomboid of land, the Drop Redoubt, cut off by deep ditches, once crossed by closable pivoting bridges, links to another fort to the east, the

Citadel, where the Immigration centre is housed. The whole area is a network of strongpoints and trenches designed to hold off and halt any enemy advance. Below this lofty vantage point lies the harbour, its piers and jetties clustered with small boats. The fortifications here were used for military purposes throughout later centuries, up to the Second World War when they housed a unit of commandos, whose role in the event of invasion would be to destroy all shipping in the harbour below. After the war the redbrick, barracks-like building of the Citadel briefly became a prison, and thereafter a Borstal, one of the old detention centres for young offenders.

And it is here, on this site that since Roman times has been the haunt of soldiers, prisoners, juvenile delinquents – a place of military defence, incarceration, legal detention – that the British state has chosen to locate its centre for the holding of refugees, its title of 'Immigration Removal Centre' indicating clearly enough that they would not be expected to stay for very long.

Ralph parks up, leaves the car and heads towards the grey, featureless building, more like a prison than a welcome centre. Bored-looking security guards challenge him at the door, and he shows them an official letter from the Home Office. He signs in, and is given an orange wristband to mark his visitor status. At a checkpoint he is instructed to empty his pockets. Then he is shown to a locker room where he has to deposit his wallet, keys and phone. At a second gate another guard opens up and tells Ralph to walk along the yellow painted path. 'Don't leave the path', he shouts after Ralph. 'Where the hell else can I go?' he wonders. At the end of the path he reaches the Visitor Centre, and is subjected to more security checks. His photo is taken, his wristband inspected and logged, in case he should try to switch it with an inmate.

Finally he is told to take a seat in the visiting room. This is a large space like a school hall, but set up with tables positioned far apart, suggesting a prison visiting centre rather than a school parents' evening. There is a coffee machine in the corner, with a few dirty cups left around it. Ralph can now here the chattering of many voices, including those of children, as the inmates queue to be admitted. People begin to file in. He waits for a quarter of an hour, though there is no explanation for the delay. At last the person he is here to visit enters through security on the other side of the room.

Ralph is here to meet an asylum seeker he has been assisting remotely for some time. His name is Salam Hassan. Salam is the son of one of the Iraqi Communist Party members Ralph had helped during the 1980s. When Salam arrived in Dover, discovered hiding under the tarpaulin cover of a lorry, he had given Ralph's name, obviously received from his father, as a friendly contact in England. He had given his age as sixteen. This is the first time Ralph has met him in the flesh.

Salam looks around, identifies Ralph sitting at one of the tables, and walks over to join him. The inmates wear high-viz sashes to distinguish them from civilians. The room is filling up with visitors and inmates, beginning to echo with animated conversation. The centre houses refugees mainly from the east and south: some South Asians, many men of Arabic appearance, and darker-skinned immigrants from North Africa. The surly guards look on with indifference. They are all white: the inmates all people of colour.

Salam sits opposite Ralph and gives him a broad smile, showing very white teeth. Up close, Ralph can see that Salam is no more sixteen then he is, and has given a false age. He's more like twenty, a handsome youth with thick, wavy black hair and brilliant dark eyes. Home Office staff are obliged to accept the age provided by the asylum seeker, and are not permitted to seek any further verification.

'Good to see you, Ralph', says Salam, his English impeccable, with hardly a trace of an accent.

'How are they treating you? asked Ralph, looking around at some emotional scenes between elderly people and their younger relatives, or between young couples hoping to be reunited.

Salam shrugged. 'It's OK. The food's not great. I watch telly a lot. Play a bit of ping-pong. Wait for the next meal'. He laughed. 'I've been in worse places. I just need to get out of here. Get back to my studies. Just live a normal life in England'.

'There's good news on that score. I've been taking advice from our lawyers. They think you have a fair case'.

Salam's father, Omar, had lived in England for twenty years, and become a resident. He returned to Iraq after the fall of Saddam. He had died suddenly when Salam was a baby. The boy's story is that he was kidnapped from a nursery in Baghdad by Islamic State militants, who forced him to serve as a child soldier. They had taught him how to use weapons, even how to cut throats, indoctrinated him with their fanatical version of Islam, and plied him with drugs. He had been involved in battles with American forces, he claimed, and had shot at people, but did not know if he had killed anyone. He hated the life, he said, and as soon as he could manage, he contrived to escape, living in a refugee camp to avoid official attention. A family took him in, and with them he had travelled through Europe to France, where he had smuggled himself onto a lorry bound for Britain.

'I've made contact', Ralph continued, 'with a volunteer group called Seaweed. Heard of them?' Salam shook his head. 'They visit people here who don't have friends, find families willing to take them on, to help them get settled when they're released. They think they've found a family willing to take you. I've made representations to the Home Office, telling them your father was a victim of political persecution, and you were sucked into ISIS long before you knew what you were doing. That should be enough to swing it. You should be out in a month'.

Salam reaches the across the table to clasp his hands. A nearby guard raps on the table to stop them from making physical contact. Ralph doesn't think there is any such rule here, but the guard is probably used to working in a prison. 'Ralph', said Salam. '*Habib*. You don't know how much this means to me. I will be eternally grateful'.

Ralph smiles in return. 'Happy to help. For your father. And for you'.

Ralph makes his way back through the tedious security process, surrenders his wristband, collects his belongings from the locker. Once outside he takes a moment to breathe the sea air, and look down across the Port of Dover. To his left he can see the white cliffs meandering westwards. To his right is the forbidding red-brick façade of the Immigration Removal Centre, and beyond, rugged Ministry of Defence training land. The Channel is full of activity, with a multiplicity of ships passing one another on the calm seas, criss-crossing between England and France, or navigating the busy shipping lanes on their way to the Mediterranean or the North Sea. Ships that pass, and people who come and go. This is his England, global, intersectional, inclusive: welcoming to the stranger.

Chapter Fourteen

Exile

'The sea has many voices'
– T.S. Eliot, *Four Quartets*

North Sea. 934

Once again the Danes were at sea, this time in the depths of winter, their sails tattered by tempests, their boats assailed by storms. They had assembled a small flotilla of ships to carry that remnant of the community that wished to sail south to England. Dispersed between the boats were around a hundred islanders, men, women and children. Erik, Arne and Ulf were piloting the lead vessel, which also contained the members of Arne's household, including his consort Gretta. The unstable weather of the North Sea, rendered even more volatile by the eruption of Katla, drove them erratically here and there, dense fogs making navigation impossible. Most of the time they had no idea where they were. Some of the boats were quickly separated from the main fleet.

Day after day, in a darkness of despair, they endured heartache's hurt on the water's waste.[16] Their vigils at the mast foot were void, and empty their long night-watches. At times they found themselves washed towards the shore, where storms beat on stone-cliffs, and where their boats narrowly escaped a battering against the ragged rocks. Their hands were raw on the ropes and oars, their feet frozen, fettered with frost, cramped with cold.

Ulf and Erik had both grown to love Iceland, and to leave the island broke their hearts. There they had found a home. Arne had gifted Erik with a piece of land from his own holding, further up the mountain, needing much hard work, but it was their own, father and son. 'A farm of your own is better, even if small'.[17] Erik had found the peaceful society of Iceland congenial, free from the constant fear of invasion or blood-feud, free to work the land instead of continually having to fight for it. He liked the social organisation of the republican community, the absence of despotism, the almost universal respect for law, and the fair and reasonable means of settling disputes. During this time the desire for revenge against the Saxons for the killing of Hnaef, that had obsessively gnawed at him day and night, faded away into the distance, and seemed by now of little importance. The Saxon who killed him had fought for his king, as Erik had stood by his lord. In truth there was little difference between them. And having been able to deliver Ulf into a place of safety, Erik had gradually become reconciled to his actions at the Dannevirke. It had proved after all to be a kind of wisdom, turning his back on a certain heroic death, and choosing instead to preserve the life of his son.

---

16 *The Seafarer*, ed. I. L. Gordon (London: Methuen, 1960).

17 'Sayings of the High One', *The Poetic Edda*, ed. Carolyne Larrington (Oxford: Oxford University Press, 1996), p. 17.

What troubled his thoughts now, as the little fleet criss-crossed the weltering waves of the North Sea, was not revenge, or guilt and shame for his past actions, but a deep envy of those who still lived on the land, and prospered in plenty among fair fields. How could they know, those fortunate field-dwellers, of the poor man's pain, who woeful as winter, forlorn of a fatherland, weathers the waves of the ice-cold sea? Hammered by hail, savaged by snow, his ears heard only the sound of the sea, the splash of the surge and the seabird's song. His only glee was the clamour of gulls.

There's no loving lord to embrace the exile, or fondly befriend the friendless man. A life of luxury's made for that man who lives on his land, caressed with comforts and warmed with wine. He feels not a fraction of the seafarer's sorrow, the hateful hardships an exile endures. He'll never know, that creature of comfort, how others suffer on that vast voyage. Darkness deepened with drifts of snow, shadows of night brought sleet from the north. Hail fell hard. Frost gripped the ground.

Ulf had remained in a kind of quiet rapture at the terrible beauty of Iceland, the unquenchable fire at its heart, the clarity of the air, the vividness of colour everywhere: black rocks and white snow and green pasture against the hard blue sky. Here nature seemed a living thing, and strange forms of life inhabited its lakes and caves, its mountains and valleys. There was always fear, and anxiety, as there had always been, but born out of respect for something more than a king or a lord. Ulf would rather live in fear of Thor's hammer than of a Saxon sword: the island was awful, but holy, a dwelling of the gods.

And now they had been compelled to turn their backs on all that fierce and sacramental beauty, and take to the seas once more. Ulf now began to experience what Erik had felt on leaving Denmark, a pain of exile that shaped and formed itself into the rhythms and cadences of one of the old seafarer's songs. He did not know the exact words, and did not have the skill to craft them himself. But his thought and feelings matched the form of an elegiac poem.

And so his heart heaved to wander the waves, and taste of the tang of the salt-sea's spray, to seek the deep streams and their restless rolling. Here he could seek friendship in foreign lands, here he might find, homeless, a home on an alien shore. Again and again an impulse invites him, a peregrine urge to fare far forth. Stirring, his spirit raps at his ribs, flutters her feathers, then quits her cage, to soar on the wing, to fathom the flood-ways, the earth's expanses, the haunts of the whale. Wheeling and hovering, his heart's hawk yells, eagerly inciting the unappeased spirit to seek the sea's stretches, where the dead lie deep.

Chapter Fifteen

Brexit

'A new world
And the old made explicit'
– T.S. Eliot, *Four Quartets*

Weybridge, 2016

Since his retirement Ralph has spent more time with Martin and his family, visiting, infrequently but with some regularity, their home in Surrey. Martin lives in a suburb of the expensive waterside town of Weybridge, bounded by the Thames and the River Wey. One evening in May, the weather mild and sunny, Ralph is once again driving down the A3, but this time he skirts the Kingston roundabout and heads up Kingston Hill. He is making a detour to check in on his protégé Salam. Working with a charity that settles refugees with foster families, Ralph had managed to establish Salam with an experienced elderly foster couple in Surbiton. Entering a quiet residential area off the featureless town centre, Ralph pulls up in a street of small, pretty houses all painted in pastel colours of pale yellow and blue.

He is greeted by an elderly lady with a gentle manner, who is removing a pair of gardening gloves. The small house is full of the smell of cooking. Through the back window Ralph can see the old man, bending down over a bed of roses. He is shown to the stairs and invited to go up and find Salam.

Tapping on a bedroom door, Ralph responds to the invitation to enter, and finds Salam at a table by the window, hunched over a laptop, which he quickly switches off. He turns and greets Ralph with evident pleasure. Salam is studying engineering at the nearby university.

'So. Everything going OK?' asks Ralph, glancing round the small bedroom, with its white walls, neatly made bed and bookshelf with a few new-looking text-books. His eyes always drawn to a bookshelf, Ralph identifies chunky paperback text-books of mechanical engineering, some books in Arabic, a London A to Z, and a green-and-gold copy of the Quran. There are no posters on the walls, no photographs on the shelves. There is something strangely neutral about the room, which does not resemble the typical bolt-hole of a teenager, narcissistically plastered with the lurid posters that act as defiant personal inscriptions. This is almost like a holding cell, a sterile zone devoid of any individual stamp.

How would I furnish my room, he thinks, if I'd been a child soldier in Iraq, forcibly recruited into ISIS, trained to torture and kill, then left abandoned in a makeshift refugee camp? Once a refugee, maybe, always a refugee: one forever resting on a journey towards an almost inconceivable realm of safety and protection. Perhaps Salam would always be a traveller in life, always ready at a moment's notice to jump up, leave the house, flee the village, move on.

But Salam is clearly comfortable here, at least, and the neutrality of his room a personal choice.

'They've really looked after me', he says of his foster family. 'They give me anything I want'. He gestures towards the table, with the new laptop, printer, mobile phone. 'And I'm enjoying my studies. I can walk to the uni from here'. He draws Ralph to the window, and shows him the buildings of the university in the near distance.

As he walks down the stairs, Ralph reflects on the contrast between the austerity of Salam's room, and the cluttered prettiness of the rest of the house, which has too much furniture, and is full of bright glass and ceramic ornaments, the decorative debris of people who have lived in one place for a very long time. Having no children of their own, the foster couple have stocked their house with decades of collectable curios, and fostered a succession of young asylum seekers, giving them a start in their new life. Ralph feels a dislike of the lived-in suburban house, the legacy of a comfortable bourgeois existence, and feels more affinity for the stark, white-walled monastic austerity of Salam's room. But he is genuine in the thanks he gives to the foster parents for their care of his young protégé.

Ralph continues his drive towards Weybridge. There are road works on the A307, so he cuts through Kingston, traverses the stream of Hogsmill, passing the site of the Coronation Stone, where seven Anglo-Saxon kings – including Aethelstan himself, first king of all England – were crowned, then crosses the river at Kingston Bridge, and makes a right by Hampton Court Palace, to follow the stately progress of the river, past the round dome of Garrick's Shakespeare Temple. He drives through Hampton, then takes the riverside road through Lower Sunbury.

Surrey is something of a foreign country to Ralph, a place where the election posters are blue, sometimes yellow, instead of uniformly red. Now he crosses the Thames again, over the curvaceous span of Walton Bridge, glancing down at the brightly-coloured hulls of boats in the elegant marina below. Driving up the hill, he passes an Aston Martin showroom with a smart row of sleek grey sports cars on the forecourt. What sort of people can afford an Aston Martin? The question is answered as his route takes him down a long, straight road in which all the houses lie set back behind extensive gardens and gravelled driveways: a real millionaire's row. He drives through woodland, passing occasional private entrances to shielded and gated housing developments. Then a small collection of Georgian cottages surrounding a green, with a small village school, Victorian church and a shabby pub, and he has arrived.

Martin's house lies just off the green, in one of the more affordable areas of Weybridge, in a cul-de-sac occupied by families much like theirs, families with children, or older couples whose kids have flown the coop: young professional couples hoping to climb the property ladder, small tradesmen with a taste for rural living. Ralph had always thought derisively of Surrey as the stockbroker belt, the most true-blue of the Home Counties. These people are clearly not rich, though they seem to value their modest suburban houses, and enjoy their little patch of land, clearly taking much pride in their gardens. But they seem to lack the withdrawn possessiveness of the rich, who hide behind their high fences and thick hedges, their CCTV cameras and burglar alarms. Here neighbours chat cordially across the fence, while their kids play together at the end of the street. The social milieu is what Ralph would describe as petit-bourgeois, very different from the urban environment he is used to, where there is no sense of neighbourhood or local community. Everyone in this street seems to be amicable, approachable.

Ralph shakes his head as he pulls into the cul-de-sac. He can't remember having any particular ambitions for Martin, but he would prefer him to live in a more diverse and inclusive area. The people here remind him of his parents, and of the council estate he grew up in. The same modest pride, the same tolerance and respect, the same cheerful friendliness to neighbours and strangers alike. They combined the security and confidence of home-owners with the relaxed collectivism of people who had more in common than divided them. And indeed after he left home many of the council tenants of King Alfred's Estate became private owners. He remembers the bitter controversy of 1980 when Margaret Thatcher's Housing Act gave tenants the right to buy their own homes, and how disgracefully people rushed to take advantage of the opportunity, including his parents. This place is not for him. But he can see why Martin likes it here.

Ralph parks the Mercedes in Martin's driveway and rings the bell. Martin's wife answers, and welcomes him in. Mei is Japanese, and the house bears subtle traces of an imported cultural difference. Ralph automatically takes his shoes off, and walks through into the living room with a slightly constrained physical bearing. Mei is a Buddhist, and with an apology resumes her prayers before the Gohonzon. She is a devotee of one of the Nichiren Buddhist sects, and combines a daily discipline of chanting the Lotus Sutra with a commitment to social action and mutual support. Ralph, though militantly hostile to all religion, cannot help but admire her Buddhist faith, which seems to him to have much in common with a secular philosophy. The driving force of her world-view is compassion, for the self and for others: understanding peoples' circumstances, and trying to help them by any means possible.

He is intrigued by a faith that facilitates social action, for peace or the environment, without party politics. Mei regards the disagreements and controversies, the bitterly divided loyalties, that obsess her adopted nation as transient phenomena that require little attention, as they will inevitably pass away. Her mind and spirit seem to be focused on deeper things. As Ralph walks out through the patio door towards the garden, he can hear her rhythmic chanting resume:

Nam myo ho rengo kyo
Nam myo ho rengo kyo
Nam myo ho rengo kyo

And then, repeatedly struck in a plangent crescendo, the loud, sonorous reverberation of a bronze bell.

Martin is in the garden with their five-year old son, and calls Ralph through to join them. The garden is a quiet, private retreat from the communal busyness at the front. A wide lawn is fringed with borders where climbing plants grow in abundance, roses and clematis and sweet-scented jasmine. A long, low garden shed lies at the foot of the garden, and behind and overhanging it, a huge *Arbor Vitae* tree. It is pleasant to sit in a garden chair, drinking a glass of chilled white wine, and watch the youngster building a mediaeval castle from Lego. After a while the boy looks up and notices Ralph. 'Come and say hello to Grandad', says Martin, and the lad comes obediently over. The boy favours his mother, his features small and delicate. He looks at Ralph critically through very dark, opaque eyes. The child always seems to feel reserved with his grandfather, as if he doesn't know quite what to make of him. For his part Ralph feels at a loss, not knowing what to say, unable to take an interest in the things that occupy the mind of so young a child. He gives the boy a piece of Lego he has picked up from the grass. The boy takes it without acknowledgement, and returns to his play.

Mei brings out food. Her father is a chef working in a Japanese restaurant, so the family often inherit very high-quality dishes of gourmet food, in this case *sashimi* served in neat little bento boxes. The food is delicious. They talk about things that seem trivial to Ralph: how Martin's job is going; when the boy will be starting school; whether Mei is looking forward to getting back to her work as a language teacher. Soon it is time to put the boy to bed. Martin volunteers to take him, but Mei insists. She knows the men will start talking politics in the abrasive English fashion she finds unpleasant. She finds it better to leave them to it.

She has a fair idea of what their conversation will consist in. The popular and political movement to withdraw Britain from the European Union is finally coming to a head, and within a month or so the people will be voting in a referendum to determine the country's future: in or out of Europe. The conflict is cutting across all traditional political loyalties, and divides opinion more violently than any ideological opposition Ralph could remember in his lifetime. He has campaigned a little on the Remain side, and has had some bruising conversations with Martin, who has emerged from this process a committed Brexiteer.

&

The arguments pro and con membership of the EU have dominated political debate in the media, the universities, the pubs, and have been intensifying as the nation nears the date for the referendum, 23 June 2016. Britain has split into two tribes, the Remainers and the Leavers.

Leavers claim that continued membership of the EU restricts the international significance of a country that once exerted global influence, and argue that the UK should instead join the World Trade Organisation, and strike trade deals around the world, especially with close partners such as the Commonwealth countries. Leaving would see the UK regain sovereignty: Britain should be able to control her own laws, rather than having laws imposed from the increasingly aggressive and power-hungry European Court of Justice. With independence British trade could become much more agile and flexible, slashing red tape and bureaucratic restrictions imposed by the EU. Ending freedom of movement would give Britain more control over its own labour market, and have a positive effect on wages. Britain could repossess the vast sums of money contributed to the EU, which far exceed the value returned in subsidies. And finally the country could regain control of its own borders, admitting the people we want to have, and keeping out those we don't.

Remainers argue exactly the opposite. The UK can have greater international influence as part of a community of five hundred million people, than alone. Participation in the EU does not preclude some measure of independence. The UK is continually opting out of EU policies: the Euro, or the Schengen agreement which created open borders within the community, or the migrant quotas imposed by Brussels. Britain and the EU are stronger together on security and crime. The UK has unrestricted access to the European single market, the free movement of goods and services across borders. Prices are lower from tariff-free trade. Millions of jobs in the UK depend on co-operation with the EU, and some of our sectors – health, social care, agriculture – depend absolutely on free movement. And for socialists, there is the progress made inside the EU on workers' rights, employment practices, consumer protection. The left-wing political agenda of many Remainers prescribes further integration, working with EU unions and political parties to achieve a European minimum wage, to outlaw zero-hours contracts, to strengthen legal protections for workers. EU membership gives the UK free movement of goods, services, capital and labour. We need more controls on the banks, on currency, on speculation. But free movement of labour is the life-blood of our economy.

&

Ralph and Martin have now been arguing Leave and Remain for an hour or so. They have reached the topic of national boundaries, and Ralph had just been advocating for open borders.

'You can't walk into the States, or Canada, or Australia, without permission or security clearance', Martin argues, 'the way the Europeans can walk in here. You can't immediately take up work in one of those countries, receive state benefits, free healthcare, social housing, without having contributed anything in taxes or national insurance. Why should we be any different?'

'The Americans are dead against Brexit', says Ralph with a narrow smile. 'They think we're stronger and safer in Europe'.

'That's something I've never understood. Did they tolerate a foreign power imposing laws, taxes, controls over them? No, they fought a War of Independence to free themselves from them. From us. I can't fathom why they see this this as any different'.

'Because they regard us as a diminished colonial power, pretending we can still rule the world. They prefer us inside a federation, working with others for security and peace. In any case the Americans have thrown away their moral advantage on immigration. What does it say on the statue of Liberty?

"Give me your tired, your poor,
Your huddled masses yearning to breathe free,
The wretched refuse of your teeming shore".

And now they're building a wall on their southern border'.

They have reached that most sensitive and controversial topic of immigration.

'What people object to', says Martin, choosing his words carefully, 'is uncontrolled immigration. Especially in the poorer parts of the country like the North of England. Why do you think people vote for UKIP in elections to the European parliament? UKIP got more votes than any other British party. It's not because the voters hate foreigners. They're not even against immigration *per se*. But they see these open borders as a real threat to their livelihoods, their services, their culture. They can't get work because the market's flooded with cheap labour. Their schools are overcrowded because no-one can predict the level of demand. Their health services are at breaking point. They want control of the country, that's all. Democratic control. Nothing more than that'.

Ralph is beginning to stiffen slightly under the impact of these arguments. His tone of voice assumes a kind of patronising, derisive note that Martin dislikes intensely. 'That's exactly what it says on that UKIP poster. You know the one? "We must break free of the EU and take back control". That great overwhelming tide of migrants surging towards the country. All non-white. And the only thing standing in their way – Nigel Farage'.

Martin's voice becomes a little testy. 'Vote Leave dissociated themselves from that poster. So did the government. It was like Nazi propaganda. That's not what we want at all. There's nothing wrong with migration' – here he stops himself from making the obvious point that he is married to a Japanese, but doesn't want it to sound as if he has done the world a huge favour by marrying the woman he fell in love with – 'But let's make it controlled, regulated, sensible. In the best interests of the country. That's what the people want. And they're going to vote for it. Mark my words'.

'But don't you think', observes Ralph, his manner becoming almost sneering, 'that racism is a big motivating factor in the Vote Leave campaign? Are you sure the people you're talking about aren't hankering after a predominantly white, 1950s Britain? Blaming all our society's ills on immigrants, instead of focusing on the government? A real, left-wing Labour government would set a decent minimum wage, fund education and social services, put an end to poverty. Brexit is only going to further impoverish our most vulnerable'.

There was a pause while Martin poured them both another glass of wine. And then he turns the conversation to the more vexed question of illegal immigration. 'You know, I was talking to a bloke at work about the stuff you do with Open Borders. He's a bit of a UKIP supporter. He thinks what you do is just an extension of people smuggling. Advising migrants how to enter the UK illegally. Helping to cut them loose from Border Force. Using lawyers to stop them being deported'. Emboldened, he looks his father full in the face as he delivers what amounts to an accusation. 'You're not making immigration any more popular, you know'.

'I see', says Ralph, sipping his wine meditatively.

'It's all about legality. The British are very law-abiding. Think of the Windrush scandal. Have you ever met anyone who thinks that anything other than an absolute disgrace? People who came here, from the Caribbean. Invited here. Came here to work, to settle, to raise their families. Model citizens, most of them. And the government decides to start deporting them. Because the Civil Service had lost their papers. Appalling. Universally condemned. And why? *Because those people never did anything wrong.* They never broke the law.

'But to pay people traffickers, smuggle yourself into Britain illegally, on a lorry or a train or a small boat; to tear up your papers; to pretend you're from a different country; to lie about you age … we can't tolerate that. It's wrong. It's unfair'.

Ralph is silent, staring into his wineglass. Martin feels that he may have gone too far, and wants to avoid yet another acrimonious bust-up with his father.

'Sorry Dad', says Martin in an attempt to mollify his father's silent anger. 'You know I feel strongly about all this'. But it is too late. Ralph is offended. He sets his empty glass on the wrought-iron garden table.

'No, it's OK. Honestly', he replies. 'Let's leave it there. You're a Nazi, and I'm a people smuggler. Nobody's perfect. Say good-night to Mei for me. And thanks for the meal'. He stands up and walks through the passageway alongside the house onto the front drive, gets back into his car and drives off.

Martin gathers the plates and glasses together and carries them into the house. Mei is closing her *Butsedan* for the night, extinguishing her candles.

'Has he gone?', she asks.

'Yes'.

'So rude. I suppose you upset him again'.

'Yes', says Martin ruefully.

'Don't say I didn't warn you. You should show your father more respect. You argue so violently'.

'I had a good teacher'.

Chapter Sixteen

Hostage

'What might have been, and what has been
Point to one end, which is always present'
– T.S. Eliot, *Four Quartets*

York, 934

'Who the fuck are you?'

The question was asked by Alfgeir, Earl of Northumbria. He did not look up from the table where he sat, in a chamber in his fortress in the city of *Eoforwic*,[18] chewing on a piece of meat.

Arne, Erik and Ulf stood facing him at the head of a small group of Icelanders, closely surrounded by armed guards. Arne introduced them.

'So what do you want from me?', the Norseman asked, carelessly throwing a bone sideways to a pair of hungry looking dogs.

Arne spoke for them. 'To serve you, my lord. We're Icelanders. Forced to flee our homes by the bursting of the fire-mountain. We ask only for a small piece of your land we can farm. We will pay you tribute. Keep your peace'.

'How many of you?' asked Alfgeir, swigging liquor from a drinking horn.

---

18 York.

'A hundred of us when we left Iceland. The storms scattered our ships. Only one boat reached your shores, with a dozen men, as you see, and a few women and children. We pose no threat to you, my lord. We beseech you to give us your protection, in return for our loyalty and service'.

For the first time Alfgeir looked up at them and surveyed them, critically, one by one. 'I don't need farmers'. He said, shortly. 'I need soldiers'.

As Arne had explained to Alfgeir, their ships had become separated in the storm, and as far as they knew only the one vessel had reached the Northumbrian coast. Arne's ship had made landfall at a place called *Streoneshalch*,[19] which had a small harbour, with a green hill standing above it, topped by the ruins of a monastery. Sentries were posted on the hill, and a patrol of soldiers waiting at the quay. They disembarked, unarmed and with overtures of peace. Surly troops took them in charge, saying nothing. Around the harbour and the small settlement they observed Danes, Swedes and Norse, alongside Anglo-Saxons, working together at their various crafts, fishing, making nets, trading. But all looked askance, silent and subdued. And soldiers everywhere. Arne and Erik recognised the prickly atmosphere of a country preparing for war. Their boat was impounded and moored at the edge of the harbour. The women and children were sequestered and taken off towards the town. Ulf stayed close to Erik. The men were formed into a line, and ordered to start walking towards the west, flanked by guards on horses.

19 Whitby.

Arne had made for the Northumbrian coast knowing that Danes had once ruled there without interference, and independent of English power. But the political situation had grown more complex. Incursions of Norsemen had created friction, and wildcat raids into Mercia had triggered reprisals from Wessex. Recently King Aethelstan had marched north with an army to quell a rebellion in Scotland, taken back *Eoforwic*, demanded allegiance from Danes and Norse, and appointed two earls to govern in his stead. But one of them, Alfgeir, had turned traitor, and switched his allegiance to Olaf Guthfrithson, King of Dublin, who had promised to support the Northumbrian Norse against Aethelstan. Arne and Erik had the misfortune to land themselves into the middle of this volatile situation.

&

'I need soldiers', Alfgeir continued. 'You look like a warrior', he said, pointing a finger at Erik. 'Do you have fighting experience?'

'Yes, of course, my lord', Arne smoothly replied. 'But not for a long time. Iceland, you know, is peaceful. We're farmers now, we just work the land'.

'Not any more. No land for you unless you fight for it. You can join my army. Olaf is coming from Ireland, with a great force. King Constantine of Scotland is to join us. We plan to invade Mercia, and strike at Wessex. Subdue the English, as our forefathers did. Kill the king if we can. Then you can think about returning to your ploughs. Away with you'.

As they turned to leave, Alfgeir clearly had second thoughts. 'Wait. I have a task for you two. You, the big one. And you, the talkative. Bjorn, take them to Henrik'.

'What task?' asked Erik suspiciously.

'You'll find out. Off with you'. The guards began to escort them out. Alfgeir shouted after them: 'Not the boy. The boy stays here'.

'Why?' asked Erik, turning on his heel.

'To make sure you men do as you're told'.

Arne and Erik exchanged glances as they were led out by the guards.

Now the rest of the Icelanders were taken away, and Arne and Erik placed under the command of Henrik, a big Norse warrior who sized them up, and told them to gather armour and weapons from a well-stocked armoury. They would be marching on a raid the following morning. Their orders were to march all day, some thirty miles to the east, to the hamlet of *Inderawuda*,[20] and with the help of a conscripted English guide to find a monastery. They were to hide in the woods, and in the evening to surprise the king at his prayers, and kill him. Some of the prisoners performed a strange gesture, crossing a hand over the breast, as if the order offended their piety in some way. Erik, who had seen, on the raids of his youth, both monasteries and monks, having put many of the latter to the sword, guessed that Alfgeir had some hold over all these men, like the trap that bound him, with his son held hostage. Otherwise nothing would stop them running away at the first opportunity.

Erik and Arne chose helmets and byrnies, swords and spears from the racks and shelves in the armoury. Then they were ordered to gather with a troop of other men, who sat around outside a tent, eating food that was being cooked on a big fire. They were mostly Danes, some Saxons, their

20 Beverley.

faces white with apprehension in the light of the fire. Shortly afterwards, unobserved, Arne slipped away into the gathering dusk to collect intelligence on their situation.

One of Alfgeir's warriors doused the fire with a bucket of water, and told the band of prisoners to get some sleep. Erik retired into the tent, and stretched out to rest. After a while the tent-flap opened, and Arne crept in to lie down beside them. He and Erik began a whispered conversation. As in all situations of impending war, conflicting rumours abounded. The received opinion was that Aethelstan was still gathering his army in the south, fearful and over-awed by the scale of opposition, reluctant to move north before amassing sufficient force to face a combined Northumbrian and Scottish army.

But Arne was drawn towards another story, which was that Athelstan's army was already in Northumbria, camped north of the great river, and that the king was with them. This explanation was consistent with the mission into which they had been press-ganged. Alfgeir's spies, embedded in the Wessex army, had reported that the English king was to leave his troops in the field, and to visit the monastery at *Inderawuda*, where he intended to pray for a victory. The task assigned to them by Aelfgeir was to surprise the king's retinue as they arrived at the church, fight their way through his bodyguard, and kill him.

'That's suicide', whispered Erik.

'Exactly. That's why these poor bastards look so glum. Alfgeir knows there is no hope of success: he just wants to frighten Athelstan a bit'.

'Using our lives to do the frightening. But there's no chance of getting out alive, is there?'

'None. Which is why we have to get ourselves out of it'.

'But how?'

'I'm working on it', said Arne. 'Let me sleep'.

In the morning the men were woken roughly by the guards and instructed to arm themselves.

'Your plan?' asked Erik, as they buckled sword-belts over mail-shirts.

'Get ready to ride', was Arne's only reply.

The band was formed into a square, and their armour inspected. They were well-equipped with helmet, byrnie and shield, with sword and spear and axe. They were at best reluctant soldiers, but at least they were well armed. Two guards on horseback rode with them, one ahead and one in the rear. Arne leaned close to Erik, his eyes peering through the bronze cheek-plates of his helmet, and gave a sharp nod towards each of the guards. Erik understood immediately. The little band was marched out of the camp and onto the road.

They had been walking for an hour or so over a flat plain, but now found the road leading through a small wood of oak trees. As they entered the shade of the overarching trees, Arne suddenly fell sideways out of the column and fell full length onto the ground, apparently writhing in pain. The guard at the rear shouted to him, but Arne gave no response. Erik stood close to him, ready to act. Shouting irritably, the warrior pushed his horse from the rear and approached the contorted figure on the ground. Leaning over, he poked at Arne with his spear. Erik grabbed the shaft and pulled him down from his mount. The guard collapsed in a clash of armour. Arne was on his feet, sword drawn, striking at the fallen man, who lay still. Meanwhile the other guard at the front of the column wheeled his horse and began to gallop towards them, scattering prisoners to the right and left. Erik hefted the first guard's spear in his hand, waited until the charging man was almost upon him, and launched it at his chest. Luckily the man's shield was still strapped to his back. The spear flew unerringly towards him, punched through his byrnie and swept him from his mount. Arne was upon him as he lay in a tangle of limbs and armour, cutting with his sword at the man's neck. But he was already dead.

Erik had grabbed the startled horse by the bridle, leapt into the saddle and chased the other horse, which had cantered some way into the woods, and then stopped. Catching up with it, he grabbed it by the bridle, wheeled it round and returned it to Arne. Once mounted, the Danes pulled their horses round to take the road they had been travelling back towards *Eoforwic*.

'You're free now', Arne shouted to the rest of the conscripted platoon, who still stood irresolutely in the road. 'He has our wives and children', one of them said simply. And they turned and resumed their march to the east.

Erik and Arne slowed their pace as they neared the city. They were confident they would be able to wander the streets without attracting attention. But finding where Ulf was being held would be more difficult. They tied their horses behind a building close to Alfgeir's hall, and wandered into a crowded throughfare It was a simple matter to blend into the press of people crowding the populous streets. In no way did Arne and Erik look out of place among the multi-ethnic population of Saxons, Danes, Norse and Irish, warriors and tradesman, craftsmen and monks.

Eventually Arne found what he was looking for, a group of Danish men, recognisable by their dress and accent, sitting alongside a disreputable, ramshackle building, and drinking mead. Initially they were incommunicative, trusting no-one, but they made no objection when the strangers joined their group, and the convivial Arne soon had them talking. They exchanged reminiscences about Denmark, people and places, campaigns they had fought in, raids they had conducted. Eventually Arne learned what he wanted to know: where Alfgeir kept his hostages.

It was an obvious and easily accessible place, an outbuilding behind the earl's hall. Quickly Arne and Erik made their way there, and could see only one sentry standing guard at the door. There might be other guards inside, but they surmised that the hostages were probably lightly guarded, since they were of no value to anyone except those they had been taken from, who were all dispatched on errands from which they were unlikely to return. Arne walked up to the guard at the door and asked him a question. Meanwhile Erik sidled alongside him, got a strong arm round his neck and cut his throat. Before the mute, lifeless body had hit the ground, they were inside the building looking for Ulf. They soon located him, sitting among a crowd of women and children, called him over to them and scanned the vicinity for more sentries. Seeing no-one, they sprinted to the horses, quickly mounted, and were on their way without any pursuit.

Once past the city's fortifications they pushed the horses to a gallop. Ulf rode behind Arne, the lighter man. Thundering down the same road they had taken earlier, they passed through the woodland where the two dead guards lay in their blood, and continued in the same direction. They expected to overtake the little band of prisoners they had accompanied earlier, but found no sign of them.

By late afternoon they reached the monastery, tied their horses in a thicket, and hid in a dense copse, from which they could observe the entrance. The place was quiet, with just a few monks with tonsured heads and brown robes, coming and going on everyday domestic tasks, gathering firewood, drawing water from a well. Ulf noticed their strange robes, and shaved heads, and that each one wore upon his breast a metal symbol in the form of a cross. Smoke rose from the roof of the building, and the smell of cooking drifted across and into the trees where they lay hidden. A feast was being prepared.

As the sun began to set, they were rewarded by the sight of a small retinue of Saxon warriors who rode into the clearing before the church, dismounted and checked out the area. They were welcomed by the brothers. Finding all clear, the soldiers signalled to another group of horsemen, who Erik guessed to be the king's personal bodyguard, and then disappeared into the interior. The entourage approached, exercising keen vigilance, and delivered the king safely into the monastery and to the care of the troops already inside. They caught a glimpse of Aethelstan, flaxen-haired and bearded, a slight and slender figure, below average height.

'So much for our mission', said Arne under his breath. 'We wouldn't get as far as the door'.

'What do you think happened to our comrades?', breathed Erik.

'Gone. Run away. The Saxons don't know that, of course.' Then after a brief pause, Arne said decisively: 'Come on. If we're going to do this, let's get on with it. Leave your weapons here'.

And the three of them rose up from the copse, and began to walk slowly towards the monastery, their hands on their heads. The sentries at the gatehouse saw them immediately, and shouted for them to stop where they were. The three walked out into the clearing, and fell to their knees.

'We have information for the king', Arne shouted, 'concerning his own safety'.

The Saxons quickly surrounded them and took them into custody. They were dragged before a nobleman who looked them up and down suspiciously. The king's presence here, separated from his army, was a closely-guarded secret, and the evidence that it had somehow leaked to the enemy was to say the least disconcerting. Arne told him the whole tale, truthfully except for the evident disappearance of the assassination squad. The nobleman looked at him for a space.

'Get hold of him', he said to two of the guards. Arne was seized from behind by the arms and hoisted to his feet, a strong mailed arm about his neck. The Saxon lord drew an expensive-looking dagger from his belt and placed the point under Arne's chin.

'Now', he said, evenly. 'What makes you think the king is here?'

'You have spies in your ranks, my lord', said Arne, writhing his chin away from the pricking of the knife. 'It's common knowledge over there. Alfgeir thought a surprise attack would scare you'.

The Saxon looked into Arne's eyes, withdrew his dagger and thought for a few minutes, then rose to enter the monastery. After a few minutes they were surprised to see him re-emerge with no less a companion than the king himself.

'Why are you telling us this?', Aethelstan asked directly. 'Just to save your skins?'

'We owe no loyalty to Aelfgeir', said Arne. 'And no enmity to you. He has treated us unjustly. We asked him only for the use of his land, and offered to pay him tribute. He compelled us to serve as soldiers, and sent us on a hopeless mission. We would rather serve you, my lord'.

Aethelstan looked unconvinced.

'He took my son hostage', said Erik. 'And that I could not accept. We freed the boy, and came straight to you. Do with us as you will. We will serve you, fight for you if that is your wish. As long as my son is safe'.

The king looked from the man to the boy, and regarded the latter with some growing interest. 'Where is his mother?' he asked.

'Dead, my lord'.

'Then you are both mother and father to him'. He came closer, and cupped Ulf's chin in his hand. 'You are young to be in the midst of all this', he said, almost to himself. Then after a moment's consideration: 'Fight for me, then', he said to Erik and Arne. 'I need soldiers.[21] You will both have to take the sign of the cross. And if it's is safety you want for the boy, I could give him to the brothers here: to be a novice. They would teach him to read and write, and make him a monk. Safety he would have, and eternal salvation'.

Erik looked at Ulf. The son could see in the father's face how tempted he was by that prospect of sanctuary for his son. But for Ulf the thought was devastating. He felt that this was their one chance to redeem the disgrace they had endured in Denmark, and the failure of their attempt at relocation in Iceland. Here in England they had the opportunity of fighting for the right to a homeland. If they were to fall in the battle, they would do so with honour. If they emerged victorious, they would have won the right to live. Ulf shook his head at his father, and implored him with his eyes.

21 *Egil's Saga*, trans. Bernard Scudder (London: Penguin, 1997), p. 89.

The king was observing Ulf, and did not wait for a reply from Erik. He saw how it would be. Some of the monks gathered around the Danes, and bade them kneel. One pronounced words in an unintelligible language, at the same time performing again that same cryptic sign, not across his own chest, but rather in the air and above their heads, as if conferring on them a blessing. The other monks showed them how to cross themselves, and the ceremony was over. Ulf felt strangely protected by the invisible sign. Erik rubbed his chest, as if trying to erase any trace left by the illegible signature.

Meanwhile detachments of warriors had been sent out to patrol the area, looking for the reported assassins, and wary of an ambush from the direction of *Eoforwic*. They had found nothing but the two horses left in the woods by Erik and Arne. These were returned to them, along with their weapons, and they were ordered to mount and ride along with the Saxons. They were to ride through the night to rejoin the army, encamped further south, lying in wait for an expected invasion from the east.

Chapter Seventeen

Terror

'The agony of others, nearly experienced,
Involving ourselves'
– T.S. Eliot, *Four Quartets*

Putney, 2017

It is a Friday morning. Ralph sits in his kitchen drinking coffee and reading the paper. He has already taken his morning walk, across Putney Bridge and into Bishops' Park, where his routine is to stroll along the river, then down to the Fulham Palace, a largely Tudor building that contains remnants dating back to Saxon times. Some of his retired colleagues, with whom he retains fleeting contact, have adopted rigorous regimes of exercise, running intimidating distances, spending arduous hours in the gym. He much prefers the more relaxed constitutional of a long walk, often following the Thames for miles, up to Hammersmith and Chiswick, Kew and Richmond.

Returning, he may stop for a moment by the monument to the local men of Hammersmith and Fulham who enlisted with the Republicans in the Spanish Civil War, tracing with his finger the gold lettering etched on the surface of polished pink marble:

INTERNATIONAL BRIGADE

In honour of the volunteers who left Hammersmith and Fulham to fight in the International Brigade, Spain, 1936-1939. They fought alongside the Spanish people to stop Fascism and save liberty and peace for all.

Often he will take a book, and linger in the old Tudor courtyard of the Fulham Palace, with its diamond-patterned polychromatic brickwork, round central fountain and small clock tower. The Church Commissioners have an office here, marked by gilded lettering on an old black wooden board. It is a space suffused with ancient history, where it would be eminently possible to escape from the pressures of the contemporary world. Ralph doesn't really switch off like that: he prefers to sit in this tranquil spot, hallowed by time and piety, and incongruously ruminate on the urgent pressing problems of modernity. Today however he has kept his walk short, as he has errands to run.

Although, to a retiree, one day is much the same as another, Ralph still tries to keep the weekend for leisure, and Monday to Thursday for work. Friday was always in any case an interlude between the two, a day to be avoided for teaching and meetings, a day for long lunchtimes in the pub, where he and his comrades would reconstruct the syllabus, and argue the finer points of dialectical materialism, and set the world to rights over a succession of pints. For that reason Friday still remains his favourite day of the week.

He reads the news of the day, and finds it encouraging. The EU referendum in the previous year had delivered what, in his view, was the wrong result, with a majority decision to Leave. But now, a year later, departure from the EU seems no closer than it was before. David Cameron's resignation catapulted the Remainer Theresa May into the Conservative leadership post on a promise to 'honour the result' of a referendum in which she had chosen the losing side. She proceeded to select like-minded Tories for her cabinet, resulting in a bias in government towards Remain, and the isolation of the Leave party. The opposition parties are also, overall, anti-Brexit, the Liberal Democrats and Scottish National Party fanatically so. The Labour Party is led by the ultra-Leftist Jeremy Corbyn who, like Ralph himself, had formerly been implacably opposed to the European Union, but is no more capable than Theresa May of controlling the Remain elements in his own party.

Ralph himself has of course enacted the trajectory from Euroscepticism to reluctant Europhilia. So he is particularly enjoying the current shenanigans in Parliament, where a Remain majority of MPs is systematically wrecking all attempts to begin the process of withdrawal. Following a legal case initiated by a businesswoman, Gina Miller, the Supreme Court has ruled that parliament must enact legislation in order to trigger Article 50, and begin the withdrawal process. But the House of Commons has a majority for Remain, and so enacting legislation is far from straightforward. Hence, a year on from the referendum, where the people clearly delivered their wishes, the process of leaving the European Union is bogged down in parliamentary antics, legal interference from pro-European judges, and calls from all sides for a second referendum. The clamour in today's liberal press is for the latter, for a 'Peoples' Vote', as if in 2016 the people had not voted, or as if the people who did vote were not really 'the people'.

Ralph gets up from the table to get some more coffee, and the phone rings.

The alert is coming not from his mobile, but from the landline out in the hall, which is hardly ever used, and the number of which he never gives out to anyone. It is probably a scam, from some fraudster after his bank details, or a cold call, offering improved broadband, from a call centre in Manila. He tries to ignore it, but the handset keeps on ringing, a shrill, demanding summons that echoes insistently in the hall and up the stairs. It could be someone who doesn't know his usual telephone habits, he thinks. Someone who hasn't called him for years. Better answer it.

He walks out to the hall and picks up the phone. The voice on the other end is familiar, but not immediately recognisable, and is not making any obvious sense. A woman's voice, distressed, distraught even, breaking with emotion into inarticulacy.

'Ralph? Is that you?'

He realises the voice is that of Mei, his son's wife. He begins to feel a vague sense of alarm.

'Mei? Is everything all right? Is it Haruki?'. He naturally thinks the child may be ill. Martin will be at work by now.

'No. It's Martin'. Her voice retreats again into inarticulacy.

Now Ralph begins to worry. 'Mei, speak clearly. I can't understand you. What's the problem?'

'It's the train. Martin's on the train. His mobile's not responding. Have you seen the news?'

An unexpected chill strikes through Ralph's stomach, and his hand on the phone trembles. He is surprised at the immediacy of his own physical reaction to a still ambiguous threat. 'Martin? Is he ill? What train?'

Suddenly the line goes dead. He goes to the living room and switches on the television. On the screen he sees, at a distance, the vivid red, yellow and blue outline of a South Western train, standing at a station. The camera zooms in on one of the carriages. There must have been a fire, since the outside of the carriage is charred and blistered, adumbrated with smoke, the paint blistered and peeling. The windows are blackened and cracked, some smashed altogether as if passengers had broken them in order to get out.

He listens to the commentary. The 0703 from Portsmouth to Waterloo, Martin's usual commuter train. Many casualties, some serious. The TV camera pulls back, and Ralph can now see a cordon of police surrounding the station, and a fleet of emergency vehicles, fire engines and ambulances. Paramedics are kneeling down beside patients stretched on the ground.

He listens to the commentary, and gathers that the incident involved an explosion on the train, somewhere between Esher and New Malden. The train is stopped at a station called Berrylands, which he has never heard of. At the bottom of the screen appears a phone number with an invitation for people to call in with their inquiries after passengers. Ralph grabs his mobile, and thumbs the numbers, then puts it to his ear. Engaged signal. He dials again. Engaged. And again. Engaged. Frustrated, anxious, Ralph looks up Berrylands station on his Google maps. Somewhere around New Malden. He runs through the hall, grabbing his keys from the side table, and slams the front door behind him.

Luckily there is little traffic through Putney, enabling him to take the hill at speed. He overtakes a lorry, causing an oncoming car to brake. On the A3 he smashes the speed limit, overtaking everything in sight, pushing the Mercedes to unaccustomed velocity. The route to Berrylands Station involves looping around the Tolworth roundabout, and here he meets some traffic, and wishes he'd taken the more direct route through Wimbledon. At last he's there, pulling up in a side street close to the perimeter of the police cordon. Walking up, he addresses the first policeman he sees, and explains that his son was on the train.

'All the casualties have gone to Kingston Hospital', says the officer, gesturing to the north. 'Quickest way is back to the A3 and next left'.

Ralph runs back to the car, turns around and performs the suggested manoeuvre. The hospital is not far away, at Norbiton. He listens to the radio for news of the incident. A number of casualties, some serious, some critical. Exact number not known. More serious cases being taken to local hospitals. Still no word from police on the causes of the explosion. Eyewitnesses report hearing a loud bang, and the train slowing, then slamming to an abrupt halt. Others describe hearing a detonation, and seeing billowing clouds of smoke rolling through the carriages. People lying on the floor covered in blood. His hands are sweaty on the steering wheel. Reaching the hospital, he drives to the front entrance and leaves the car in the car park. Ambulances stand around, their doors still open. Anxious relatives throng the doorway, waiting for news. He pushes through them, and heads for the Reception desk.

'Martin Ravenswood. Is he here?' The Receptionist consults her computer. 'Sorry, sir. Nobody of that name. But we're full here, so some patients were sent to Charing Cross'.

Charing Cross is north of the river, in Fulham. He gets back in the car, swings to the right, and is soon coasting down Kingston Hill. The radio newsreader reports that counter-terrorism police have joined the investigation of the incident. They are not ruling out a terror attack. They urge people to remain calm, and let the police do their job. Anyone anxious about a relative on the train should call …

Once again Ralph is back on the A3, steering harshly left onto Putney Hill. this time speeding north, through Putney High Street, over the bridge, into Fulham Palace Road, approaching the tall grey-and-white concrete tower of Charing Cross Hospital. He leaves the car in a resident's parking bay across the road, and runs towards the hospital. To his right is the big Henry Moore sculpture that stands among water-lilies in its own pool in a concrete basin. The statue, of oxidised green bronze, is of a reclining figure emerging from the water, its knees protruding separately, like a figure seen in a bath. Ralph has seen the statue often, but on this occasion finds its representation of a dismembered human body a questionable subject for decorating the forecourt of a hospital. He enters under the big blue sign, *Charing Cross Hospital, Imperial College*, and inquires at the desk. At last, a result: Martin is here. Where? Hang on a moment, please. Admitted to A and E. No, he's not still there. Already on a ward. Eleventh floor.

Ralph strides off to the lift. Around him people engage in animated discussions about the explosion on the train, speculating on what has happened. He keeps quiet, containing himself, not inviting conversation. The lift stops at the eleventh floor, and he asks a passing nurse where he can find Martin. She fetches the Ward Sister, who directs him down to the end of the ward. He passes a row of beds containing patients with bound-up wound injuries, lacerations and punctures. One man lies silently in the bed, his face covered in bandages, obviously hiding burns. At the end of the ward one bed is shuttered off with the regulation green plastic curtains. He pulls open the screen and looks in. Martin is lying on the bed, propped up on pillows, an oxygen mask over his face, his eyes closed. Ralph observes a saline drip over the bed with a tube connected to a cannula at the wrist. A vital signs monitor stands on a trolley beside the bed, showing blood pressure, heart rate, oxygen levels. Martin looks pale, thin, and strangely small in the bed.

A nurse enters the screened-off cubicle, asks Ralph who he is, tells him to sit down while she checks on the patient. She explains that Martin was admitted with severe breathing difficulties, and some superficial burns, but has no other injuries. He's sedated. The doctor will be examining him later. She leaves Ralph sitting beside the bed. Ralph pulls out his mobile and calls Martin's home number. There is no answer. Mei has probably already left for the hospital. He doesn't have her mobile number.

There is nothing he can do, and the feeling of impotence grates on his nerves. Having feared the worst, it should be a relief to find Martin alive, in one piece, getting medical attention. But seeing his son lying helpless in a hospital bed, unconscious, his breathing assisted, his vital signs under constant observation, affects him with unaccustomed emotions. Looking at the pinched, white face, he recalls the boy's childhood illnesses, when he would sometimes sit with him at night, watching over him, giving his mum chance to rest. He has long forgotten such moments of tenderness and solicitude, but now they return. Suddenly he feels moved to take his son's hand, careful not to disturb the cannula that is feeding his unconscious body with vital fluids. Martin's hand is insensible, but warm.

Ralph hears Mei's voice out on the ward, and exits the cubicle to meet her. Her face is crumpled with crying. He tries to reassure her, though he has nothing on which to base such reassurance. He shows her into the cubicle, and lets her sit down beside the bed.

'I'll go find the doctor', he says.

Ralph wanders the ward, making inquiries of nursing staff, and eventually tracks down a very young, harassed-looking junior doctor who examined Martin when he was admitted.

'We've still got a lot of tests to do', he says, 'but I don't think you should be too worried. Smoke inhalation. Breathing difficulties. The paramedics sorted him out on the scene and got airway control. We don't know the extent of the lung damage yet'.

'Lung damage?' asks Ralph. 'How serious could it be?'

The doctor is non-committal. 'Wait till we run some more tests. We've done laryngoscopy and fiberoptic nasopharyngoscopy. He's down for chest radiography, when there's a machine free. We'll probably do MRI and CT as well. He's not in serious danger. But there may be some damage to the lungs that'll need further treatment'.

Ralph's anxious concern is not satisfied, and he wants the doctor to provide more information. But the stressed and overworked young man is impatient, even irritated, and already on his way elsewhere.

'Doctor, if you could just explain..'

The doctor turns and comes back to him. 'Look', he says, 'he's lucky. He survived. Some didn't. He's intact. We've got people in intensive care with life-changing injuries. Now I'm sorry to be so direct. But I've got to get on'.

'Of course. I'm sorry, doctor. Thank you', says Ralph,

and wanders back to the cubicle. Mei is leaning over the bed, wiping Martin's forehead with a tissue. 'He hasn't woken up yet', she says.

'I spoke to the doctor. They need to do more tests. His lungs may be affected. But he'll be OK. I'm sure he'll be OK'.

There is only one chair beside Martin's bed. Ralph could go find another one, but he prefers to hover on the threshold, neither in nor out of the secluded space. He asks Mei if he can get her anything, but feels that all she wants is to be left alone with Martin. 'You come back later', she says, dismissing him. And he is only too glad, Martin being in good hands, to get clear of here for a while.

Ralph leaves the ward and takes the lift down to the ground floor. He takes a wrong turn at the bottom of the elevator shaft, and finds himself walking through a maze of corridors towards the back of the hospital. He passes various departments with unintelligible names; some glass cases containing dusty-looking antique medical instruments; an erstwhile chapel that is now a multi-faith prayer-room. Eventually he comes across the rear door of the hospital, and finds himself back in the open air.

Across the road he can see the old Margravine cemetery. He crosses the road and enters through the stone gateway. Ahead of him stretches the wide central walkway that leads down to Baron's Court, surrounded on either side by stone memorials, some dating back to the 1860s. They are large and small, ornate and simple, some still standing erect, others slipped and subsided to a crazy angle. Overall the graveyard is well-maintained, the grass kept short and trimmed, the cemetery bordered by trees and bushes, and a haven for wildlife. Squirrels chase one another among the gravestones, and birds chatter in the trees.

Looking at the monuments he reflects on the polarised attitudes to death they represent. Some are well-tended, cared for by people who treasure this reserved space of memory where they can keep the name of a loved one alive: cut grass, fresh flowers, the headstone cleaned and polished. Others lie forgotten and neglected, graves of the ancestors of people for whom death is finality, oblivion, best forgotten, literally laid to rest. Here, he realises, in this same small spot of earth, there is a convergence between people who, like himself, think of death as the end of everything, and others who cling to religious notions of immortality, or at least try to keep alive abiding memories. His thoughts are clearly triggered by the fact that today, for at least a couple of hours, he has been forced to face the possibility that his son might be dead.

He stops by one memorial he has seen before, a rough-hewn granite wheel-head cross, commemorating a famous local disaster. The cross bears the names of thirteen munitions factory workers, almost all women, killed in an explosion in November 1918, just before the Armistice. The blast occurred at Blake's Explosive Loading Company in Wood Lane, Hammersmith. The inscription reads:

TO THE MEMORY OF THOSE
WAR WORKERS
WHO DIED FOR THEIR COUNTRY
IN THE EXPLOSION
AT BLAKE'S MUNITIONS FACTORY
NOVEMBER 1918.

Ralph recalls reading accounts of the blast. 'A fire occurred at the filling factory at about 3.30pm on the 31st October, 1918 … in the shed used for the filling of thermalloy caseless bombs … when suddenly a dull thud was heard coming from the filling shed followed by flames'. Some of the staff were taken to hospital with burns and shock. Eleven women, aged between 21 and 46, were killed, and two men. The coffins were taken to the cemetery in army lorries.

A dull thud, followed by flames. For a moment Ralph imagines what it must have been like for Martin, standing insouciantly in the train carriage, glancing at the headlines, ducking to peer out of the window. Then without any warning, a dull thud, flames, a thick cloud of impenetrable smoke. The munitions workers who lie here died for their country, packing caseless incendiary bombs, front-line workers exposed to the same dangers as the soldiers in the trenches, even though the war they were all fighting was already effectively over. Martin and his fellow passengers were just going about their everyday business, heading off to work, concerned only to house and feed their families, doing harm to no-one. But they were struck at with merciless spite by a concealed and inscrutable enemy.

Ralph glances back up at the windows of the hospital. What must it be like, he thinks, for some patient, living in fear of death up there, to look down at the dense rows of crosses and funerary monuments below? The connection is accidental and contingent, since the cemetery was here for over a century before the hospital was relocated from the Strand. Who knows, perhaps the prospect is soothing and consolatory: it is a lovely spot.

Every hospital has one kind of entrance, the portal of fear and pain, and two kinds of exit. There is the sunlit doorway back to life and health; and the dark passageway that leads to dusty death. That morning he had passed the sign for the Mortuary, and glanced through a glass panel at a blank corridor, with an empty trolley standing abandoned beside a closed door. Perhaps this Victorian graveyard, so pleasant in the morning sunshine, affords a better prospect than the autopsy table and the incinerator. Surely, just as the dying soul yearns to escape from the body, that decaying mesh of suffering and pain; so the liberated spirit, if there is such a thing, must yearn for open spaces, as a bird that is caught in a building flutters desperately against window glass to regain the empty air.

Ralph sits down on a bench and consults his phone for news of the blast on the train. The police have designated the incident a terrorist attack. An explosive device appears to have been left on the train, possibly in a rucksack. The bomb may have contained projectiles. Officers are interviewing witnesses and studying CCTV footage in an effort to locate the perpetrator. Members of the public are asked to come forward with any information they consider might be useful to the police. The public should be assured that everything possible is being done to apprehend the terrorist and bring him or her to justice.

A call comes through to his mobile. The number is not recognised. It is Mei. 'Please come now', she says.

'Is he awake?'

'No. The doctor says he will sleep until tomorrow. But they are pleased with the tests. I need to get Haruki. Come please'.

Ralph stands up and with alacrity obeys the summons. Martin's condition seems to be unchanged. Mei looks composed, her emotions under control: but she is suffering some slight embarrassment.

'I must collect Haruki', she says.

'Yes, run along'.

'Can you stay here?'

'Of course'. Ralph is slightly surprised by the question. 'Yes of course I'll stay'.

'I mean … I can't come again until tomorrow. I don't want him to wake up and find nobody here. Will you stay with him?'

In realising that Mei seriously thinks he might be reluctant to stay at the hospital, Ralph suddenly senses the huge gulf between their understandings, and how much things have changed since this morning. It had not occurred to him that there might be anything important enough to call him away from his son's bedside. He is shocked that Mei should ascribe any reluctance to him. Here is his son's wife, the mother of his grandson, embarrassed to ask her husband's father to sit with his injured son.

Ralph tries to make himself comfortable in the hard, straight-backed chair. There is nothing he can do for Martin. But he is glad to be there. From outside the screen he can hear the usual noises of a hospital ward dedicated to serious cases: the quiet hum of electronic monitoring devices; the clattering of metal pots and pans; staff talking quietly to one another. One man in a nearby bed has a whooping, racking cough. A TV monitor on the wall, the sound turned down contributes a barely audible whisper.

In hospital time moves very slowly, but for the watcher there is also a strange feeling of release from responsibility, since everything possible is being taken care of, and there is nothing to be done except watch and wait. Ralph dozes off in the chair, then gets up to go to the lavatory and to stretch his legs. In the corridor outside the ward there is one of those bookshelves displaying a motley collection of old paperbacks, with battered covers and amorphously-shaped spines. There is one larger cloth-covered volume, the title obscured by years of wear. He pulls it down, and finds it to be a 'James Bond Omnibus' edition of Ian Fleming's thrillers.

Ralph takes the book back to his seat. It may not be the worst of companions in the long night ahead. He had loved the Bond books when he first read them in the 1960s, starting with a tattered paperback copy of *From Russia with Love* that a friend of his had brought to school. It was passed around the class so they could take turns to read the notorious sex scene that takes place in the stateroom of the Kristal Palace in Istanbul. After that he had borrowed all the books he could from the local library, and relished the early 'Cold War' novels.

But he had been obliged to revise his view of Bond in the 1970s, encountering them again with an altered perspective, and realising that they are in fact iconic embodiments of capitalist ideology, chauvinistic, racist and sexist. After Britain's imperial destiny had foundered and collapsed in the debacle of Suez, national liberation movements were throwing off their shackles, and feminist movements transforming the role of women. The world was making itself new, but Bond continued to represent the values of the old. Fleming, he came to believe, had promoted a myth of British superiority at a time when British influence in the world was waning; promoted British class snobbery in an age of increasing social equality; and revelled in the new consumerism that was extending capitalist power over a larger constituency. Above all, Ralph had been indoctrinated by a political party, the CPGB, that still harboured a grudging affection for the USSR, so Fleming's grotesque villains of SMERSH seemed to him nothing more than the clownish bogeymen of anti-Soviet propaganda.

Now he finds himself, after a long absence, revisiting Bond with a strangely altered perspective. Bond, he had been taught to think, was a typical poster boy for the establishment, typifying all the upper-class vices of British snobbery and privilege. Here however, in the foxed and mildewed pages of an old copy of *Casino Royale*, he reads of a different Bond: one whose occupation of his aristocratic territory is marginal, provisional and temporary. Here he is, in the glittering surroundings of Blades club, but he doesn't look like an insider, more like a battle-hardened soldier than a member of the establishment like M. 'Doesn't look like the sort of chap one usually sees in Blades'. He is as much an outsider as the former Nazi Drax: 'there was something alien and un-English about him'. He is a professional among amateurs: 'Against the background of this sparkling stage Bond felt his mission to be incongruous and remote, and his dark profession an affront to his fellow actors'.

Ralph devours one book after another, filling the long hours, while his son lies breathing regularly and peacefully beside him. Here in *Moonraker* he finds Bond standing, as he himself had recently stood, under the cliffs of southern Britain, 'the snarling milk-white teeth of England', until an explosion brings them collapsing down onto his head. Reading in these pages about the threat of nuclear catastrophe, Ralph remembers how real it was in the 1950s, and how anxieties about the Bomb merged in the minds of his own people with memories of the Leeds Blitz of 1941. He remembers the Civil

Defence leaflets telling the populace what to do in the event of nuclear attack. He remembers the air-raid sirens that routinely sounded in practice, and the manifest vestigial terror of those for whom they had recently sounded for real.

Of course the action-man Bond, with the help of the scientist Gala, saves the day. But how close it all came to disaster. 'How nearly it had come, thought Bond, to being stilled. How nearly there might be nothing now but the distant clang of ambulance bells beneath a lurid black and orange sky, the stench of burning, the screams of people still trapped in the buildings. The softly beating heart of London silenced for a generation. And a whole generation of her people dead in the streets among the ruins of a civilisation that might not rise again for centuries'.[22]

He raises his eyes from the page and is surprised to realise that it is night, the ward illuminated by subdued lighting, darkness black against the windows. A brisk and efficient Filipino nurse enters to check on Martin, and scribbles some notes on his chart. 'He doing OK', she says. So far as Ralph can judge, her observation seems genuine. Certainly Martin's face has more colour, and perhaps his breathing is easier, though it is hard to tell past the oxygen tube and face mask. 'He wake up soon'. She gives Ralph a blanket and a cup of tea, and he settles into the chair to try and get some sleep.

A voice disturbs him. 'Dad'. He has no idea where he is. The voice is familiar, but distant: subdued, a kind of hoarse whisper. It must be Martin, trying to wake him up, but keeping his voice down so as not to disturb Hannah. Why's he out of bed? 'Dad!' The call is more imperative, but still in the same constricted whisper. Ralph opens his eyes, expecting to see the

22 Ian Fleming, *Moonraker* (Pan, 1956), p. 185.

lineaments of his familiar bedroom, but instead encounters green NHS curtains. And the voice of his son is not an echo from the distant past, but an urgent contemporary summons.

'Dad, for Christ's sake wake up. Where am I?'

Ralph starts awake and finds Martin sitting up in bed, trying to remove his oxygen mask.

'Let me help', says Ralph. 'Not sure if you should be taking it off'.

'I can breathe OK', says Martin, pulling the mask free of his face. 'My chest hurts a bit, that's all. Where are we? Kingston?'

'No, Charing Cross'.

'Where's Mei?'

'She went home to take care of Haruki. Left me holding the fort. I'll call her for you, let her know you're awake'.

Ralph puts in the call to Mei. It's still very early, before sunrise, but she answers the phone immediately. He can hear the relief in her voice. She'll come in the morning, and bring Haruki.

'What can you remember from the train?' Ralph asks.

'Oh, not much. We were somewhere around Surbiton, I think. There was this almighty bang. The other end of the carriage. Then this ball of fire swept down the aisle. Then smoke, thick choking smoke. Everything went black. That's all I can recall'.

'You've been unconscious ever since. They doped you up and assisted your breathing. Give your lungs a chance to recover'.

'What was it?'

'A bomb. Someone must have planted it. They haven't said much else'.

'So were people – killed?'

'Yes, quite a few. The ones unlucky enough to be near the blast. The bomb was charged with projectiles, I think. Made to maim and kill. Thank God you weren't too close'.

'Found God, have you? That really would be a turn up for the book'. He tried to laugh, but clutched at his chest with pain. 'Don't make me laugh'.

Ralph puts a hand on his shoulder to still him. The touch seems unfamiliar. 'I was worried about you. For a while'.

'So you've been here the whole time?'

'Yes. Mei phoned me. I drove down to the station, then to Kingston Hospital, then here. Mei came in and stayed. Then she went back to get Haruki home. She'll be here first thing'.

'Good'. Martin looked at his father critically, as if detecting some change in him. Then his face creased with pain. 'Ow. My fucking chest hurts'.

'I'll get the nurse'.

The ward staff are pleased to see Martin awake. They had perhaps been more anxious than they were letting on. A nurse administers some pain relief, and makes him comfortable. He relaxes against the pillows, and close his eyes.

Ralph sits and looks at him, valuing the simple sight of his son recovering.

'Think I'm going to sleep again', says Martin. 'What the hell are they giving me? Must be good stuff. You get home now, Dad. Get some sleep. Mei will be here soon. Can you come back later?'

'Of course', says Ralph. 'I'll be back this afternoon'. He rises to leave.

As he pulls back the curtain to leave the cubicle, Martin calls him back. 'Dad. I wanted to say one thing. Well two.

First of all …' his mind retreats a little as the strong painkiller reaches his brain. He struggles to concentrate. 'I wanted to say … just… well, thanks. Thanks for being here'

'No need', says Ralph. 'Where else would I be?'

'Lots of places'. Martin clearly remembers the acrimonious terms on which they last parted, and the long silence that has persisted between them. 'I'm really glad you're here. And maybe … we can be better friends now?'

Ralph returns and clasps his son's hand. 'We've always been friends. The best of friends'. Then with an incongruous recollection of *Great Expectations,* which he remembers Ralph reading, with little enthusiasm and even less understanding, while at school: 'Ever the best of friends. Old chap. I guess I'm just not that good at friendship'.

Martin tries to laugh again, and clutches his chest.

'I'm off', says Ralph, 'before I do you some more damage'.

'What was the other thing?'

Martin's voice is reduced to a sibilant whisper, with a slight creaking and wheezing like the breath of an asthmatic. 'I sound like your Grandad. Maybe I'll wake up and find myself still in the trenches. What other thing?'

'OK. Think of it later', says Ralph. And once again he moves to depart.

'Oh I know', comes Martin's voice, again hushed into that rasping whisper that reminded Ralph so forcefully of the boy's childhood. 'I remember'.

'What is it?'

'Take that fucking DNA test'.

Ralph smiles. 'I will'.

Ralph walks back through the ward. Most of the patients are still sleeping. The man with the hacking cough has gone.

He finds the lift, glides down to the ground floor and walks through the lobby. Out on the forecourt, still in darkness, he can see an ambulance starting up, its blue light flashing and turning. Beyond are the street lights of Fulham Palace Road.

As he nears the exit, he glances up at a TV screen bracketed to the wall. The newscaster is announcing some breaking news, and Ralph pauses to read the sub-titles. Police have apprehended the Berrylands bomber. The image of a face is flashed up on the screen. A handsome face, shapely features, thick dark hair. A familiar face. Ralph stands in the doorway, staring up at the screen, oblivious to a group of paramedics who have to impatiently push past him.

The face is the face of Salam Hassan.

Chapter Eighteen
Brunanburh

'History may be servitude
History may be freedom'
– T.S. Eliot, *Four Quartets*

Humber Estuary, 937

Ulf and Erik stood on the shallow slope of a small hill and surveyed the flat marshy ground between themselves and the River Humber. They had been enlisted in Aethelstan's army, which was drawn up in formation along the estuary. Thousands of men from Wessex and Mercia had flocked to his standard as he marched north to meet the Scots under King Constantine, the oath-breaker, and the rebel Northumbrians who followed the traitor Alfgeir. Acting on the information given to him by Arne, Aethelstan had ordered a strong detachment of the Mercian army north to attack *Eoforwic*. Arne had been deployed with them. The main force of the Wessex troops, to which Erik and Ulf had been assigned, was waiting to defend the coast against the expected arrival of the Norse fleet from Ireland, led by Olaf, King of Dublin, intent on recovering the city of *Eoforwic*, ruled by his family for generations until its recent conquest by Aethelstan. Another host was drawn up a few miles further north, expecting the arrival of the Scots.

Ulf shivered as a cold morning breeze blew in from the Humber. He concealed the reaction quickly, not wanting to betray the fear he felt. The worst thing was the waiting. Every man there wanted the enemy to appear, so the fight could begin. Anything, even death, was better than this soul-sapping apprehension, that lay as cold and wet on the spirit as mist on the dreary mud-banks that lay between them and the black waters of the Humber.

Suddenly Ulf looked up, at what he thought was a small black cloud, coming fast and straight towards them, but which resolved into a huge flock of ravens, heading for the battlefield, grim and greedy, hungry for human flesh. The sky grew dark above their heads as the birds wheeled and swooped in undulating formation, and loud in their ears was the raucous concatenation of their uncanny clamour.

Ulf pointed them out to Erik, who grasped anxiously at the silver hammer of Thor suspended around his neck. 'Odin's birds', he said. 'Watch which way they fly'.

A Saxon next to them in the line overheard this exchange, and shook his head as if in disapproval. Ostentatiously, and as if in riposte, he drew the sign of the cross with his hand across his breast. Erik looked back at him aggressively.

'No senseless bird can foretell the future', the man said. 'You will not find your fate written in the sky, in signs such as these'.

'You speak bravely', said Erik fiercely, 'to disrespect the gods. Everyone knows the ravens whisper in Odin's ear, and tell him tidings of all they see and hear'.

'There is only one god', replied the Saxon simply. 'Believe in Him, and He will protect you from the might of the heathen.

But let's not quarrel, brother', he said, adopting a friendlier tone. 'We may need one another before the day is out'

Erik turned his face away. 'Come and find me, when this is done', the man called across to him. 'Let's see whose God is more powerful, yours or mine. In the meantime, may the Lord protect you. And your boy'.

Sourly Erik resumed his watch over the river. All eyes were on the lower reaches of the estuary as the tide began to flow landwards. At last the watchers were rewarded for their waiting. Peering east along the riverbank, Ulf could see the tall prow of a beaked dragon-ship sliding along the estuary, its red and white sail bellying in the breeze. It was followed by another, and another, and another, a great fleet of ships, carrying a formidable host of armed men. The first ship shelved onto the shallow mudbanks at the river's edge, and dozens of fighting men leapt over the side, carrying their painted linden-board shields and brandishing spears, axes and swords. Ulf swallowed hard, hoisted his shield and gripped his sword.

As the Norse streamed across the marsh towards them, a shouted command from an officer ordered them to form the shield-wall. Ulf dropped his shield to the ground and knelt behind it. Erik shoved his out over the boy's head, balancing it on the edge of Ulf's, and crouched down behind the boy. The line held against the first shock of battle, when Olaf's army fell on them, hacking at the wooden wall with sword and axe, splitting shields and cutting down men. A sharp spear was thrust through the gap between Erik's shield and Ulf's, and grazed the boy's temple. Erik returned the thrust with his spear, and the Norseman fell.

Out on the river some of the Norse ships were having

difficulty beaching in the marshy shallows. Many men had jumped over the side and found themselves stumbling in thick mud and tangling reeds, or floundering with their weapons in the fast-running water. The Norse army was not reinforcing as quickly as it should, and the shield-wall was holding. Another shouted command told the English force to begin advancing, using the slope of the hill to force the enemy back into the water. Ulf stood up and pushed his shield forward, unable to see what lay ahead. Resistance against their forward movement was giving way as the invaders fell back. Erik came beside him, pushing with his shield and delivering deadly strokes from behind it with his shining sword's edge.

The Norsemen were faltering, giving way, falling back, crushed by the inexorable weight of this great English army. As the enemy faltered, the line broke up, and warriors extricated themselves for hand-to-hand fighting. Again and again Erik's sword rose and fell. Ulf found himself stumbling over the bodies of the slain.

Out of the corner of his eye he saw a man running towards him. Finding his feet, he swung his sword back and over his head, slamming it down on the head of the attacking warrior, crushing his helmet and forcing blood from between his broken teeth. All along the line sword rang against shield, axe and spear clashed and crunched against mail and flesh. Some of the enemy began reboarding their ships, having not even reached the bank. Some turned and retreated for the safety of the water. Others tried to hold their line, standing firm and still dealing deadly strokes.

Many West-Saxons fell before the onslaught. A huge warrior stood unmoving at the water's edge, laying about him with a broad-bladed axe. Erik moved towards him and launched his spear, but the point glanced aside from the Norseman's shield and splashed harmlessly into the river shallows. Erik fumbled at his belt to draw his short axe as the man came towards him, raising his blade high above his head. But Ulf was on him, thrusting the point of his sword into the warrior's armpit. The man shouted in pain and rage, but his axe-arm fell, and in seconds Erik had buried his axe in the Norseman's neck. With a great splash he fell into the water and straightaway the tide began to take him, bearing him back out to sea.

The Saxons fought bravely, and as they had been trained defensively, staying behind the shelter of the shield-wall, minimising the risk of casualties. A man fallen in battle might earn glory for himself, but would be one less soldier left to defend the homeland. Erik, on the other hand, fought like a Viking, taking the fight to the enemy, rushing into the melee with a berserker ferocity, laying about him, cutting at the faces of the foe, inspiring terror in the opposing ranks. The Norsemen began to fall back before his onslaught, and the Saxon army soon swelled forward to enclose Erik and continue their tactic of pushing the enemy back into the river. Again and again Erik broke free from the defensive wall and cut a swathe through the invaders' ranks. His courage and ferocity were noted and approved by the senior commanders, who kept ordering their troops to close up and support his full frontal attack. The Norse warriors were demoralised by meeting an opponent who displayed their own merciless savagery in battle, and found their will and fighting spirit beginning to ebb away.

All day the men of Wessex pushed onward, driving the enemy into the river.[23] Troop after troop pursued the hostile invaders. Grievously they hewed the fugitives from behind, with swords sharp from the grinding. Nor were the Mercians reluctant to hand out harsh punishment to the warriors who had accompanied Olaf over the sea-surge in the bosom of their ships, seeking land, but fated to fight at the water's edge. By the end of the day five young kings lay dead on the battle-field, put to sleep by swords. Seven of Olaf's earls lay with them, and countless warriors of the invading army. The chief of the Norseman, Olaf himself, had been put to flight, forced to seek the safety of his ship's prow, his army broken, his retinue dispersed, blessed with little company. His ship turned on the fast-flowing current; away the king went on the dusky flood-tide, anxious to save his life.

On the breeze drifted the sound of another battle, some miles to the north. The army of Constantine, a veteran campaigner, a grizzled warrior, was clashing with the remainder of the English troops. This was one fight the King of Scots lived to regret, seeing so many of his friends fall on the battlefield, killed in the strife. He too found himself bereft of kinsmen; even his young son, green in battle, was left in that place of slaughter, hacked to pieces with grievous wounds. Constantine, that wily and grey-haired warrior, author of many a deceit and betrayal, had no reason to boast of the sword-slaughter he witnessed that day. Neither did Olaf have any reason to rejoice when he saw the ragged remnants, what was left of his army. Neither commander could boast that they excelled in deeds of war on the battlefield, where beneath their streaming banners troops collided, in a splintering of spears,

23 *The Battle of Brunanburh*, ed. Michael Livingstone (Liverpool: Liverpool University Press, 2011).

and a splitting of shields. Not when they came up on the field against the sons of Edweard.

The nailed ships of the Vikings turned in flight, desperate to regain the open sea, to sail back to Dublin over the deep water, returning to Ireland, their spirits quelled, their warlike hearts ashamed. Behind them the Scots too were turning tail, hammered into submission by the might of Mercia. But the brave brothers, Athelstan and Eadmund exulted, victorious in their valour.

The enemy fled, and the victors began to withdraw from the field. Behind them they left those dark-coated scavengers, the horny-beaked ravens. They flocked down on the battlefield before the slaughter was over, exulting in carnage, ravaging and tearing at still warm human flesh. There too could be seen the white-tailed eagle, swooping majestically down on his broad wings, whetting his bent beak, flexing his sharp talons. And there too, sidling along the edge of the battlefield, that fierce grey beast who roams the forest, the wolf of the weald, threw back his head and howled to his companions, eager to join the grim banquet. Together those beasts of battle were left to feast on the corpses, carouse on carrion, supping on slaughter.

Never before, on these islands, had there been seen such homicide. Never before were as many killed, so many fallen beneath the sword's sharp edge. Never before, so said the old wise men, since the Angles and Saxons came here over the broad sea: those same glorious warriors who had defeated the Welsh, and took possession of the land. Now they had successfully defended that same land in glorious battle against challengers from land, and invaders from the sea.

So it was that King Aethelstan, lord of warriors, ring-giver to men, and his brother Prince Eadmund, won eternal glory in battle with sword edges around Brunanburh. They split the shield-wall, they hewed and hammered the battle shields. They were truly the sons of Eadward. It was their solemn duty, by their noble descent, to protect their land by battle against hostile people: to defend horde and home, treasure and land. Before their combined might the seafarers perished, fell as they were fated to do. There lay many a warrior, by spears destroyed; many a Northman, shot with spear that had sung over shield; there lay many a Scot, wasted by war. From the dawn, when that glorious orb rises from his resting place, all through the long day as he glides over the ground, to the evening when he sinks down again to his rest, did the field flow freely with the blood of warriors.

Ulf trembled with a kind of aftershock as he watched the last dragon-ship of Olaf's fleet slide along the estuary, its beaked prow riding the incoming tide, eager to meet the open sea. His knees felt weak, and he could not feel his hands. The din of battle and the slamming of blows against his shield had made him partially deaf. All along the river Saxon soldiers were callously dispatching the wounded Norsemen; he could just hear the short sharp shrieks of pain as the swords and axes rose and fell.

Erik found Ulf among the press of men, and wound his strong arms tightly about him. Both were impasted with blood, some of their own, shed from cuts and grazes inflicted by sword's edge and spear's point, but mostly spurted from the open wounds of their slaughtered enemies. Ulf's face was encrusted with blood from the wound on his temple; Erik had sustained a blow to the head from a war-hammer, his face was bruised and his helmet buckled and bent. Ulf felt sick, and dizzy, but also buoyed up with a liberating thrill of joy. He had redeemed his shameful act of cowardice at the Dannevirke. He was able to leave the field with honour. He had even saved his father's life.

'Brother!', a voice called over the heads of the surrounding troops. 'Brother! Wait for me'. It was the garrulous Saxon who had talked to them before the battle. 'Now', he panted, coming alongside Erik, 'whose god is the stronger?' Erik remained sceptical, though more subdued, and less disposed to argue.

It was true, thought Ulf: they had invoked the help of Thor and Odin when they met the Saxons at the Dannevirke, defending their own homeland; but fate had been against them, and they had lost their leader. Here, fighting for an adopted country in which they were virtually strangers, marching under the banner of a king they hardly knew, surrounded by men who believed in this strange new god, they had won. Perhaps there was something to it, after all.

The Saxon went on to tell them the story of St Oswald, King of Northumbria in years gone by. Fighting against the Welsh, faced with insurmountable odds, greatly outnumbered, Oswald had fashioned a crude cross from sticks of wood, and called upon the Lord. His faith was rewarded, and the Lord spoke to him:

> Be strong and act manfully. Behold, I will be with thee. Your foes shall be put to flight, and Cadwallon your enemy shall be delivered into your hands. You shall return victorious after battle and reign happily.

'And so it befell, exactly as the Lord foretold. You see, Dane? He is with us, always, even to the end of the world'.

Again Erik shook off the importunate evangelist, setting his face forward and avoiding further speech. But Ulf was fascinated by the man's fervour, and impressed by the strength of his faith. Was it not true, what he claimed? Had their fortunes not turned when they enlisted in the ranks of this pious king, and marched into battle under the banner of Christ? Was there perhaps some mysterious power in the sign of the cross itself?

As they followed the press of soldiers heading back towards *Eoforwic*, they came upon a group of men, standing on a low hill and looking back towards the river. Thinking the enemy might be returning, Erik stood with them, and followed their gaze.

Seeing nothing but the flat marshland and the broad river, he asked them 'What are we looking at?'

The men were silent, as if struck by some momentous discovery or realisation.

'We are looking at England', said one man, in an awe-struck voice.

The others agreed. They used different names: *Saxon-land, Anglia, Engla-lond*. But they all meant the same thing: a united kingdom.

Chapter Nineteen

Ancestors

'Not one life only, but many generations'
– T.S. Eliot, *Four Quartets*

Weybridge, 2017

Once again Ralph sits in the back garden of Martin's house in Weybridge. Summer jasmine is blooming against the fence, diffusing a sweet perfume across the lawn. A big rose bush hangs heavy-headed, incandescent with brilliant white blossoms. Hardy Begonias, vivid red and yellow flowers, cluster clumsily across one another in the flower-beds. Martin is in the kitchen, audible through the patio doors as he clatters around making coffee. He is still recovering from the damage sustained in the blast, and Mei has been working full time while her husband is off sick. Ralph is reading a book with his grandson.

Since Martin was injured in the bombing of the train, Ralph has been a much more frequent visitor, so the boy has got used to him. He stands close to Ralph's knee and points out details in the pictures. The initial catalyst for this closer relationship between father and son was Ralph's profound sense of guilt at his role in facilitating Salam Hassan's entry into Britain.

It had emerged that far from being forcibly recruited into the Islamic State, as a child soldier, Salam had, as a teenager, pledged allegiance to the Caliphate, and enlisted as an agent in their war of terror against the West. It appeared that he had blamed British intelligence officers for betraying his father to the Baathist authorities, and held Britain responsible for his mysterious disappearance and assumed death.

Salam had indeed been trained by ISIS, but not as he claimed as an unwilling conscript, but rather as an enthusiastic volunteer. His hatred of the West, fuelled by the Salafist teachings of his religious mentors, and enhanced by the continued unwelcome presence of Western troops in Iraq and Afghanistan, knew no bounds. Indoctrinated by the ISIS Mullahs, trained by intelligence officers of the Caliphate, he had organised his entry into Britain with a clear and single mission: to infiltrate an environment of hospitality and trust, and to strike at the chosen moment with merciless force against the hated infidel.

His attack had been meticulously planned. He had built an explosive device in his bedroom, using basic knowledge from his engineering studies, and blueprints clandestinely supplied by his masters in ISIS. He had loaded the bomb with razor blades and nails, to achieve maximum human carnage. He had chosen to travel towards London on a busy commuter train, knowing it would be packed with passengers travelling to work. He had boarded the train at Surbiton station, planted the bomb in the carriage where Martin happened to be travelling, and jumped off at the next stop. He had then somehow made his way back to Dover, hoping to board a cross-channel ferry and perform his initial journey across Europe in reverse. But counter-terrorism officers had struck lucky with CCTV footage obtained from TFL, and picked up images of Salam boarding the train with a bag, and leaving at the next station without it. They were helped by a vigilant ex-army officer who had seen Salam deposit the bag shortly before the blast, and was able to corroborate the CCTV evidence. When Salam arrived at the Port of Dover with his ticket to freedom, counter-terrorism officers were waiting to arrest him.

Ralph felt a heavy responsibility. He had returned to the hospital the following day, and confessed to Martin the whole story, expressing a profound contrition at his unwilling contribution to his own son's narrow escape from death.

'Oh, come on, Dad', was Martin's response. 'You can't blame yourself. That guy fooled everyone: Border Force, police, Home Office, the foster family. He's obviously a master of deception'.

'I know. But if I hadn't helped him settle here – he wouldn't have been on that train, at that time …'

'Oh Christ', said Martin. 'I don't believe this. I get blown up, and you succeed in making it all about you. Look, you know I haven't agreed with everything you do. And I do think you sometimes seemed to care more about your – projects, than about me. But I know you've always done what you thought was right. You've helped, I don't know how many, people to escape from real persecution. Like Salam's father. People who really wanted to come here and live with us. Make their lives here. But there will always be others who come here to destroy us. The solution is to be more careful about who we let in. Not for you to decide that everything you've ever done has been ruined by one evil bastard.'

Ralph knew his son was right. Every year thousands of people come into Britain: refugees, asylum seekers, economic migrants, EU citizens entering via freedom of movement rules. Some simply want to avail themselves of opportunities to work, putting down no roots, always intending to return home, such as the seasonal migrant labourers who worked in agriculture. Others are attracted by the British way of life, its political and economic freedoms, the vibrant richness of its culture, its world-class education, and want to make their home here. Some arrive with the opportunistic intention of benefiting from the welfare system without contributing to it. They are probably in a minority, and the UK has the choice whether or not to cater to their demands. And then there are the rare cases, such as that of Salam, of people who infiltrate themselves into the country with an agenda of hatred, and with the clear intention of harming her citizens, wrecking her way of life. Ralph was already persuaded, by bitter personal experience, that much more care needed to be exercised over such sworn enemies of democracy.

Martin emerges from the patio doors carrying a tray of coffee and a juice for the boy. He puts the tray down and returns to the house to fetch something. He returns carrying a big fat lever-arch file filled with papers.

'Your DNA test result came through', he says. The result of Martin's test had been sent online to Martin's account. 'Everything is in here', he says, slapping the file down on the table, with a touch of excitement in his voice. 'I wanted you to see the whole picture'.

&

Ralph had returned home after that first day at the hospital, and immediately started rummaging around in his desk drawers to find the package. He had opened it, and studied the instructions. The box contained a glass vial, a label to wrap around it, and a self-addressed envelope to return it. Following the directions, Ralph spat into the vial, filling it to the recommended level. Then he screwed the cap back on, tightly as directed to release a stabilising solution. The saliva turned blue, indicating the sample had been correctly prepared. Ralph shook the tube, placed the vial inside the collection bag and sealed it with an adhesive strip. He placed the package in the mailing box, and the test was ready to go.

At the time Ralph had felt a surprising sense of release, as if the untaken test had irked and irritated him in some way. To have completed it felt like a turning point. It was the first time he could recall ever having done something he didn't want to do, simply because his son had asked him to.

Once he had taken the test, he felt it necessary to find out more about how the operation worked, and read up on the system. He knew something of genetics, having read a few books by Richard Dawkins and Steve Rose.

But his understanding of the relationship between DNA, evolution and population studies, especially with respect to race, proved to be substantially out of date. He recalled the debate as having been largely about DNA testing as a means of assigning people to the five 'races', European, Asian, African, Oceanian and Native American. Wedded as he was to a political philosophy that regards race as largely a social construct, ideologically designed to create and weaponize otherness, he expected to have no truck with the idea that a saliva test could measure a person's ethnic identity. The whole concept seemed to him more useful to those on the political right, desperate to prove their Aryan heritage, than to those on the left who, like him, work to dismantle barriers of race, as well as class and gender.

In fact, he had discovered when revisiting the field again, that after bioscientists had completed the Human Genome Project in 2003, the examination of human ancestry with genetics had entered new territory. The new genomics appeared to suggest, he read with interest, that there is no evidence that races have distinct, unifying genetic identities. Two people of European descent may be more genetically similar to an Asian person, than they are to each other. Scientists, he found, had moved the debate on to describe human diversity in terms of ancestry, connecting human variations with geographical origins. Thus the methods used to measure ethnicity – comparing an individual's DNA to that of population groups in particular regions – began to seem to him entirely reasonable. Most users were probably happy to believe that the trace of, for example, German ancestry detectable in their DNA indicated a long Teutonic lineage. In fact, since the comparisons were being made only between users of the service, and not against the DNA of long-dead generations, the evidences of kinship related to people now living in Germany, irrespective of how long they had been there. To demonstrate that one's ancestors came from the Middle East was not at all the same thing as claiming that one possesses an element of Arab, or Persian, or Semitic ethnicity. The project is more about connecting people with places, than it is about racial and ethnic differences.

Martin takes Haruki indoors for his afternoon nap, leaving Ralph to peruse the file. The first page is a long strip of paper that folds out to reveal a conventional family tree, descending chronologically, roots at the top, branches at the bottom.

The ornate styling and formal presentation seem to Ralph to suggest a professional production, with the impersonality of a printed and published work. But the content is personal. At the foot of the page, the final branch of the tree, is Martin's own name, and above it his own, with dates and places of birth. Above Ralph's name is that of his father Eric, and above him grandfather Walter. Beyond, climbing up the page, stretches a succession of unfamiliar Christian names, all linked by the same surname, Ravenswood. Each holder of the patronym is shown connected to a marital partner, with the date and place of the wedding, and the date and place of the spouse's birth.

Ralph starts leafing through the rest of the file, which proves to be a compilation of photocopied documents, mostly birth, marriage and death certificates, baptismal records, census returns, newspaper cuttings, pictures of gravestones. There is a section corresponding to each name on the family tree, giving a complete delineation of the person's life, from cradle to grave: when and where he or she was born, their parentage, where they lived and what they did for a living, when and where they died, where they are buried. The list of documents proceeds in reverse chronological order, and grows thinner as they reach further back into the past.

For the very last entry, a Richard Ravenswood, there are only a couple of documents, a page from an old baptismal record, a printed tabular register of some kind, and the picture of a grave. The latter gives the date of death as 1756, the name engraved on a sandstone tablet, in copperplate writing, with a florid inscription that is hard to decipher. The second he recognises as a printed electoral roll, dated 1741. The list of baptisms, written of course by hand, is difficult to decipher, but Ralph works out that the date is 1693, and that the ceremony was solemnised in St Wilfrid's Church, Otringham. He has never heard of the place. He notes that on the church baptismal record the surname is misspelt, given as Ravensrod.

Martin returns, observes Ralph scrutinising the file, and looks pleased with himself. He sits down beside his father, so they can peruse the records together.

'What do you think?', Martin asks.

'You did all this?'

'Impressed?'

'Well yes. It's a huge project. Take me through it'.

'OK. Start with yourself. There's your Dad, born in Meanwood, Leeds, 1928. His Dad, Walter, also born in Meanwood, 1899. He worked in printing, as you told me. A compositor at the Yorkshire Post. There's a newspaper article about his death, look at the back' – he turns to the section of the file relating to Walter – 'died at the age of 39. There's his picture'.

Ralph puts his fingers on the blurry image of the grandfather he had never known. He had never seen the photograph, or the obituary. 'It is with regret that we learn of the death of Mr. W. Ravenswood of the "Yorkshire Post" machine room, who was 39 years of age, died after a long and painful illness ... His death came as a shock to his colleagues, for the more recent reports of his illness had given rise to hopes that he had at last turned the corner, and was on the road to recovery'.

'But look, see what happens. There's Walter's dad Charles, 1860-1932. He worked in printing too: look, there's his census record: 'Pressman'. But his father, now, Thomas, 1830-1895: see, there – he was a Cloth Dresser. So he worked in a woollen mill. A machine operator, presumably, servicing the dreaded shear frames that upset the Luddites. He must have worked in the Oatlands Mill, up in Woodhouse'. Martin eagerly turns over another page, which gives information about the work of a Cloth Dresser, or Cropper. Ralph is of course familiar with the croppers, whose job was to cut the surface of woollen cloth after raising it with shears. At the beginning of the 19th century they were prominent among the Yorkshire Luddites who destroyed the shearing frames, faced off against 4000 soldiers, and saw seventeen of their number hanged at York. He realises that he knowns much more about the rebels who resisted industrial progress, than he does about his own great-great-grandfather, who had turned his hand to operating the machinery, moved with the times and facilitated industrial progress. 'But now', Martin continues, 'look back at the tree. This is where it gets interesting. Up to that point, your people were all living in the same place, Meanwood. Working in a woollen mill, then in the printing trade. The men married women also from the same area, usually the same parish. The family was rooted in that same place for over a century. But now, look. Thomas's father, John. He was a Cloth Dresser too, died 1867, in Meanwood. But he was born' – Martin turned again to the documentation for John Ravenswood – 'in Bubwith. East Yorkshire. In 1803'.

'Bubwith?' The name rang a bell, but Ralph would not have been able to locate it on a map. Handily Martin, thinking of everything, had included a modern map of East Yorkshire in the folder, with a small number of villages pin-pointed. 'Bubwith is there, south-east of York'. He points to a village on the plain of York, close to Selby. 'So John moved to Leeds, some time in the mid-19th century, I guess for work. But his father, Thomas (1771-1807) was born and died in Bubwith. His father John (1727-1786) born and died in Otringham'. Martin places a finger on a village that lies far out on the narrowing promontory that thrusts out into the North Sea from the East Yorkshire coastline, forming the estuary of Humber, and which Ralph knows to be Spurn Head.

'And that's where our first known ancestor was born and died. There he is' – pointing to the name at the root of the tree – 'Richard. 1693-1756. I can't get back any further than him. And here's where it gets interesting. There's a document at the back – wait a minute – here it is. Look at this'.

Martin shows Ralph a copy of a printed table, the orthography suggesting an 18th century historical source, four columns to a page. On the left, a list of names, in Roman type; followed by two columns of places, in Italic, and finally a series of initials, T or F. There is Richard Ravenswood, listed as resident in Otringham. The second column gives Wellwick. The final column shows the letter T.

'Wellwick? And what do the T and F stand for?' asks Ralph, who knows the document to be an electoral register. 'Tenant and Freeholder?'

'That's what I thought at first'. Martin is clearly enjoying knowing more about something than his father. 'But it's not. Look at the heading of the second column'.

Obediently Martin looks. '*Freehold lies in*'.

'This is a page from the register for the General Election of 1741. Richard is here because he was a freeholder, a landowner. The letters in the last column are the initials of the two parliamentary candidates. He voted for the Whig, Cholmely Turner. So your 6th great-grandfather was a Whig-voting member of the landed gentry'.

'Well, well', says Ralph softly, feeling his world turning upside down. 'Who knew that?'

'Now', says Martin, taking a tiresome pleasure in

explaining his research. 'Did you notice anything about the surname?'

'Yes. In the baptismal register it's misspelt. Ravensrod'.

'Misspelt? Perhaps. But the same form appears on the gravestone'.

Martin shows Ralph a magnified print of Richard's funerary monument. And here the name and date can be seen clearly, *1693, Ravensrod.* 'You think it's not a misspelling? A variant of the name?'

'I think it's the original name. Ravenswood is a modernisation. The name was Ravensrod'.

'Which means?'

Again Martin finds the map in the folder. 'OK. Here's the East Coast of Yorkshire. There's Spurn Head, above the Humber estuary. There's Richard's freehold land, Wellwick, out on the promontory. But here' – picking out a point just on the inside of the headland – 'there was a village, settled by Danes around the 10th century. You know what it was called? *Ravenser Oddi.* The raven's tongue. Because the headland curves, see, like the tongue of the bird. *Ravenser Oddi.* Ravensrod. Ravenswood. Our name belongs to that place' – stabbing his finger on the map – 'and to that time. Four centuries ago'.

'So what happened to the land?', Ralph asks. 'Are you thinking of reclaiming your birthright?'

Martin laughs, holding his chest, but continues his exposition. 'They were still paying land tax in 1798. But then with John, who moved to Leeds in the 19th century, it's gone from our line. John had a brother who stayed put, Thomas, lived in Fangfoss, and he's listed as a craftsman and small businessman – a cobbler, but also a draper. So my guess is he started with some capital. But the land disappears from the record. John must have had some money too, to set up in Leeds. That area, bottom of Meanwood Road, is still called Little London: because it was full of grand houses, so it looked metropolitan. I guess he bought a house. So the money didn't last long down the generations.'

'Yes', says Ralph thoughtfully. '*Sic transit gloria orbis*. A long farewell to all my greatness, as Cardinal Wolsey is supposed to have said'.

'But they applied their skills. You assume, as farmers out in Wellwick, they would have had sheep. A short step from there to working in a factory with wool. Then learning about machines, and moving on to printing presses. From there to literacy, and you. I guess it's not an uncommon story'.

'Just one more thing. While I've got you in a receptive frame of mind, and before you start analysing, and disagreeing with everything. Think about this. We can trace our name through a male line back to the 17th century. In between of course there are myriads of other people – some of these guys had 6 or 7 kids, boys and girls – most of the women married and took other names of course – so this is just a single thread pulled out of a much bigger tapestry, connecting us to that place, four centuries ago. We know back then the family were gentry, part of the landed elite, even if it was in a small way. And they bore a name rooted in the place.

'So: where were they before that? Do you think it likely that, prior to the 17th century, someone with the name Ravensrod travelled up to Yorkshire from somewhere else, and decided to settle there just because of the accident of the name? "Ravensrod! What a coincidence, let's stay here, we'll fit right in". No. The family, and the name, must go right back to the days of the Danelaw. And this', he announces with some pride, 'is where the DNA test comes in. Look at mine first'.

Martin reveals a print-out of another map, showing Britain, Northern Europe and North America. Alongside is a pie-chart with slices of different colours, yellow, green, brown. On the map there are blotches of the same colours over the UK, and stretching into Northern Europe.

'OK. So this is me. Two distinct centres, with links to different areas of Europe. There's Mum's contribution: south-west England, shading off into Northern France. And here's yours: East Yorkshire, shading off to the east, Germany, Scandinavia'.

'Scandinavia?' says Ralph, puzzled.

'Yes. So they assess me as 80% British and Northern Europe. Some Scots, Welsh and Irish. And traces that show those different roots, going north and south, into Europe. Now look at yours'.

This is the big reveal. Martin senses that he has Ralph in a state of expectation and curiosity he has probably never known before. He takes his time to find the right document, letting the suspense build, enjoying the showmanship, master of the situation. At last he puts the document down in front of Ralph.

Ralph sees a similar map, with the same pie-chart, differently marked. 100% British and North European. 80% English. 5% Scots. 5% Irish. And last of all, and most extraordinary, 10% Danish. The map visualises the same pattern of ethnicity, a blob of bright yellow centred on East Yorkshire, a penumbra of brown catching Scotland and Ireland, and a net of green stretching out across the North Sea, and capturing the Jutland peninsula of Denmark.

'So let's put it all together', says Martin, with the triumphant air of one who feels his argument to be irrefutable. 'You happen to bear a name that's rooted in a place with that same name. So there must be a connection. The name happens to be Danish. It just also so happens that the Danes ruled Northumbria in the 9th century, when *Ravenser Oddi* was settled. And it appears that your ancestral DNA retains traces of a Danish origin. You have an ancestor who was a substantial landowner in the 17th century, right on that promontory. Now what are the chances? Accident? Coincidence?

'Dad. I'd like you to meet – yourself. As you've never seen him. Ralph – Ravensrod'.

Chapter Twenty

Settlement

'The life of significant soil'
– T.S. Eliot, *Four Quartets*

England, 938

Notwithstanding the January cold, most tangible in the sting of the biting easterlies that came over the North Sea, Ulf was sweating as he manipulated the heavy plough. He gripped two long handles that steered the machine, consisting of a single wheel supporting a big iron ploughshare, shaped like the prow of a ship. Ulf had watched the smith forge the share on his anvil, heating the iron to a white incandescence, hammering it into shape, throwing off streams of bright sparks, and finally dousing it, with a great vent of hissing steam, into a bucket of cold water. The plough was harnessed to a team of four oxen, which was treading a slow, heavy path across the fields. Erik led the team, in his hand a switch to tap the beasts if they paused to graze.

Clumsy as the instrument felt in Ulf's hands, it represented a technology far beyond anything he had used before, and never failed to astonish him in its capacity to slice open the damp, clay-impacted soil of their farmland. Two men could traverse a whole field, ripping up the soil to cleave deep furrows, in a fraction of the time formerly taken by men working with their hands. The plough cut deep into the soil, opening the earth to refreshing rain, rooting out weeds and leaving them exposed to wither in the open air. As the oxen trod their ponderous gait, heaving the plough behind them, their dung dropped ripe and rich over the fields, manuring the soil as they passed.

After the battle, Erik had thought it prudent to stick with the detachment of warriors to which they had been deployed, having nowhere to go, and without friends, and followed them back to the city. The troop, a local *fyrd* from York, welcomed them warmly into their midst, since they had fought bravely, helped to hold the shield-wall firm against the invader, and Erik in particular had played a significant part in the repelling of the invading army. He knew that these Saxons would eventually need to return to their homes, farms and occupations, where there would probably be no place for a couple of supernumerary Danes. Fortunately for them, on arriving back in York the *fyrd* was kept under arms to ensure security in the still volatile and divided city.

The work of a peacekeeping force was not onerous, and they were regularly fed. They searched for Arne, who had advanced on York with the Mercians, but he had travelled back to *Streoneshalch* to find Gretta. They were given to understand that Arne had also made something of a name for himself among the Saxons, by supplying useful intelligence, and fighting bravely to relieve the city, finding favour even with the king. Erik hoped that if they could be reunited with Arne, they might be able to petition the king to reward them for their service. Aethelstan himself however had ridden north to secure fealty from any remaining rebels, and to pacify the northern territories, so any such entreaty would have to wait.

For a matter of weeks father and son served on security details, keeping order and preserving the king's peace. During this period, quickly getting used to the different language spoken by the Saxons, they learned about the momentous nature of the battle they had fought in, which had acquired the name Brunanburh, and was everywhere spoken of with reverence, as a great victory that in the future would be sung and spoken, in poems and chronicles. They learned of the ambition of the kings of Wessex to unite the British isles and its petty kingdoms – Scotland, Northumbria, Mercia, East Anglia, Wessex, Cornwall – under one king, an aspiration initiated by Alfred the Great, and inherited by his heirs Edward the Elder and Aethelstan; of how again and again their plans were blocked and thwarted by successive attacks from Danes and Norse, overlapping waves of reconquest and recolonisation; and how it was only after the triumph of Brunanburh that the king was able to style himself, as he now did, *rex totus britanniae*, king of the whole of Britain, and claim the historical distinction of being a nation's founding father.

The Danes' experience of monarchy in their own lands, with kings like Harold Fairhair and Eric Bloodaxe, had not been encouraging, and they had quickly become accustomed to the republican society of Iceland, especially under the guidance of Arne, who was a great enthusiast for the island's democratic polity. They had had to admit, on the other hand, that Iceland's popular self-government had utterly failed in the face of a great crisis, and that the islanders had been left by the *Althing* to their own devices. Here on the other hand the centralised organisation of the commonwealth, especially its military deployment, was awe-inspiring, and they heard nothing but praise for Aethelstan, as a king who ruled his realm fairly and equitably, and was motivated chiefly by piety, learning and a passion for justice. He seemed to be a different kind of king, one who easily and readily commanded loyalty. Whether or not he would find it possible to reward them for their service, giving them some means of livelihood in this land, remained to be seen.

Ulf could not rid his mind of a suspicion that this new religion, the worship of Christ, which seemed ubiquitous in this country, and into which they had perforce been inducted, must have something to do with the quality of Aethelstan's kingship. In Ulf's experience kings ruled by fear, and secured loyalty by reward. But here thousands of men and women supported Aethelstan because they trusted him, and believed in his leadership. The Danes prayed to gods who were stronger and wiser than human beings, but whose appetites and desires were really no different from theirs – they were lustful, and angry, and treacherous, and jealous; whereas this thin, pale god known as Jesus brought a message of peace, and renunciation of desire, and universal love among the whole of humankind. The Norseman Erik Bloodaxe slew his half-brothers so they could not challenge him for the throne. Here in England Aethelstan and his half-brother Eadmund Aetheling rode into battle together, side by side as kinfolk should, showing to their people the power of unity, spreading throughout the land a gospel of love and peace.

A few days later Arne returned with Gretta and the other women and children impounded on their arrival. The remaining Icelanders who had sailed with them, who had also fought for the king, had sought them out, and the whole expatriate community regrouped in York. By this time Aethelstan had returned from the north and began to hold his court. Long files of people queued for an audience, and the Icelanders took their place and waited their turn. Arne was appointed to speak, when their turn came, on behalf of all. At last they were shown into the hall, and once again faced the king in whose cause they had risked their lives. True to his reputation, Aethesltan dealt with them justly, recognising their service, as attested by his own officers, and asking them what they wished for as reward. Most of them asked for money or treasure, as was the custom, and received from the king's own hand silver and gold. In recognition of his exemplary service, Arne was given a jewel-encrusted sword, and a helmet decorated with scenes of battle.[24] When Erik reached the king's throne, one of Aethelstan's advisors whispered something to the king, presumably an account of Erik's military exploits at Brunanburh. As Erik knelt in silence before the king, Arne reminded Aethelstan of how they had first met at the monastery at *Inderawuda*, and of how they had alerted him to the conspiracy against his life.

'Ah yes', said the king, 'I remember. The boy with his father-mother. You wanted land, I believe, rather than treasure?'

'Yes my Lord', replied Erik respectfully.

The king thought for a moment, and consulted with his advisor. 'There is a vacant post I would like you to take. We need a watchman to guard the promontory of the river, near where the battle was fought'.

The previous incumbent, a Norseman, had disappeared shortly before Olaf's forces landed, and his body had not

24 *Egil's Saga*, trans. Bernard Scudder (London: Penguin, 1997), p. 100.

been found. It was assumed that he had thrown in his lot with the invaders, and probably returned with them to Ireland. If Erik assumed the position of coastguard, he would also take over the renegade's house and all his property in the port of *Ravenser Oddi.*

'Watch the shore for us', said the king. 'Guard the promontory. Hold the ness'.

Erik leaned forward and placed his head on the king's knee, according to the old custom. Aethelstan laid a hand briefly on Erik's head, then bade him rise and be about his business, for the kingdom had need of good men like him.

Arne congratulated Erik on his promotion. Erik was not quite sure what it all meant, and had been hoping simply for the tenancy of a farm.

'It's a test of loyalty', Arne explained. 'It's what they do: he probably learned it from his grandfather Alfred. When Danes show up on the shore, you'll be called upon to show your loyalty by opposing them. They're afraid there might be – a conflict of interest. Someone will be watching you, and reporting back. For a while at least. Do the king's bidding, and you can hope for further reward'.

And so Erik became a watcher on the wall, guardian of the coastline from *Flenneborg* to *Ravenser Eyr*, and the north bank of the River Humber as far inland as the upriver settlement called by the Danes *Vik*, and by the Saxons *Wic.*[25] Some of the other Icelanders enthusiastically threw in their lot with Erik, and agreed to serve him as labourers, and as warriors to defend the king's land. Others joined Arne and Gretta, who announced their intention of travelling south with the king's entourage, hoping to find employment in Wessex.

25 Hull.

Erik and Ulf assumed occupancy of a fine house in the port, and took over a large staff of house-carls, labourers and servants. Using his companions from Iceland as a base, Erik soon assembled a troop of warriors capable of defending the territory. He sought out veterans, some of whom had fought alongside him at Brunanburh. These men were given the task of keeping the local *fyrd* suitably armed, well trained and kept in a state of readiness.

Within a short space of time the small community of *Ravenser Oddi* was once again flourishing. Every day its fishermen launched their boats and spread their nets on the sea, seeking herrings and sturgeon, flounders and lobsters, or set their basketwork traps along the banks of the estuary to catch eels and pike, minnows and burbot, trout and lampreys. Every day the field-workers trooped out onto the land to plough and sow, to reap and harvest, the shepherds tended to their flocks and the herdsmen to their cattle. Every day ships arrived in the harbour with trade goods from overseas, and departed laden with exports. Every day Erik took his militia out to scour the estuary and the sea-coast for any sign of raiders.

Sometimes they would spot a ship coming in to land, the lookout would observe weapons and shields loaded on the deck, and Erik would ride down to the shore with a few hand-picked men to confront the strangers, flourishing his spear and issuing a formal challenge.[26] He would ask them what kind of men they were who had sailed over the sea-lanes in their deep-hulled boat, equipped for combat with mail-coats and sharp swords.

He would tell them that he was the coastguard, stationed here, watching the waves for raiders who come to hurt and to

26 *Beowulf*, ed. C. L. Wrenn (London: Harrup, 1969), 229-300.

harm the king's peace. Why should he allow them safe-passage, if their intention was, as interlopers, to march inland?

'Tell me who you are, and what business you have in King Aethelstan's realm'.

If the strangers gave a good account of themselves, and seemed to come in good faith, they would be granted safe passage, escorted to *Wic* and handed over to the king's authorities.

'A wise man', Erik would say, 'takes account of two things: what's said, and what's done'.

He would accept what they had told him, that they professed loyalty to the king. Now they must prove their words true in action. 'Follow my men', he would say, 'who will escort you to town to meet with the king's thegn. We'll watch over your boat, down on the strand, ensure she's safe, until the time comes for her beaked prow to cut through the waves, and haul you heroes back to your homes'.

The broad-beamed ship would ride on the waters, securely moored and anchored fast, while the English escorted the newcomers to their destination. At other times a boat would beach and betoken danger. Erik and his men would ride to the shore in force and demand of them their business. If the strangers proved shifty, and elusive, and were seen secretly drawing their weapons and preparing to fight, Erik would order his men to be ready for battle. The raiders would look up and see a band of stern-faced men sitting high on their horses, boar-shapes glittering above their cheek-guards, the brightly forged work of smiths. And above them, on the clifftops, a much larger troop of infantry, shields at the ready, spear points bristling against the sky. Then the invaders would think twice, and set to their oars, and push their long ship back out to sea.

Chapter Twenty-one

Headland

'Old men should be explorers'
– T.S. Eliot, *Four Quartets*

Yorkshire, 2020

Ralph stands on the utmost tip of a green and white, grassy and sandy promontory, looking out to sea. Little more than a sandbank, this is Spurn Head, the ultimate extremity of the Southumbrian peninsula, where the tapering, attenuated point of the region known as Holderness divides the Humber Estuary from the North Sea. Yorkshire's Land's End, they call it. From the air the Head resembles a tear-drop, linked to the mainland by low and level sands that are washed over at high tide by the scouring, irrepressible ocean. From above you can see why the Danes, who used to rule here, called its elegant curve *Ravenser Eyr*, the raven's tongue. Round the bend of the estuary the port of *Ravenser Oddi* had stood on the shifting sands, only to be inundated as coastal erosion undermined its foundations. Perhaps it was the same submerged mediaeval town he had dreamt of, after that first conversation with Martin about the past. But he did not believe in déjà vu.

The end of the promontory is accessible only at low tide. To reach the point you have to negotiate a treacherous isthmus of sand, where the surface crumbles beneath your boots, where your feet give way and constantly slip into water. The trip can only be accomplished on foot, and requires caution and vigilance. The tides are swift and merciless: it is all too easy to get cut off.

There is nothing here, really: two disused lighthouses, half buried in sand, and a lifeless life-boat station. But Ralph feels in some inexplicable way that in this place of liminality, this threshold between land and sea, poised between the elements of earth and water, this dead end that could be also a locus of embarkation, that he has found – somewhere. Something.

But what? Across the waves is Denmark; perhaps – if his DNA make-up is to be believed – the original home of his putative ancestors. It doesn't seem that far from here. Six thousand years ago you could have walked across. But his forebears, if indeed they existed, came here the hard way, over a harsh sea, sharp with the sting of spray and the scream of the gull. They came in square-rigged clinker-built boats, crafted of unseasoned wood by their own tools; propelled by the strength of their own hands; blown by the power of winds expertly caught in their own handmade sails.

Who knows why they left Scandinavia? Were they the story-book Vikings of legend, who came to pillage and raid, slaughtering churchmen and looting their shrines, raping and enslaving, putting men and women to the sword and villages to the torch? All these things happened. Or were they rather, like many who have arrived on these shores, refugees, fleeing perhaps from some catastrophic war, or some cataclysmic disaster, seeking shelter, sanctuary, a place to call home? People who wanted only safety, space, soil; to settle, to raise their families, to plough the land?

If the family history constructed by Martin, and the corroborative DNA test, were accurate, then somewhere along the line Danes came here and decided they would belong. They took their name from the port that once flourished here, *Ravenser Oddi*, and passed it on to their descendants, along with the lands they had occupied and somehow come to own. Ralph searches his senses and emotions for some evidence of affinity, some feeling that connects him back, through the land, to those distant generations. But there is nothing there, no emotional basis for claiming kinship with the past.

&

Ralph had nursed for some time the idea of revisiting Yorkshire, but had been impeded by a stubborn reluctance, probably born out of fear. Not since his youth had he regarded the place as home, and he had shamefully neglected to maintain any connection with his extended family. He felt that if he made contact, they would quite rightly want nothing to do with him. But with the impetus of Martin's discoveries urging him on, he decided to take courage and embark on a journey into his own, largely disowned, past.

All the people of his parents' generation are dead. He knew he had a number of cousins still living in Leeds, or scattered around the East Riding. One in particular, Roger Ravenswood, son of his father's brother, had, to his surprise, suddenly sprung at him out of his family tree. Comparison of Ralph's DNA with that of other members had thrown up Roger's name and photograph, defining him as a first cousin. Ralph made contact with him, was immediately invited to visit, and was made unreservedly welcome.

He discovered that Roger, a successful lawyer, lived in Fangfoss, an East Riding village close to the place Ralph had come to call, ironically, the family's ancestral seat, Wellwick. This proximity to the site of an ancient family history seemed too much of a coincidence, but Roger confessed to knowing nothing about it when he first decided to live there. He just liked the place, and had unconsciously gravitated back towards what turned out to be the resting place of his ancestors.

Roger lives in a stone cottage, once a farm building, next door to the old National School where, in the mid-nineteenth century, a John Ravenswood was the headteacher. His grave is there in the well-maintained graveyard of St Martin's church, a grey stone tablet spotted with lichen. The church has been there since the 12th century, but the building restored in the mid-19th. Roger had not thought to explore the churchyard, and had discovered the affinity through genealogy. Only then did he realise that he lives near neighbour to the dwelling of his own long-deceased great-great-great-great-great-uncle.

With their shared interest in ancestry, the two men joined forces to probe deeper into the more distant past. Together they explored the locality, combing through parish records, haunting churches and graveyards. They were rewarded by finding a couple more generations of Ravenswoods in the local churchyards, dating the family line back to 1500. They found no evidence of wealth or social prominence, no elaborate tombs inside the old churches. But the Ravenswood gravestones were solid, well-founded, clearly inscribed, indicating a sufficiency of wealth, consistent with the status of prosperous farmers, artisans, tradesmen, as they are represented in the census records.

&

Ralph found that he enjoyed this pottering about in churchyards in search of an elusive past. Unconsciously the quest drew him, unawares, towards the threshold of the church itself. Usually the buildings were locked up during the day when he did his foraging. But one late afternoon, as he was hunting in the grounds of a village church for more Ravenswood tombs, he found the doors unlocked, and heard the faint sounds of an organ. Preparations were being made for Evensong. Through the stained-glass windows he could see the flickering light of candles. Something drew him to the door, though he had not attended a church service, excepting for funerals, since his boyhood. The candlelight, and the breathy wheezing of the old organ, reminded him of Oxford, and suddenly he saw himself, walking through a college quadrangle in a November twilight, observing coloured light filtering from the chapel windows across the lawn, hearing the vibrating tones of an organ, sometimes the unearthly sound of a choir. He had always resisted any attraction he might have felt for whatever superstitious ritual went on in such places. Religion was the opium of the masses. If he had been honest with himself, he would have recognised that what was emanating from that chapel at dusk was in fact a summons, almost a calling, that he had chosen to ignore. Secretly he had envied the confidence of those who thought it worthwhile to perform such rituals in what to them was a sacred space.

Another memory struck him: once he was in Venice, trying to find information in his guidebook about some echoing, cavernous church on the Dorsoduro. A girl walked past him, her head demurely covered with a white silk scarf, with a face out of a Botticelli painting. She stood by the wrought-iron votive candle-rack, lit one of the small night-lights, placed it back on the rack and uttered a silent prayer. The candle glowed red and yellow. Ralph had watched her in fascination, and felt literally sick with envy at her certainty. Notwithstanding his ideological antipathy to any supernatural belief, he could not help wishing that he too could offer devotions to a deity, pray on behalf of others, honour the dead. As he left the gloomy church, regaining the hot pavement, seeing the harsh sunshine reflecting from the Giudecca beating back against his eyes, he felt it unfair that he was condemned to live in this harsh, material world.

He realised that throughout his life, apart from a few years of his boyhood, he had resisted emotions, sensations, perceptions that were clearly religious in nature. Once in the cathedral of Notre Dame in Paris, almost blinded by the clouds of incense and coloured light, he had heard the organ playing Bach's *Toccata and Fugue in D Minor*, and was obliged to sit down under the access of emotion. He had entered the Duomo in Florence, and found himself fighting back irrepressible tears. And once in St Peter's in Rome he had stood before Michelangelo's Pieta, sensed in the air the palpable presence of millions of whispered prayers, and felt the unmistakable, resisted touch of an inexplicable blessing. As he enters through the porch of the old Northern church, he wonders if such elusive feelings might once again come almost within his grasp: here, in this secluded chapel, now, and in England.

ȣ

Through his reacquaintance with Roger, Ralph had learned that the family still held him in high regard, and stood in admiration of his talents and abilities, as the only member of the family to attain such success, so far away from home. They seemed to see him as a kind of envoy or ambassador, who scaled the dizzy heights of academia, distinguished the family name, even put it into print by writing books.

Again this discovery was a source of shame to Ralph. Their residual appreciation of him was hardly justified by his mediocre academic career, or whatever infinitesimal contribution he might have made to the socialist revolution. It was abundantly clear to him that this legend was something established and maintained, across the extended family by his parents, long after he left. They had obviously continued to think about him during the years he had tried to forget about them, and to lodge in the family consciousness that myth of his status as a working-class hero. In every respect, he did not deserve it.

It was his parents who had made him into a legend, and in return he had shamefully neglected them. Newly anxious to avoid repeating the same mistake, he has booked a parkhome on a site by the east coast, a village of white plastic cabins sitting above the cliffs near Scarborough, and invited Martin to bring the family up for a week. His son was only too glad to oblige, and soon he and Mei were off taking long walks along the windy cliffs, while Ralph tried to show Haruki how to light a barbecue in an East Coast wind. Together they toured the East Riding in Ralph's Mercedes, visiting cousins and revisiting his old haunts. Everywhere they received a welcome, and much was made of the little boy, whom they have of course never seen before. Ralph notices that nobody reacts at all to his Asiatic appearance.

One day the family accompanied Ralph down memory lane to King Alfred's Estate in Leeds, where his parents had lived. They drove up to the old house, which is barely changed from the last time he saw it. The 'castle' was the same, except that the birch trees were taller, and the rocks rewilded with clambering undergrowth. Ralph could not repress a feeling of sadness when he looked at the house, occupied by strangers, empty even of ghosts. But up on the hill the air was bracing, the wind audible in the branches of the trees, and the buildings of the city could be seen, miles away, sharply clear despite the distance. The little boy slipped and clambered over the rocks, much as he had done as a young lad, squeezed himself into cracks and fissures, fell and skinned his knees on the tough Millstone Grit. Any melancholy thoughts were soon dispelled in the need to comfort him, clean and put a plaster on his wound, then chase him through the brambles trying to stop him from doing it again. Ralph was glad he had brought him along.

This excursion is Ralph's first trip behind what has recently come to be known as the 'Red Wall': that bulwark of Northern parliamentary constituencies traditionally guaranteed to return Labour members in every General Election. It wasn't of course called the Red Wall when he knew it first-hand: nobody thought it could be any other colour. Now, mainly in his view because of the Brexit crisis, the Red Wall has collapsed, and in the 2019 General Election blood-red Northern constituencies deserted their traditional Labour loyalties, in droves, in favour of Boris Johnson's Conservative government, giving the Tories an 80-seat majority. The Red Wall has turned blue.

It was crystal clear to Ralph that the vote was very largely about withdrawal from the EU, and that the people of the North were casting their ballot for the only party that could be trusted to 'Get Brexit Done'. While people of his political stripe found the result incomprehensible, Ralph was not even surprised. He knew that people like his parents were always instinctively Conservative; he himself had belonged to a left-wing movement that never wanted EU membership in the first place; and he had watched with amusement the desperate machinations of the 'Remainer' political class to block, thwart or even reverse the result of the EU referendum. An unwillingness to be in any way associated with the despicable undemocratic tactics of the Remainers had the effect of pushing Ralph even further towards, and beyond, the political centre. His roots in left-wing politics had weakened considerably since his retirement. He belonged to no political party. Since Martin almost fell victim to a terrorist bombing, he had discontinued his work with Open Borders.

As he became reacquainted with these Northerners, the extended family he hardly knew, Ralph began to understand them better. They had voted for Brexit: but they were not racist, or xenophobic, or nostalgic for the long-lost days of Britain's imperial greatness. They wanted, for their country, independence from a foreign bureaucracy. They wanted the UK to become again a sovereign nation, making its own decisions, going its own way in voluntary co-operation with allies. They wanted their own parliament to make their own laws. They wanted their own government, chosen by themselves, to control the country's economy, trade policy and borders. In 2019 they cast aside traditional habits and voted for the party that promised to deliver on what they had already demanded: Brexit.

Increasingly Ralph is beginning to find himself more at home with the people of the North. Many of his extended family could still be designated as working-class, while others have entered the professions, and the younger ones begun to attend university. They all seem to live comfortable lives, owning their own homes, sporting some impressive cars, even perhaps owning a boat, moored on the river close to York. They seem like true descendants of the ancestors he had discovered: ambitious for their family, struggling to do the best for their children. Above all they had remained attached to the place he had deserted, an ancestral homeland of which they were inordinately proud, and content to possess just enough of it to live a decent, comfortable life. A few years ago he would have castigated their trajectory as bourgeoisification. Now he felt despondent that he was not like them. He was the one who was the outsider, the wanderer, the exile.

The tide is rising. Ralph realises that he's leaving it dangerously late to get off the spit.

He cannot honestly say he has found what he sought. But still, as his feet sink into these dangerous, treacherous, shifting sands, he begins to feel that he knows as much as one ever does about where he came from. He remembers Bede's anecdote about the sparrow that flies into King Edwin's mead-hall, out of a great windswept, snow-filled darkness, flits through the brightly lit space of the hall, and disappears into the darkness again. Of all places, this perilous spot, on the margin of the land, on the perimeter of the sea, feels like a good place to start your journey. Who knows, perhaps his forefathers landed here, their feet splashing into the shallows of these waves, after their long journey from over there, across the gannet's bath.

You think of belonging to a place as a matter of standing firm on supportive, unyielding soil, your feet rooting down towards the earth, your position fixed and stable, your possession secure, like a tree. But perhaps this formless, dissolving composition of sand, diluted by the water that tries to wash away everything in its path, is as good a place as any to shape a new identity out of a land, out of a past. Everything speaks here of the imperative need to find some foothold, some little patch of land to stand on and call your own. Here you feel like a man caught in quicksand, struggling to extricate himself from a clinging, sucking yesterday, grasping at the nearest tenacious root to pull himself out of the vortex, haul himself onto the shore, make himself a new tomorrow.

Truly there is nothing here. But standing here, that nothingness feels like an invisible platform on which to construct something monumental, even though that too will soon be washed away. Here everything that is solid really does melt, at first into water, and thence into air. Life is a process of decomposition and renewal. Vacancy is plenitude. Stasis is movement. The past becomes future without ever pausing over the present. Being is becoming.

It is time to take hold, even though the present can never be grasped. This moment is possibility, and possibility now seems to him, in some way, infinite and endless.

Chapter Twenty-two

Death

'The time of death is every moment'
– T.S. Eliot, *Four Quartets*

England, 939

While Erik was diligently performing the duties of watcher, Ulf sometimes rode with his father on coastal patrols, sometimes worked around the homestead at whatever tasks needed doing. He had soon got used to the new country, which resembled in many ways the lands he had left, with one exception, and that was religion. Ulf had encountered nothing like the Christian faith that functioned as a national religion, and pervaded all aspects of life in the land. It was all new and strange – churches, monks, tithes paid to the church, prayers in some unintelligible language, ceremonies of baptism, and marriage, and the burial of the dead. Many aspects of social life that he had grown up to think of as normal – drunkenness, violent anger, unbridled lechery – were stigmatised as sins, punishable in this world by public opprobrium, and in the next, it was said, by the pains of hellfire. The worship of their gods, Odin and Thor and Frigg, was sternly condemned as blasphemy, idol-worship, paganism. But it could not be denied that life here seemed all the better for the influence of the church and the Christian piety of the rulers.

Erik stubbornly refused to have any part in it, and kept his old allegiance to Odin and Thor. Ulf found the English religion fascinating, and wanted to know more. Instruction was readily available, since as he soon learned, people were expected to attend church, at least once a week on Sundays, and to participate in an intriguing ritual known as the Eucharist. He had heard rumours that Christians were cannibals, who gathered together to eat the body of their dead god, but this proved to be a misunderstanding, since all the worshippers did was to eat some bread from a special plate, and drink some wine from a silver chalice, while the monks said prayers. It was explained to them that the bread signified the body of Christ, which had been given up for humanity, and the wine signified the precious blood that the saviour shed on the cross, which redeemed us all. By eating and drinking these tokens the faithful were enacting the Passion of the Lord, when He delivered Himself into captivity, and suffered death on the cross, and shed His blood freely to cleanse us from our grievous sins.

Ulf found one church service, or Mass as they called it, particularly enlightening. Although there were many aspects of the service that were simply unintelligible – the language used by the monks, which was called Latin, their hieratic, stylised gestures, the elaborate vestments worn by the officiants – the atmosphere never failed to captivate his senses and provoke his imagination. He loved the music, the melodious sound of monastic chanting; relished the sweet smell of incense, so different from the rank stench of animal sacrifice; and found the liturgy of the Eucharist in some mysterious way moving, as if, when he consumed the bread and the wine, something really did enter into him, some delightful and potent spirit that thrilled his senses and clarified his vision.

On this particular Sunday the clergy processed, wearing their flowing white albs, and some of them the stole. They approached the altar, singing a psalm in Latin, bearing candles and incense. On the altar stood the chalice and the paten, and between them a cross, laminated in silver and decorated with jewels that gleamed in the candlelight.

After more prayers and chanting, the priest gave a speech, in English, which they called a sermon. He spoke, in a kind of quiet rapture, of a dream, that had come to him in the dead of night, when all earth-dwellers slept, in which he had seen the cross of the Saviour.

&

'Beautiful it was,' he said, 'soaring into the sky, beams bathed in the brightest of light: joyfully jewelled, shining in splendour, the cross of Christ.[27] But then the vision shifted, altered, and the rood became a cross of wood, splintered by nails, wet with blood, foul with excrement: a gangster's gallows, the cross of a criminal.

'But the strangest thing', the priest went on, 'in the dream, is that the cross began to speak to me, and told me the story of its life. How it grew in the woodland as a tall tree, branches reaching up towards the sky, roots digging down into the depths of the earth. How one day its trunk was toppled, wrenched from its roots, its branches lopped and hewed. How it was hoisted, high on a hill, standing up tall, there for all to see'.

27 'The Vision of the Cross', *Sweet's Anglo-Saxon Reader*, ed. C.T. Onions (Oxford: Clarendon Press, 1965), 143-147.

Then the Priest raised his eyes towards the back of the church, as if staring into the distance, and pointed his finger at some invisible apparition, as if seeing something approach. In an altered voice, he took the part of the cross, and spoke the words the cross delivered to him in his dream.

&

'Then in the distance, a young hero approached from afar. Fearless and firm, keen for the combat, he laid down his life when he clambered upon me. All earth faltered and flinched with fear. I'd have fallen full-length, flat to the ground, but was forced to stand firm. I'd have crushed all His enemies, if only He'd let me: but by Christ's command I had to stand fast. Though the warrior wound his strong arms about me, I daren't stir: more forbidding than fear was the Lord's word. Crude and rough-hewn, a cross of wood I was: yet I lifted on high the Lord of Hosts; I held aloft the might of majesty. Black nails battered through me, opening wide the wounds of wickedness. When they scoffed at the Saviour, their spit spattered me. When they thrust a spear through His side, and his precious blood sprang, then was my splintered surface soaked. A fearful fate I endured on that high hill, a dreadful destiny. There was darkness at noon, and thunder in the air. I saw the Almighty in agony racked, the corpse of the Ruler covered in clouds. All Creation wept at a king's killing; all creatures cried for Christ on the Cross. At the end of the day they came to relieve Him. I surrendered the Saviour to their outstretched arms. They took Him up tenderly, torn from his torture, left me blood-boltered, impaled by the points of annihilating nails. They stretched out his limbs, wounded, war-weary, and laid the exhausted hero to rest'.

'Thus spoke the Cross' the Priest resumed in his own voice, and his eyes settled again on the hushed and bowed heads of his listeners. 'But He rose again, the Lord of Hosts, from the dead; and by His sacrifice, paid the price for our sins. Now He sits in glory at the right hand of the Father. His faithful retainer, that cross of wood on which He suffered, appears before us now, here in this church, gorgeously dressed in raiment of silver, garments of gold'.

And here, with the utmost reverence, he picked up the silver cross that stood on the altar, and held it high above his head.

'Behold', said the priest, 'the elevation of the cross. This rood held the Lord aloft to complete His Passion. And He will return, the Lord of Hosts, at the day of doom, to this middle-earth, to deliver His judgement. But no-one who bears, bright on his breast, this best of all signs, need feel any fear. The Cross will intercede for us, take our part, and help us to Heaven'.

Ulf was profoundly moved by the sermon. Here he was shown a god he could relate to. This was not the pale god he had heard tell of in the scriptures, who would not fight for his people, and prevented them from defending him, and laid himself open to abuse, and humiliation, and a painful death. This was a god who was also a hero, young and brave, advancing into combat fearlessly, as a young warrior should. He was not stripped of his raiment, as Jesus is stripped in the gospel, but doffs his own garments to gird him for battle. He did not surrender himself to the power of his enemies, but by clinging to the cross fought a battle, a trial of strength and courage against Death itself. He died like a man, of warlike wounds; but rose like a god, victorious, reborn from the dead. By some miraculous power he transformed the cross from a malefactor's crucifix, to a sign of victory. His resurrection resembled that of Baldr, most beautiful of all the gods, who after the cataclysm of Ragnarok returned to remake the world anew. His voluntary death on the cross reminded Ulf of Odin, who hanged himself from the world ash-tree, sacrificed himself to himself, in order to gain wisdom, the secrets of the runes. Jesus died, not to acquire wisdom for himself, but to pay the price of human sin, to redeem mankind, to rescue us from death, and bring us to eternal life in his heavenly kingdom.

At the back of the church, propped against a wall was a sandstone tablet depicting what the brothers called the 'Harrowing'. There, carved on the stone, stood Christ, big as a giant, muscular and powerful, a god in the form of man. In his outstretched hands he held the cross, upside down, and its end he lowered into a pit that was like a grave, and from the pit came swarming the hosts of all the men and women he came to save, and they clung to the cross, and with His power he drew the cross out of the pit, and with it the forms of the dead who clung to it, and brought them back into the light of a living world.

It was in the church that Ulf came to be acquainted with Agnetha. Her father was the carpenter in *Ravenser Oddi*. He saw her first in the church, and while the priest fulminated against lechery and carnal lust, he could not stop looking at her, the head demurely bowed under her cap, her nose slightly tilted upwards, her jaw pleasingly rounded to contain large, even teeth and a full-lipped mouth. Feeling his stare, she turned towards him, and gave him a mischievous glance from eyes that seemed at once sky-blue, sea-green. After the service, as her family walked on towards the village, he followed, and she deliberately hung back, pretending to pick some flowers by the wayside, so Ulf could catch up with her. He was so tongue-tied as to be literally speechless, but she seemed confident and self-assured. She pulled off her cap to reveal a crown of auburn hair, almost orange in places, that shone around her face like an aureole. Glancing around, she took his hand and led him away from the path and into the adjacent woodland.

At first they simply walked in the forest, Ulf gradually gaining enough courage to speak to her and exchange stories of their separate and very different lives. Sometimes they played like children, running and hiding from one another, one leaping out of the bushes to ambush the other in a flying tackle that swept both off their feet and sent them rolling into the undergrowth. Panting they lay there, she on her back and he leaning over her, and with her orange hair and smiling teeth she seemed to him like an angel from one of the frescoes in the church. Then she closed her eyes and pulled his head down towards her, and he was deep in his first kiss. Her mouth opened to his, their tongues intertwined and he was lost in a swooning darkness.

Quickly she jumped up and said she had to go home. The next day he made sure to pass her house, and there she was in the yard washing clothes. She signalled to him to meet her later at the same place in the woods. Thereafter they kept assignation after assignation, at first kissing and embracing, then gradually becoming more adventurous in their explorations of one another's bodies. For the first time he felt what it was like to slide a hand inside a girl's smock, and feel the yielding softness of a breast; to run a hand down her spine, and feel her back arch in response and her lower body begin to cleave to his; to touch her ankle, her calf, her knee and finally the inside of her thigh in a slow, tentative journey of exploration. Here she drew the line, pushing his hand away, but as their courtship deepened so did her receptiveness to his probing curiosity, and he found himself licensed to slide his fingers between her legs, and experience the soft, wet hospitality of an aroused female body. Then one day as his fingers caressed her there, she pushed her hand into the top of his hose, seized the shaft of his penis and tried to pull it towards her. In a matter of seconds he had freed his cock, rolled between her legs, let himself slide into her, thrust a few times and ejaculated, his mind exploding in a blinding riot of colours and sparks that seemed to set the universe on fire, leaving him exhausted, like a singed and smoking rock tossed from the crater of an erupting volcano and left to cool on the charred earth. When he opened his eyes, the world was still there, but changed, since she now occupied its centre, with her laughing eyes and auburn hair, and he wanted nothing more in life than to hold her body and keep it close to him.

Both aware that something significant had happened, as they walked home in the twilight they talked earnestly of what they should do, if she became with child, as neither of their families were even aware of their courtship. To her surprise Ulf had no hesitation in agreeing to marry her. He could think of nothing better in life than having her close to him, and being able to join with her sexually whenever he wanted. Since his mother had died when he was very young, and being an only child, he had no knowledge of family life. She knew better, having both parents and older sisters, a family environment which made her much more knowledgeable about sex than Ulf, but also with fewer illusions about the harder aspects of people living together. She decided however to let Ulf find out for himself, and with the willing consent of both households they were married in the same church where they had first met, before the swelling of her pregnancy even began to show.

Ulf had no idea how to be a husband. Agnetha had a much better idea not only how to be a wife, but how to shape her raw young Viking spouse into a decent marital partner. Thanks to her family's wealth, they enjoyed possession of their own house. When Ulf came home late, drunk in the traditional Danish manner, she refused to have sex with him, waited until he was asleep and tipped him out of bed to snore on the floor, where he would wake up, sick and cold, in the early hours of the morning. On one occasion when he came home, finding she had been gossiping with her sisters and there was no food prepared, he cuffed her on the side of the head, as he had often seen men use their women. She took the beating silently, and said nothing. Later, as he came in with firewood, she waited behind the door, and as he entered hit him a clanging blow on the side of the head with a cooking pan. She supported him in explaining away to others the black eye, an act of courtesy that helped him subdue his sense of humiliation in favour, since he had been the aggressor, of a sense of shame at his own conduct.

Gradually he came to realise that all their conflicts arose from a fundamental inequality between them: though he was the clearly the stronger of the two, the more courageous, the more skilful with his hands, she was quite simply cleverer than him, more capable of thinking through problems and solving them, more knowledgeable about the intricacies of domestic life. He was acutely conscious that she, a Saxon, had been brought up in the Christian civilisation of England, while his origins lay in what the church excoriated as the primeval darkness of heathenism. He perceived this difference, together with her family's wealth, as a sense of superiority on her part, as if she were better then him, an inequality that manifested itself sometimes in mockery, or superciliousness, or even apparent dislike of his manners and customs. He had no experience of being disliked, and at times felt that this was an unbearable indignity. He often thought of leaving her, and going back to his father's house.

But in time, as he became accustomed to the culture of England, he came to understand that the tensions between them were social, not personal. Over and again she proved and demonstrated her love for him, forgiving him for intolerable behaviour, making allowances for his inexperience. For example he knew nothing at all about sex, other than what he had seen in the farmyard, and for a long time she put up with his clumsy love-making, which was modelled on the quick and quivering way a cock would cover a hen. It fell to her to show him what could be done between a man and a woman. Above all she never criticised him publicly, but always showed to family and community a rock-hard solidarity. He grew to realise that they could live happily together, if he was more tolerant and accepting of the differences between them, and if he acknowledged that in some ways she was, quite simply, his superior. In the end, he found nothing in life to be sweeter than simply being together with her, talking by the fire, or working side by side in the yard, or walking in the woods where only a few months previously they had played like children. Nothing better than to go to bed together, and to relish the long slow sweetness of married love, with all the intricate contortions entailed in working around her swelling child-filled belly, free from fear, having no-one to please but themselves.

But the real test of Agnetha's value as a marital partner came in a moment of crisis.

Erik served as coastguard for a year. His loyalty commended him to the king's favour, and he was given as tenant a small grant of land around a place called Wellwick, within the wapentake of Holderness.

And so it came about that Erik and Ulf were ploughing their own furrows over the land they held from the king. A flock of gulls swooped and scavenged among the clods of turned earth, screaming and fighting among themselves, then soared again to wheel and cry as the plough inscribed its steady progress across the field. In the distance the hard blue northern sky met the softer grey-blue of the North Sea. Ulf paused for a moment to catch his breath and to look around at their own little corner of England.

At Brunanburh Erik had sustained a heavy blow to the head, hard enough to buckle and crumple his helmet, and to leave a dark bruise that for a long time disfigured the side of his face. He had shown no sign of any lasting damage or impairment. As time went on, however, Ulf noticed signs of increasing weakness in his father, who often had to stop to catch his breath, and often struggled with the lifting of a particularly heavy weight. Although furious at any suggestion of debility on his part, Erik finally had to accept that some tasks should fall to younger hands. This was why Ulf was handling the heavy plough, while his father guided the team of oxen. Today even this task seemed laborious to Erik, since he stopped often, and leaned against the flank of an ox to take a breather. Ulf waited patiently, though he was anxious to continue with the ploughing. Just as he was considering fetching a boy from the farm to take over from his father, Ulf saw Erik suddenly slump and sit down in the field. He put a hand up to one side of his head as it lolled forward onto his knees. As Ulf ran towards him, Erik leaned over and vomited, tried ineffectually to wipe his mouth, and then fell sideways, rolled over and lay still.

Erik lay on his face in the field. Ulf shouted across in the direction of the village for help. Men came running, and together they picked him up and carried him back to the port. Erik was unconscious, his eyes glazed and unseeing, one side of his face dropped downwards as if the muscles had given way, one arm hanging loosely by his side. They laid him in his bed, where he lay oblivious, breathing heavily, unmoving. His eyes were open, staring but sightless. Ulf had no idea what to do, but Agnetha made him sit by his father with a wet cloth to lay on his forehead, and went back to her parents' house to seek help. Her mother arrived, in the company of a monk skilled in physic. He examined Erik, pulling up his eyelids and looking into his eyes, feeling the heat on his forehead. He noticed the asymmetry of his face, and the obvious paralysis in one of his arms. Satisfied, he moved around behind Ulf so the boy could not see him, looked at Agnetha and shook his head.

Ulf was unaware that his father was dying, although to those around him it was painfully obvious. All knelt, and the monk led them in prayers for the sick man. Shortly after, Erik had what was obviously another stroke. His respiration became more laboured, his chest heaving and gasping for air. His breath was foul-smelling, as if his lungs were corrupting. His sweat was cold.

Ulf was helpless, and could only hold his father's hand and weep. He tried to gulp back the tears, to put on a brave face, but the emotion was too strong for him. He buried his face in the sodden bedclothes, and cried, as he had cried when a baby, for his father.

Ulf was lost in the horror of the moment, but Agnetha remained cool and calm. She got her mother to draw Ulf away from the bed for a moment, so she and one of her sisters could tend to the dying man. He went outside and took his first look at world that did not contain his father. The women cleaned Erik up, where he had fouled the bed, washed his body and face, turning him over. Then they called Ulf back in. As he entered, he saw Agnetha standing over the sick man, holding one of his hands to her belly, as if she hoped Erik might feel the strong, regular rhythm of his grandchild's heart. As Ulf drew near, Erik gave a great sigh, almost of relief, like a man at the end of a hard journey. Quickly the women stepped back, and drew Ulf back to the bedside, and again he took hold of his father's hand. Erik felt cold now, to the touch. His features were pinched and drawn, the nose thin and sharp.

But then suddenly, as often happens before the end, Ulf felt Erik's hand tighten on his, and saw the glazed eyes focus and stare at him, and the wry mouth give the ghost of a twisted smile. For a brief moment of transient joy, Ulf believed that his father would recover. But one long, last sigh, expelling all the breath Erik had left in his body, marked the end. His father was dead. Ulf put out his hand and closed the eyes, now fixed and vacant; not because it was appropriate, or customary, but only because he could not bear to see them open, now the light in them had gone.

Erik's death left Ulf filled with a dull anger that kept flashing into violent rage. He was angry with Erik, for leaving him alone; angry with himself, for failing to keep his father alive; angry with death, the unconquerable enemy. Agnetha seemed to understand his condition, and simply held him to her. In the night's stillness he was able to bury his head between her breasts and shed a few unadmitted tears.

Ulf had as little idea how to manage Erik's funeral as he had shown in the management of his father's death. By the next day his anger against everything had subsided, and his thoughts become clearer. Agnetha remained a strength and stay, keeping him grounded, his emotions in equilibrium.

The monks were adamant that Erik should have a Christian burial, and be interred in the churchyard. As a servant of the king, he deserved a memorial ceremony, a requiem mass, and a gravestone provided by the church. These observances would convey Erik's soul swiftly into the next world, to stand before Christ our redeemer and judge.

Erik's old Danish comrades, who had accompanied them from Iceland, were equally positive that he should be cremated on a pyre, in the traditional manner, his spirit released quickly to travel to the afterlife, not laid in the cold ground, bound to a decomposing corpse. Notwithstanding his acceptance of the sign of the cross, Erik had remained loyal to the old gods of his distant homeland, and it was to their care his body should be entrusted.

Agnetha prayed constantly for Erik's soul, but insisted that Ulf should decide what obsequies to perform for his father.

On the third day Ulf made his decision, and confided it to his wife. And so that evening they carried Erik's body, sewn tightly into a white shroud, up to a headland overlooking the sea, facing the distant shores of Denmark. There they built a pyre from logs of timber, strong enough to support the corpse, but lined with soft branches of evergreen to lay him to rest.[28] On the pyre, high-up, heavenward, they hung his helmet, still bent from the blow he received at Brunanburh. Then weeping, the warriors gently laid him in the midst, honouring the memory of a famous fighter. Quickly they kindled a blaze on the barrow, fuelled a fire of baleful flame. Up went the woodsmoke, black on the brightness, windswept and woven with woe and with weeping, till the blaze in its burning bored through his breastbone, and hissed at his heart. The fire burned like a beacon on the clifftop, visible to sailors across the wide waves.

Heart-heavy, woe-weary, the warriors cried at his quelling. The old woman Gudrun, her grey hair unbound, groaned out a grief-song, and keened out the calamity that would follow the fall of a hero: seasons of slaughter, sorrow of soldiers, days of disaster, hard times. The sky snuffed up the smoke. All night they stayed by the pyre, watching until the last of the flames flickered and died, and the glowing embers galled and gashed with gold, and smoke was smudging the rim of the rising sun.

Then Ulf and Agnetha doused the embers with water, and carefully gathered together his ashes, and placed them in an urn. This they bore down to a beach on the far side of the harbour, taking what was left of the hero to the ocean's

28 *Beowulf*, ed. C. L. Wrenn (London: Harrup, 1969), 3137-3182.

edge. There they laid him gently into a small boat that was sometimes used to patrol the coastline, equipped with mast and small sail.[29] Alongside the urn Ulf laid Erik's shield, and by his side his spear. In the boat he placed also a bridle from Erik's favourite horse, and a pair of stirrups from his saddle, and a flask of mead as an offering to the gods. Inside the urn with Erik's ashes, Agnetha placed a small silver cross. Beside it, Ulf laid the pendant of Thor's hammer they had taken from Erik's neck when preparing him for cremation.

The small boat bobbed on the white wave, eager to depart. The morning tide was at the full. They waited until the moment of its turning, and together pushed the boat out to sea. The sail flapped and bellied, the boat's prow slid seawards, and Erik was embarked. They let the tide take him, renounced his remains again to the deep. Side by side, in incongruous unison, husband and wife offered prayers to their several gods.

In honour of his father's stubborn paganism, in the remembered Danish tongue, Ulf offered petitions to Odin, the All-father, praising the god for his wisdom and power, offering him mead as a sacrifice, begging him to accept Erik into his hall of heroes.

Agnetha prayed, in her own English language, to Christ, the Lord, to take her father-in-law into his keeping. She asked the Lord to bless him and keep him; to make his face to shine upon him, and be gracious unto him; to lift his countenance upon him, and give him rest.

Ulf put one arm around his wife, and laid his other hand on her belly. Both knew, without a word spoken, that if the child was a boy, they would name him Erik Ulfson. The little boat drifted out to sea on the swift running tide. For a while

29 *Beowulf*, ed. C. L. Wrenn (London: Harrup, 1969), 26-52.

they could watch its progress over the water; and then it was gone.

Variously they hoped that Erik's spirit would be received into Valhalla, or into Christ's heavenly kingdom. But nobody knew, in absolute truth, neither the crafty councillor in court, nor the brave hero beneath the blue sky, who, at the last, unloaded that cargo.[30]

30 *Beowulf*, ed. C. L. Wrenn (London: Harrup, 1969), 51-52.

Chapter Twenty-three

Wager

'Here the intersection of the timeless moment
Is England and nowhere. Never and always'
– T.S. Eliot, *Four Quartets*

Putney, 2020

Ralph is standing at the back of the Church of All Saints, Fulham, which stands at the north end of Putney Bridge, during a Sunday morning service. Here the Christian faithful are exceptionally well served, since Putney Bridge is the only one in Britain with a church at both ends. It must be the safest bridge in the country, at least from a spiritual point of view.

All Saints consists of a 15th century Kentish ragstone tower, with a late 19th century perpendicular building bolted on, replacing the smaller and chronically flooded old church. All Saints is famous, or rather notorious, for one particular reason: it featured in the horror film *The Omen*, in which a flagpole is snapped, by demonic influence, from the roof of the tower, and pitched down to transfix a troublesome, inquisitive priest.

Inside the church the nave, with its big clerestory windows, seems both lofty and narrow, giving that mixed sensation of intimacy on the ground, and awe-inspiring distance above, often captured by Victorian gothic. Ralph is performing the duties of a sidesperson, welcoming people to the church, showing them where to sit, assisting anyone who needs help. He likes the position this affords him, in a liminal territory between the congregation and the church door that leads to the outside world. He is in, but not of, the company of the faithful. He joins in the hymns, singing in a passable, untutored tenor, and in some of the prayers. But shortly, when members of the congregation begin to stand and file forward, across the worn 18th century tombs, to receive the Eucharist at the Communion Rail, he will not accompany them. His presence in the building is conditional, contingent, voluntary not compelled. He is not so much a convert as a divert, having turned partially away from his lifelong belief in materialism, to confront askance, sideways, the possibility of the numinous. But he is by no means wholly inverted to face anything like a sure and certain faith.

Ralph's perhaps surprising presence in an Anglican church is explained by something that happened to him on his recent sojourn in Yorkshire. He had spent a few days taking advantage of beautiful August weather, such as he remembered from the summer holidays of his childhood, touring graveyards around these remote East Riding villages, looking to add more branches to the family tree. One church he found particularly interesting was that of St Wilfrid in Otringham, the village where Richard Ravenswood had lived, the church in which he had most likely worshipped. The church dates from the 12th century, the building itself from the 13th and 14th. He had spent hours in the churchyard, where he found a memorial tablet to a Sarah Ravenswood, died in 1769, wife to John. The stone bore the touching, almost witty inscription:

> Affliction sore long time she bore
> Physicians were in vain:
> Till God did please
> To give her ease
> And take away her pain.

There was no sign of her husband in the same grave, and he did not like to think of her lying alone, so he began scouring the churchyard among the almost obliterated headstones, looking for more clues. While on his knees, parting the grass and brambles that clung around the base of an illegible stone, someone came and stood behind him, casting a long shadow across the graves. It was the Vicar, a young man in cassock and clerical collar, much shorter than his shadow. He inquired about Ralph's interest in the graves, and listened with interest to his story.

Ralph had never actually known a minister of religion, and was guarded and wary in his presence, expecting to become the target of an onslaught of evangelical zeal. This was unsurprising, since his views of the clergy had differed little from those of the Bolsheviks, or the French revolutionaries of the First Republic. The old joke, often traded in communist circles, flashed into his mind, in which the last capitalist is envisaged hanging from the entrails of the last priest. In fact the Vicar, a Welshman with shrewd, intelligent eyes behind thick glasses, disarmingly kept the conversation entirely to matters raised by Ralph himself. He seemed urbane, highly educated, his accent more Cambridge than Merthyr Tydfil.

Meanwhile an elderly couple turned up at the church door to attend Evensong, and the Vicar excused himself to unlock the doors and welcome them in.

Ralph had wanted to look inside the church, which was usually kept locked during the day, to inspect some potentially interesting medieval gargoyles, 12th century corbel-head carvings, and other details surviving from before the Reformation. So after lingering in the churchyard for a while, he followed the old couple into the nave. No-one bothered him, so he was free to examine details of interest in the church's architecture. Absorbed in his observations, he failed to notice a few more people entering, and presently realised that the service of Evensong was about to begin. The organ struck up, and the little band of the faithful, bravely standing proxy for the whole of humanity, began a ragged chorus of *All People that on Earth Do Dwell.*

Ralph hovered on the lintel, trapped, embarrassed, wanting to make his escape but anxious to avoid a disruptive exit. And the coolness and silence of the space felt in some way reassuring. So instead of leaving, he perched on the edge of a pew and stared up at the king-post roof. The church was atmospherically lit by candles in gold candlesticks standing on the altar, which was covered by a crisp white cloth. The Vicar knelt at a *prie-dieu* in front of the altar, leading the service, which seemed to consist largely of a kind of melodic chanting of familiar biblical texts. Ralph did not know the liturgy, but detected allusions to the Annunciation, and to the old man Simeon who recognised the infant Jesus as the Messiah. There were some prayers for the parish and the clergy, for the sick and the dead, and a closing hymn. As the few parishioners left, Ralph stood awkwardly at the back of the church, not wanting to make an impolite and unceremonious exit, not wanting to stay. The Vicar spoke to him, again without any aggressive buttonholing, and asked if Ralph wanted more time to look around. He seemed to want to close the church, and Ralph demurred, unwilling to presume. But the Vicar said he had some things to do in the Vicarage, and would come back later to lock up.

'Just give me a knock when you leave – across the road, you can't miss it. You can hold the fort. Keep an eye on the candlesticks. Enjoy'.

And so Ralph found himself in the unprecedented position of being unexpectedly left, and inexplicably trusted, in charge of a medieval Anglican parish church. The silence of the place was peculiarly obtrusive, almost like a presence, heavy and perfumed with the smell of incense. Ralph wondered if this was some kind of experiment on the part of the Vicar, like consigning a sceptical ghost-hunter for the night in a haunted house: to determine if, confined in this ancient space, he would see or feel anything unusual. After all, centuries ago, members of his family had been here, walked the old stones, offered prayers into the cavernous spaces of the roof where they must have imagined God and his angels to dwell. Should he not feel closer to them, sharing this common space? Could he perhaps even hear, in the audible silence, that could be composed of thousands of whispering, praying voices, a few words from the people whose blood he shared? He could not hear them, but lines of poetry he had not remembered for years came unbeckoned into his mind. 'The communication of the dead is tongued with fire beyond the language of the living'[31] whispered the impeccable, clipped Boston English of

31 T.S. Eliot, 'Little Gidding', *Collected Poems 1909-1962* (Faber and Faber, 1966), p. 215.

T.S Eliot. And then the dull, bored voice of Philip Larkin, librarian of Hull University just down the road, could be heard describing a church much like this one – perhaps it *was* this one – as a place 'proper to grow wise in – if only that so many dead lie round'. Perhaps, like the militantly atheist Larkin, Ralph had uncovered, even at this late point in life, 'a hunger to be more serious'.[32]

But if he was expecting the dead to speak to him, it wasn't happening, even though the church was full of inaudible voices, and the very air, pungent and solemn, felt prayed in. He looked at his watch and thought that it was time to be on the road. As he opened the inner door, his attention was caught by a glass display case that had previously remained unnoticed. Inside was a text he recognised immediately as a page from the Lindisfarne Gospels. It was just a facsimile of course, placed there because the real book, the 8th century Northumbrian masterpiece, had been briefly exhibited in the church on a national tour from which it had travelled from its home in the British Library. The facsimile was open at the beginning of St John's Gospel.

Ralph studied the page more closely. It was dominated by an immense, brightly-coloured capital letter, or rather three interlocking letters from the opening text, *In principio*, in the beginning, knitted together into a statuesque form, its ends sealed by flourishes like architectural pedestals. Everywhere within the strict geometric lines of the design were fluid and mobile signs of vitality, creeping undulating plants, two-headed beasts knotted together in vibrant symbiosis, strange exotic birds with bodies intertwined in some kind of ecstasy. Even the simplest decorative motif displayed that irrepressible tendency

32 Philip Larkin, 'Church Going', *Collected Poems* (Faber and Faber, 2014), p. 49.

towards organic unity, shapes interleaved and lines interlaced, as if all creation were seeking to resolve and re-combine into some lost pristine solidarity.

The English monk who had illuminated the manuscript had introduced an interlinear vernacular translation of the Latin Vulgate text:

> *In principio erat verbum, and verbum erat apud deum and verbum erat deus*
>
> **In prima wor word and word wor mid god fader and word word god**

Ralph's eyes filled with tears. He was reading words written over thirteen-hundred years ago, but which spoke to him in exactly the accent he had learned from his parents. Phonetically the writing captured the sounds he remembered as those of everyday speech. 'Wor' was exactly how his parents had pronounced 'were'. 'Fader' sounded just like the way he used to say 'father', with the short accented vowel, indistinguishable from the Anglo-Saxon '*faeder*'. There was a continuity here, through the common language preserved in this polyphonic religious text, that connected him even further back than the Ravenswoods buried in the churchyard: back to those who spoke Anglo-Saxon, the English language crafted for these islands by the Germans and Danes and Norwegians of the first Christian millennium, and which he had learned at Oxford. This invisible chain passed from him through his parents, back through the long line of documented Ravenswoods, into a much more remote past inhabited by people he knew nothing of, except that they shared his name, and had lived in and around this place, and had worshipped here in this church. Beyond them were the others, those who had reached here from Scandinavia, probably bringing their own gods, and initially fiercely resistant to the hegemony of the new Christian faith. But they had eventually entered the common linguistic covenant, the same universal church, and begun to say their prayers to a single God, and accepted these words as the truth that had been in the beginning – '*in prima*' – is now, and would be for ever: 'word were god, and word were wi' God t'father'.

It would be an exaggeration to claim this as a 'road to Damascus' moment in which Ralph found God, 'got religion'. In truth it was more like a 'Road to Emmaus' moment, in which he met an unrecognised stranger, when the evening was far spent, and found that the words he spoke remained within him. In spite of himself, he wanted the stranger to stay, to abide, to tell him more. But he was gone, softly, soft as the wind, leaving Ralph on an empty road, with words in his ears, and the language of an ancient poetry burning in his heart.

&

If the dead could speak to him in this way, personally and in an accent he recognised, perhaps there was after all something in the religion he had long despised. If there was a chain of continuity linking him with those distant ancestors, a linear strand of common interconnection, then maybe that which had previously been invisible was now manifest, and things unseen becoming substantial. Perhaps what he had felt, in that place and through that language, was more than affinity with his ancestors. Perhaps it was a reaching out towards something numinous, something spiritual, something he had for most of his life believed impossible.

This experience, ambiguous and inconclusive as it had been, was enough to revive the spiritual longings that had inflamed his soul as a teenager, and this resurgence of long-suppressed inclinations served to remind him of what now became apparent as an unkept, overdue appointment with religion. So he decided to explore Christianity. There were many denominations to choose from, and he wondered if he would feel more comfortable in something closer to the nonconformist belief-systems of Cromwell's Independents rather than the doctrines of the established church. But he hardly felt drawn towards Calvinism; he had after all been baptised into the Church of England, the church of his ancestors; and it was in an Anglican church that his spirituality had been tentatively reawakened.

So he tried out a church in Fulham, just across the river, which proved to be a base for the Evangelical wing of the Church of England. The welcome given to him was very warm, even effusive. He had been expecting a service resembling the quasi-Anglican, *Book of Common Prayer*-based assemblies he remembered from school, but this seemed much more informal, and aspired to be up-to-date in the most outdated way. Three young people with guitars and an electric piano sat on a platform to provide the music. The hymns were set to poppy, sing-along rhythms, and the congregation had the disconcerting habit of swaying from side to side as they sang. It was like something between a Victorian music hall and a Billy Graham rally. Ralph expected a surpliced cleric to mount the pulpit and give a sermon, but instead three church leaders stood up and performed a kind of incongruous and embarrassing game-show pantomime illustrating some parable or other. Everything seemed to be aimed at the comprehension level of a five-year old. Ralph walked out, didn't look back, and it was a while before he ventured onto holy ground once more.

A little research informed him that in order to find anything resembling traditional Christianity he would have to attend an Anglo-Catholic or 'high' church. Fortunately, as he discovered, the parish church at the other end of the bridge fell into that category. He began to attend services there, and found the traditional worship, which lovingly preserved the *Book of Common Prayer* and the *King James Bible*, much more congenial. Anglo-Catholic churches go in for the full regalia of clerical dress, elaborate formal processions to the altar, clouds of incense streaming towards the rafters, candles and crucifixes. The hymns were those he knew from school. The church was equipped with a magnificent organ, and an accomplished choir of quasi-professional male and female singers. At first he would leave immediately after the service, but after a while accepted invitations to stay for coffee. Members of the congregation began to talk to him, and gradually he became accepted as one of them. After a while he was asked to take on a minor role in the church as a sideperson.

Ralph was surprised to find the society of the church as congenial as he did. He had assumed that the emphasis on traditional liturgy, worship, clerical dress and music would go with a politics too reactionary even for his new centrist views. He soon learned that the reverse was the case: in the Church of England, the more traditional the worship, the more liberal the politics. The enforced chumminess of the evangelical churches masks some extreme views on, for example, homosexuality, or at least gay sex, regarded as invariably sinful. Whereas he found that the clergy of the Anglo-Catholic persuasion tended to be on the left politically, much more hospitable towards sexual diversity, and socially inclusive. He found it refreshing to be among people who espoused a kind of emotional socialism, not of course based in Marxist doctrine, or Enlightenment principles of human rights, but on a genuine belief in what used to be called 'the brotherhood of man', a universal human solidarity he would once have dismissed as utopian socialism.

The church seemed particularly adept at recognising the different talents and abilities people brought with them, and cultivating these for their potential contribution, rather than forcing every congregant into a uniform servility. No-one asked Ralph to polish the brass, or run a jumble sale. He would often hear quoted the dictum of St Paul, that people are granted different gifts, of prophecy, or ministry, or teaching, or exhortation, or philanthropy, or leadership, and should be encouraged to specialise according to their particular strengths.

One of the assistant priests attached to the church was undertaking a study of the early English church, and was eager to discuss his work with a noted historian. Ralph was happy to render some religious texts for him from the Anglo-Saxon, and instantly recovered a taste for translation. Handling Old English seemed to strengthen that sense of connection with his distant ancestors, and he began to want to know more about their world. He re-read the Anglo-Saxon poems, finding he needed a parallel version to help with some of the dense knots of language, but determined to get back inside that primordial tongue that was at once, as the past should be perceived, reassuringly familiar, yet forbiddingly remote, similar, yet different. Once again, as he had done as a student, he repossessed the energetic rhythms of the poetry, the chiming alliteration, the musical cadences, the intricate half-rhymes. Though he had not written creatively since he was a teenager, something prompted him to turn the Old English lines into a modern equivalent, and he embarked on some verse translations of the ancient elegies and poems of battle.

One Sunday he attended a service of 'Veneration of the Holy Cross', in which the crucifix was not only processed and displayed and bowed down to, but kissed, worshipped, adored. A natural iconoclasm, and all the Reformation strictures of the *Thirty-nine Articles*, set out in the very prayer-book in his hand, against 'Romish doctrine' held him back from what seemed an excess of devotion, verging on idolatry. But later he rummaged among his old books and found his undergraduate copy of that great Old English devotional poem *The Dream of the Rood*, or *The Vision of the Cross.* Here religion was as solid and material as everything else in the Anglo-Saxon world. The cross in the poem is many things, 'a shifting sign': a real historical weapon of execution; an emblem of victory, such as that seen in the vision of Emperor Constantine; a symbol of personal resurrection; and a badge of commitment, of belonging. But as he recalled from his undergraduate studies, this poem had been taken out into the world and embodied in physical objects, in metal and stone. Its lines are to be found inscribed on the great Northumbrian Ruthwell Cross, an image to be knelt down before, and prayed to; and a fragment of its verse written on the small silver-laminated devotional Brussels Cross, an icon to be touched, and held, and kissed in adoration. Fascinated by the poem's syncretic blending of heroic and devotional poetry, its catholic merging of secular and religious pieties, he embarked on a translation, and produced a convincing modern version. He showed it to the Vicar, who promptly arranged to have it read from the pulpit by a prominent actor who was also a member of the congregation. Hearing the imaginative splendour and emotional depth of the old poem conveyed, through his own words, and in the sonorous voice of a fine reader, convinced Ralph that he must have some kind of vocation within the church, a calling that could not be resisted for ever, and would one day claim him for its own.

Service over, Ralph is walking across the churchyard and through the elaborately-cultivated Tudor garden to the Bishops' Palace, to deliver a message to a sick parishioner who lives in the adjoining lodge. From there he strolls, unhurried, towards the river, and pauses by the monument to the International Brigade volunteers who fought in Spain, 'to save liberty, and peace for all'. Standing with a hand on the pink marble, he mutters a prayer for the dead, and remembers how enthralled he once had been by the purity of heroism that drove those young men to travel to Spain in 1936, to risk everything for socialism. They seemed to him to represent an ideal of humanity, their achievement unblemished even in defeat. When he had begun to look more closely at the historical record, at the evidence of brutal intolerance practised by, and on behalf of, the Republican cause – over six-thousand religious, bishops and priests, monks and nuns, callously murdered in the Red Terror; the torture and mass executions of non-communist Republicans by the Stalinist PSUC – he had simply refused, still under a residual pro-Soviet influence, to accept it. Even when he read George Orwell's sombre, disillusioned, first-hand account of those events, he had pushed it all aside, refusing to let any of it touch him, or contaminate the memory of the Republic. Only Fascists could commit atrocities.

'Peace for all'? Now he no longer believed, as he once had, in that political language of peace, which is so often on the left accompanied by enmity and division, and which was predicated, just as much now as it had been in the 1930s, on the annihilation or 'cancelling' of oppositional viewpoints. The International Brigade volunteers were still heroes to him, ordinary people who had put their lives on the line for liberty. But their cause had been contaminated by cruel intolerance, and their idealism shamefully betrayed by their own political leaders.

On his way back he passes the west door of the church. Through a low mediaeval arch, a survivor from the old church, can be seen two glass doors, etched with white images of protective and welcoming angels, and an inscription from the Sermon on the Mount: 'Blessed are the Peacemakers'. This was a different kind of peace, based in forgiveness, tolerance, reconciliation. There is no space for forgiveness in the model Republic of contemporary ultra-left socialism: a single error placing the heretic on 'the wrong side of history' damns him to excommunication. Historical figures are consigned to oblivion on the basis of their shortcomings, even though these might have been the universal practices of their day, and with no acknowledgement of their virtues or achievements. Everything that has been is anachronistically viewed from a dogmatic standpoint of absolute faith in contemporary opinion. The past can never be forgiven for not being the present.

But the peace offered by the church, the peace that passes all understanding, acknowledges the frailty and fallibility of humanity, and comes out to meet it with tolerance and absolution. When the Prodigal Son returns, there is neither judgement nor blame, but only welcome, and relief, and a father's embrace. Ralph had himself made enough mistakes to feel that he needed such forgiveness. Like the Prodigal Son, he had wasted his possessions, and found himself in want. Perhaps it was time to arise, and go to his father, and tell him he is not worthy to be called his son. He has been lost. It is time to be found. Blessed are the peacemakers, for they shall be called the children of God.

Ralph walks back across Putney Bridge in the direction of what is now his own house. In response to the great ideological shift he has undergone, he had made the decision to buy the property with his pension lump sum and redundancy benefits. Thirty-five years ago he could have bought it for a fraction of what it cost him today, but he is reconciled to the loss. As he passes St Mary's church, he remembers his reflections on the Putney Debates, and realises that once again, simply by walking fifty paces across the bridge, he has retrospectively changed sides. The Levellers were wrong, and Commissary-General Henry Ireton was right: all citizens of the commonwealth should aspire to establish, by whatever means, a 'fixed permanent interest in the kingdom'. Not of course, as Ireton intended, in terms of a property qualification for the suffrage, or even involving ownership at all: but a virtual interest, an obligation, a dedication to the country and its communities. Patriotism, perhaps: a wish to keep the country and its citizens prosperous and safe. In his case it meant a home, a little patch of ground, shared with others, a place to cherish, and improve, and convey to his heirs.

&

He lets himself into the house and goes through to the garden, which he has had developed into a pleasant retreat, laying out a lawn and flower-beds, planting ornamental trees, even installing a small pond in which he keeps a few small Koi carp, protected from predators such as foxes and herons by a cover he fashioned himself from chicken-wire. The garden was no more than a little patch of ground, but it had given him a new kind of pleasure, and even a portal into the insights that become visible once you are inside your own territory.

Meanwhile the mind, from pleasure less,
Withdraws into its happiness;
The mind, that ocean where each kind
Does straight its own resemblance find,
Yet it creates, transcending these,
Far other worlds, and other seas;
Annihilating all that's made
To a green thought in a green shade.[33]

Ralph had come to think of Andrew Marvell as an ancestral neighbour, since he was a contemporary and compatriot of his seventh great-grandfather, born in the picturesque and deliciously named village of Winestead-in-Holderness, near Hull. His fragment of red-brick wall, reputed to survive

33 Andrew Marvell, 'The Garden', *Selected Poems*, ed. Bill Hutchings (Taylor and Francis, 2002), p. 60.

from the Putney estate of Marvell's patron, Thomas Fairfax, suggests another transhistorical connection. This tiny plot scarcely measures up to the grounds of Nun Appleton House: but it was to exactly such a garden as this that Marvell, veteran of the English Revolution, Cromwell's Latin Secretary, having lived through great earth-shattering events, retreated and withdrew to contemplate the richness of interiority.

Ralph too had at last learned to withdraw from the world, to seek alternative, parallel universes within, where he could in turn recreate the external world into a new form, a world repainted in the colours of imagination. He begins to lay out the garden table: Martin and Mei are coming for lunch. At the bottom of the garden, under the shelter of General Fairfax's wall, a pet rabbit lives in a hutch, also enclosed by a wire fence. The rabbit is Haruki's, and was acquired to give the boy some special reason for wanting to visit his grandfather. The lad would spend hours sitting in the little compound, feeding the rabbit torn-off sprays of grass, laughing at its twitching nose and languid, blinking eyes. He would also stand and watch in fascination the slow, antediluvian motion of the fish as they swam around the pond, their sliver and orange scales flashing into view, and as quickly disappearing into the shadows. Ralph would observe him, absorbed in his childlike wonder.

The man had come to a place where he could acknowledge, without rancour or resentment, that his significance to the world was inevitably diminished, and that it was time to begin ceding power to the young, to shake all cares and business from his age, conferring them on younger strengths. He had never thought of Haruki as his heir, since he had never thought of himself as mortal, or managed to venture sufficiently deeply into another's experience to think seriously about succession, of what he might be able to transmit to another generation, living to live in a world of time beyond him. Yet here he is, in a garden he has made for the pleasure of someone else, happy to be pushed to the side of his own existence, content to see the little boy assume the centre of the picture. He thinks of T.S. Eliot's poem about Marina, daughter of Shakespeare's Pericles, the lost and found.

> … let me
> Resign my life for this life, my speech for that unspoken,
> The awakened, lips parted, the hope, the new ships.[34]

After a long process of intellectual struggle with doubts and reservations about his ancestry, Ralph has finally come to rest on something analogous to Pascal's wager. The great 17th century French philosopher and mathematician had confronted the one question that could not be resolved by reason: does God exist? The church offered Pascal faith in place of reason. 'To the man of faith, no explanation is necessary' wrote Thomas Aquinas. 'To the man without faith, no explanation is possible'. But for him the rational mind, even when facing so insoluble a conundrum, could not stop reasoning.

His solution was to lay bets. Do I wager that God exists, or that He does not? Every individual must place a bet. 'You must wager. It is not optional. You are embarked'.

If I bet that God exists, I may win or lose. If I win, my gain is infinite, the possibility of heaven. If I lose, I lose everything, for heaven too does not exist.

If I bet that God does not exist, I may win or lose. If I win,

34 T.S. Eliot, 'Marina', *Collected Poems 1909-1962* (Faber and Faber, 1966), p. 116.

I lose everything. If I lose, again I lose everything: for I have turned my back on God, and my path to heaven is barred.

Thus the only rational choice is to wager that God exists. All other options lead to loss. Only a fool would bet against an eternal life of happiness, for the possibility of gaining nothing. The wise decision is to wager that God exists, since 'If you gain, you gain all; if you lose, you lose nothing'.

Despite his international politics and professional cosmopolitanism, Ralph has spent his personal life firmly if metaphorically on land, peering out across the waters that separate him from other people, even those closest to him. Now he is all at sea, 'embarked', as Pascal put it, '*en route*'. He has taken the decisive step, jumped off the jetty onto the boat, felt the deck dip sharply under his weight. The tide has turned, the boat has left the harbour. The journey has begun.

His ingrained habit of scepticism, a Northern unwillingness to be hoodwinked or cheated, hardened by years of immersion in dialectical materialism, counsel mistrust and suspicion. He is naturally inclined to bet that the DNA test, the family history, even the survival of his name, actually mean nothing.

Say, for the sake of argument, he has some kinship affinity with people in Denmark. But so, in all probability, does everybody else. To fully map any individual's heritage would be practically impossible, since every conception fuses two biological entities already formed from a bewildering multiplicity of similar unions. If you go back just a few generations, and include the proliferation of grandparents and great grandparents, two becoming four, four becoming eight, eight becoming sixteen, and so on *ad infinitum*, even mathematically the equation defeats calculation.

Historically, then, the biological net widens as it sinks into the past: but the shoal of human fish it aspires to catch reduces in size. There are far more of us than there are of them. In 1700 the population of Britain was about five million people. In the year 1000 it was a little over a million. It would be counter-intuitive to believe that traces of that tiny fraction are not embedded somewhere in all those whose ancestors have been, as his appear to have been, on these islands for millennia. During the centuries of Scandinavian incursions into Britain the geographical extent of Nordic settlement, and the relatively small size of the population, meant that mathematically everyone from Europe, and even beyond, must retain some trace of Viking ancestry.

Other objections crowded his mind, as he exercised that long habit of over-analysing every problem in order to keep it at a distance, maintain his objectivity. He and Martin had succeeded in tracing a family line back to the fifteenth century by following the paternal name into its eponymous geographical location. But why should that patrilinear line be privileged over other possible cartographies? Where were the women in this scenario, given the obvious fact that there could be no conception or birth without them? Every male Ravenswood in the family tree had a wife, or partner, and each mother contributed equally to the inherited DNA mix of her children; every female participant in the process had her own story, her own background, her own chronicle of inheritance. Was he himself not an overdetermined product of that great multiplicity of influences, all pointing backwards through a widening family circle towards a steadily reducing reservoir of human progeny, eventually even to some remote common ancestor? Ultimately, according to this logic, there is nothing in his DNA to differentiate him significantly from anyone else on earth.

Thus he is naturally inclined to bet against the significance of ancestry. But like Pascal's predication of unbelief, the wager can only end in loss. If he wins the bet, and there is nothing to it at all, then he has no tangible link with the past, and becomes once again what he had been before, the free radical particle, the atomised element of the great field of humanity, stamped only by what he has in common with others, possessing no character of his own. If he loses the wager, and the DNA thread connecting him to the past is real, he has lost the possibility of a formative connection to his country, its history and its people.

Suppose then, he was to bet that ancestry is genuine, authentic, real? The evidence collated by Martin is after all incontrovertible. Somewhere in his body lie ineradicable traces of those men who share his name, father to son, who like his own father, worked with their hands, shaping reality, forming their environment, making their world: tilling the soil, growing crops, husbanding sheep, shearing and cropping and tanning, constructing and operating machines, generating the staples of social life, food, and clothing, and print. Somewhere within him there is a biological bond that, along with his name, connects him to a place, to a windswept promontory of broken cliffs and shifting sandbanks, out there on that wild eastern coast, facing across the sea towards his ancestral Scandinavian home. And with that bond he inherits a debt, to those men who first came to this country as migrants, fleeing from persecution, warfare or famine, from cataclysmic social change or natural disaster, came here to seek a home, a little patch of land, to settle, to belong. They came, and they stayed, and cultivated the soil, and made it their own, and fought to defend it, land and treasure, against those who would take it from them.

If he loses the bet, if the ancestry craze proves to be based on unscientific principles and flawed methodologies, what will he lose? Nothing but the tattered fabric of that professional dignity that used to be so important to him, that obsession with being always right, with winning every argument. He would be proved wrong. So what? One of the greatest gains he takes away from this life-changing episode is that he no longer thinks that matters.

&

One Sunday Ralph is approached by an earnest young man who has just taken up the post of curate. He had studied History at Cambridge before entering theological college, and was familiar with some of Ralph's work. He tells Ralph he is undertaking work with a Christian fellowship, affiliated to the church, which is offering educational services to refugees and asylum seekers. Some of these recent migrants are also proposing to convert to Christianity, in which case they are receiving religious instruction from the church. But Stephen was keen on providing them with a broader cultural education. He knows that Ralph has done work with refugees in the past, and wonders if he would be interested in contributing some classes in British history. Stephen hands him a text-book, written by academics for use in such situations, while making it clear that Ralph can have a free hand to devise his own course.

The young curate is also in charge of supervising the religious education of the few members of the group who have expressed a wish to convert. He is clearly very nervous about this responsibility, since the role of the Church of England in facilitating refugee conversions, and simultaneously helping their applications for asylum, has very recently come under intense scrutiny. One such convert, attached to Liverpool Cathedral, had on the previous Remembrance Day built an explosive device, taken it in a taxi to Liverpool Womens' Hospital, a maternity unit full of mothers and babies, and there accidentally blown himself up. It was not clear whether the bomb was destined to explode in the hospital, or at the nearby civic Remembrance Day commemorations. Either way a terrible tragedy had been narrowly averted, and the terrorist's identity as a Christian convert, together with the church's role in encouraging public conversions to strengthen asylum applications, became the object of much negative publicity.

'I don't think any of my lot are anything like that', the curate confides in Ralph. 'But how are you supposed to tell?'

Ralph has no illusions about the plausibility of a terrorist who could pose as a Christian convert, or the difficulty the church must encounter in recognising such a covert motivation. Ralph is reminded all too forcibly of the Berrylands Bomber, and his own innocent facilitation of a terrorist outrage that had almost killed his own son. How can the church turn away dispossessed people asking to be received? How can they really tell if a malicious intention lies behind an apparently innocent and genuine supplication? There's no art to find the mind's construction in the face. He feels it his duty to help.

This is the first occasion that Ralph has taught anything since he retired, and much has changed in the meantime. There had been his betrayal by Salam, the bombing, and the injuries sustained by Martin. There had been the discoveries about his past, and his revised understanding of his place in history, and in his country. There had been Brexit, and the emergence of a renewed sovereign Britain, claiming his loyalty. And there had been his uncertain and tentative turn towards religion. He is a man suspended between old and new beliefs: no longer confident in dialectical materialism, but by no means sure that religion provides an equally firm foundation for understanding the world. He participates in the life of the church, but will not take communion, and resists the gentle encouragement to seek confirmation. He has become disenchanted with socialism, watching its increasingly rapid perversion into an ultra-leftist dogma. Political liberalism seemed little more than organised indecision, the triumph of apathy. And he can hardly think of himself as a Conservative, like his father, even though he had in 2019 voted for Boris Johnson's government with their promise to 'get Brexit done'.

So he has to think long and hard about how to approach the task of teaching history to refugees. What do such people need to know about the history of what they hope will become their adopted country? He takes out the text-book Stephen had given him, and studies it. It is positioned at the educational level of GCSE, and has been thoroughly influenced by progressive forces in the culture wars. It starts in the 18th century with Britain's role in the slave trade. The British movement for the abolition of slavery is glossed over, and the emphasis placed on the Civil Rights movement in America, as if Britain had no traditions of political freedom, and no-one here had lifted a finger to free the slaves. He has heard of such perversions of historical truth: he remembers having read in the *Daily Mail* a letter from a concerned parent whose daughter knew all about Martin Luther King, but had no idea who he was named after.

The text-book reflects the standard mainstream history

syllabus, dominant in universities and schools. It highlights Britain's shameful part in the transatlantic slave trade; the brutal excesses of Empire; the postcolonial retreat after Suez, and the imprudent enlistment in more recent quasi-colonial adventures like the invasion of Iraq. It assures students that British society is thoroughly contaminated by racism, rotten with institutional inequality, run by wealthy white men in their own interests. Its default position is a hatred of the capitalist system that allows it the freedom to offer such tendentious criticisms in the first place. It expresses a wholly negative view of British history.

Ralph knows very well that this 'woke' history is likely to confirm, if not exceed, everything these people might have brought with them from their own post-colonial culture in terms of anti-western hatred. If anything was calculated to encourage, or maintain, a loathing of their adopted society, to turn them against what they hoped would become their own country, this was it. Ralph remembers how in 1984 a KGB defector, Yuri Bezmenov explained on American television how for many years the KGB had waged a war of 'ideological subversion' against the USA by exploiting the self-hatred of the counter-culture generation. The long-term objective, he explained, was 'to change the perception of reality of Americans to such an extent no one is able to come to sensible conclusions in the interests of defending themselves, their family, their community and country': to replace patriotism, commitment and responsibility with disillusion, resentment and self-loathing.

Ralph decides he will tell them a different story. He will go back to a much earlier stage in British history, and explain how different cultures and civilisations arrived on these shores in successive waves, and shaped the country we know today. He will begin with the Romans, then the Anglo-Saxons, the Viking invasions, and the Norman conquest. He will share with them what he had learned about his own remote past, that trace of DNA that linked him back to Scandinavian settlers in the North of England. He will show to the refugees that his own ancestors may have arrived here in much the same way they did, uninvited and often unwelcome. How they came, in all probability, expelled from their own lands by war, or famine, or natural disaster; how they travelled long distances in hardship and privation; and how they found their place, not without struggle and resistance, a spot where they could remain, stay, belong. He will offer his own experience and that of his ancestors as a narrative that parallels rather than opposes their own stories. White people, he will tell them, whose roots lie deep in the soil of Britain, are not simply the bloated beneficiaries of exploitation and privilege, grown fat on the profits of slavery, grinding the faces of the destitute and the poor. They are also people who once, like them, perhaps long ago, came here from a far-distant shore, and fought and struggled and worked, to make this place a home. Together they had helped to fashion a nation, rich enough to welcome the stranger; strong enough to protect its own people; powerful enough to defend the wretched of the earth. A nation that could command pride, without arrogance; confidence, without xenophobia; love, without hatred of others. A nation defined as a people with a fixed permanent interest in this community, this England, this United Kingdom.

And so he enters the church, not without trepidation, to take his first class. The student refugees are waiting for him in a glazed side-chapel converted into a meeting-room, thus losing the atmospheric gothic gloom of the nave, but retaining the magnificent Victorian stained-glass windows, that cast their coloured images of teaching and healing across the tiled floor. The group consists entirely of men: the women are taught separately by a member of the female clergy. Ralph makes a mental note of this segregation as a problem to tackle at a later date. Let us take people as they are, not as we would want them to be. He looks around the circle at the anxious, expectant faces; draws in a breath; and embarks.

'Let's start in the beginning …'

THE END

Acknowledgements

I am grateful to my son Tristan Holderness for pointing me towards genealogy, DNA testing, Norse mythology and much more; to my nephew Lee Stephens for acting as my guide to the East Riding; to Father Kevin Morris for inducting me into Anglo-Catholic Anglicanism; and to the late John Burrow, who taught me Old English. My wife Marilyn Holderness has been, as always, my first and most constructive reader. The book is dedicated to my friend Bryan Loughrey, who passed away in 2021, and whose spirit hovers over many of the following pages.

Footnotes may cite direct quotations or indicate adapted sources. Some of the writing is based on verse translations of Anglo-Saxon poetry published in my *Anglo-Saxon Verse* (Liverpool University Press, 2000), and *Craeft: Poems from the Anglo-Saxon* (Shoestring Press, 2001).

By the same author

Criticism

D. H. LAWRENCE: HISTORY, IDEOLOGY AND FICTION
SHAKESPEARE'S HISTORY
THE SHAKESPEARE MYTH
THE POLITICS OF THEATRE AND DRAMA
SHAKESPEARE RECYCLED
ANGLO-SAXON VERSE
SHAKESPEARE: THE HISTORIES
CULTURAL SHAKESPEARE
TEXTUAL SHAKESPEARE
VISUAL SHAKESPEARE
SHAKESPEARE AND VENICE
GENDER AND POWER 1500-1700
NINE LIVES OF WILLIAM SHAKESPEARE
TALES FROM SHAKESPEARE: CREATIVE COLLISIONS
RE-WRITING JESUS
THE FAITH OF WILLIAM SHAKESPEARE
SHAKESPEARE AND MONEY
SHAKESPEARE AND BIOGRAPHY
SAMURAI SHAKESPEARE

Fiction

THE PRINCE OF DENMARK
BLACK AND DEEP DESIRES: WILLIAM SHAKESPEARE VAMPIRE HUNTER
'ECCE HOMO'
MEAT, MURDER, MALFEASANCE, MEDICINE AND MARTYRDOM: SMITHFIELD STORIES

Poetry

CRAEFT: POEMS FROM THE ANGLO-SAXON

CPSIA information can be obtained
at www.ICGtesting.com
Printed in the USA
BVHW052246230522
637882BV00002B/18